TRAPPED
IN
ICE

New York Times & USA Today Bestselling Author

CYNTHIA
EDEN

This book is a work of fiction. Any similarities to real people, places, or events are not intentional and are purely the result of coincidence. The characters, places, and events in this story are fictional.

Published by Hocus Pocus Publishing, Inc.

Copy-editing by: J. R. T. Editing

PROLOGUE

"Madelyn? Madelyn Lake? Yo, Madelyn!"

A strong hand closed around her arm, pulling her to a stop. With her heart thundering in her ears, she swung to face—

A handsome boy frowned at her. "Didn't you hear me calling your name? Because I swear, I think I did it like fifty times."

Her breath shuddered out. "I—" *Forgot*. She was still getting used to that name, but she wasn't supposed to say that to anyone. Another secret to keep.

"You left your English book in class. I was just bringing it to you."

She saw that he was gripping her textbook in his right hand. His left still curled around her arm, and his touch felt funny. Like it made her skin too sensitive. Too hot. Too...*something*. Hurriedly, she jerked away from him.

His brows immediately shot up. "Jeez. Get over yourself already. I'm not chasing you down to ask for a date."

Of course, not. Her heart needed to stop its crazy thundering, but when he'd grabbed her...

Fear. Would she ever get over the fear?

Her gaze darted around. She wasn't trapped in some hell. Or, maybe she was. All about perspective, right? She stood in a bustling school hallway. Everyone wore the same preppy uniform. Her pleated skirt scratched a little over the tops of her thighs, and she could swear she felt everyone watching them.

"I'm doing a good deed," he growled. "Despite what you may have heard, I can do one. Occasionally." He extended the book toward her.

She reached out for it. Her fingers touched his and that crazy too hot, too sensitive, too...*something* feeling darted over her again. Her hand snatched back—with the book—as if she'd been burned.

Giving a disgusted shake of his head, the boy turned away.

"I haven't heard anything about you." The words rushed from her. "I don't even know your name." How could she? This was only her second day. Sure, yes, she'd met plenty of people, but their names were all blurs to her. *This* boy? With the thick, dark hair that fell rakishly over his forehead and his intense dark brown eyes...no, she didn't remember him. Tall, with shoulders that were already plenty wide. He stared at her with a kind of knowing confidence, and she was—

And I'm scared. But she was always scared. Her mother said the trick was to act as if she wasn't.

Her chin darted into the air. *Do not act scared.* She'd be the opposite of scared.

"I'm Smith Sanders." His head tilted to the right. He had loosened the blue tie that all the boys were supposed to wear. Loosened the tie. Turned up the collar on his white dress shirt. He flashed her a wide smile. "And now you know my name."

That smile was...gorgeous. Charming. *Scary*. Dang it, she had to stop being afraid! She backed up a step. "I do."

His gaze fell to the floor. Noted the distance she'd put between them. When he looked back up, there was curiosity in his gaze.

Oh, no. She didn't want anyone to be curious about her. She was supposed to be flying under the radar at this swanky school. The last thing she wanted was attention.

"I lied to you."

"What?" Caught completely off guard, she gaped at Smith.

"I do want to ask you for a date."

This wasn't happening. She'd never, ever been asked out before.

"The book gave me a chance to talk to you." A shrug of those oddly powerful shoulders. "A buddy of mine is having a party this Friday. Want to come with me? You can learn lots of names there."

An immediate shake of her head. *No.* She didn't do parties. Wasn't allowed to do them. "I-I need to go." Clutching the English book to her chest like it was some kind of shield, she whirled away.

"I don't bite."

Oh, no. He had *not* just said that, had he? She looked back. "I certainly hope not."

His lips twitched at her response. "You *will* hear stories about me."

A bell rang. Time for class. She couldn't be late. She couldn't attract attention. Couldn't do anything that would get her noticed.

But this boy is noticing me.

"Only believe some of those stories, Madelyn Lake."

Her heart slammed into her chest. "Wh- which ones should I believe?"

But the headmaster appeared behind Smith. Dr. Griggs slapped a hand around Smith's shoulder. "Mr. Sanders," Dr. Griggs growled. "We need to talk in my office, *immediately.*"

Uh, oh.

Smith winked at her. "Only the good ones," he told her. "Just those..." He turned toward the headmaster with an innocent smile. "Would you believe that snake slithered out of biology class on its own?"

Her feet felt rooted to the spot as she watched Smith Sanders leave.

She realized that while she might not be able to remember her own name, she would never forget his.

***

"I was asked out today," she blurted the words as soon as she got home. The big, cold, massive house that was their new home.

New house. New life. Everything will be different.

This was the third new home in three years. But this was supposed to be the last move. No one would ever know them here.

Her mother turned toward her. "No."

"I didn't say yes." *But I wanted to.* "I just..." Her words trailed away because she didn't know what to say.

Her mother rushed toward her. Her hands flew out and clamped around Madelyn's shoulders. "You can't."

"I..." A click as she swallowed. "I wasn't going with him."

"You have to stay close. School and home. That's it. I don't—" Her breath expelled. "We can't start again. *This is it.* We're safe. You have to stay—"

"Below the radar," Madelyn finished. "I know." Why did her chest feel so heavy?

"Tell the boy you aren't interested." Her mother's hands dug into her skin. "Tell him he's not your type. Tell him whatever it is that girls say these days. You can't be like the others, baby. You know it. It's too dangerous."

Dangerous...for the boy. For anyone who got too close to Madelyn. Because of what had happened before. Madelyn blinked away the tears that wanted to fill her eyes. "I'm not going to let anyone close, don't worry."

Her mother's lower lip trembled. "Sweetheart..."

She pulled away. "I didn't like him anyway. Not my type." She stepped around her mother. "There are stories about him. I'm sure he was just playing with me, anyway, not really interested in who I am at all. He probably just asked because I'm the new girl." *One foot in front of the other, just keep moving and put one foot in front of the other.*

"Madelyn."

She put her left foot in front of the right. Headed forward.

"*Madelyn.*"

Her steps froze. "Sorry. I keep forgetting that name." This time, she had an official new name. First name and last name.

"You can't forget anything. If you slip up..."

She looked back at her mother.

"He'll come for you," her mother whispered. "You have to stay hidden."

Right. She knew the rules. *Stay hidden. Don't act scared.* And...

Don't get close to anyone. Madelyn swallowed over the lump that kept trying to rise in her throat. "I'll make sure Smith gets the message. I'm not interested in him. Not now. Not ever."

Smith's smile flashed in her mind.

"Not ever," Madelyn whispered as she reached for the gleaming banister that would take her upstairs to her new bedroom.

New bedroom. New life.

Same old terror.

CHAPTER ONE

The elevator doors opened, and Madelyn Lake found herself staring straight at a ghost from her past. A very handsome, very dangerous ghost. One who flashed her a devilish smile.

"Going down?" Smith Sanders inquired with a slow lift of one wicked brow.

Her chin lifted. She'd known he was in the building. Mixing it up with the rich and famous who'd been partying on the floor below hers. But that party should have ended an hour ago. It was nearing two a.m., and even the party boys had to stop at some point. And the man had *no* business being on this floor. Her floor. She'd been working late on an authentication project that had to get finished, and she had not—

"Still think you're too good to talk to me, hmm?" Smith held a hand out to stop the elevator doors from closing. "How many times do I have to tell you, Maddie, I don't bite?"

Her shoulders straightened. "I never thought I was too good for anything." She didn't get on the elevator. "Why are you up here? This is a private floor."

A lazy shrug of shoulders that had grown even more powerful over the years. "Must have hit the wrong button. My mistake. Meant go to down to the lobby after the party ended, but I wound up here, with you."

The party. Right. Smith had been partying it up with his boss and best friend, Aiden Warner. Aiden had been celebrating another major acquisition—she was pretty sure Aiden owned half the world at this point—and she'd been invited to the festivities. More of a courtesy invitation than anything else, Madelyn was sure. She'd popped in a moment, seen Smith, and...

Gone running back up to my office.

"I'm sure you're ready to get home," Smith continued in the rough and rumbly voice that made her think of things she shouldn't. "Come on in the elevator, and I'll see you safely down to the parking garage. Consider it yet another of my endless good deeds."

"Shouldn't you have a date?" she blurted. "Someone else to see home?"

That smile of his stretched. His dark eyes gleamed. "I'm flying solo tonight."

Her gaze darted to the hand that still pressed to the side of the elevator door. Long, tanned fingers. Strong. That was the thing about Smith. He *always* seemed strong. Powerful. Like he was a caged beast waiting to leap out and attack.

"The building is pretty much deserted," he continued. "You really shouldn't be here so late by yourself."

"There's a security guard downstairs. Actually, I think there are *two* security guards."

"But no one up here with you."

Because she wasn't supposed to be working, but she'd really wanted to finish her project and slipping out of the party had seemed like such a fine idea since making small talk was something she *never* excelled at doing. "You're here."

"So I am." His gaze swept over her. "Gorgeous dress, by the way."

She wore a black dress made of lace, one with two-inch-wide straps that slid over her shoulders, then dipped toward her cleavage. The feather-light material slid down her body, hugging her hips, and ending just below her knees. Black heels completed the look. No jewelry. Her hair was loose around her shoulders, mostly because she'd been running late earlier and hadn't taken the time to put it in a twist or something more sophisticated.

As he studied her, Madelyn's own gaze dipped down his body. The suit looked like it must have cost a fortune. It fit his body perfectly. Sculpted to Smith's shoulders and broad chest. He wore a crisp, white shirt, and a thin black tie. His hair was just as thick as it had been when he'd been in high school, but now it was swept back from his high forehead.

Handsome. Dangerous. But all grown up.

A true blast from her past.

"So, not to rush you, but are you planning to stand there staring at me all night?" Smith asked her.

Madelyn felt heat stain her cheeks. "Certainly not." *Get on the elevator.* This was hardly some life-altering event. It was a ride that would last moments, nothing more. Then they'd go their separate ways. As they always did.

Because their paths had crossed over the years. Mostly because she did a whole lot of business with Aiden Warner, and Smith *was* the guy's right hand. He'd been hired by Aiden after Smith had spent years doing some rather covert work for the military. During those years, Smith had vanished from everyone's radar.

Then he'd reappeared. Taunting grin in place. Secrets in his eyes. And seemingly inseparable from Aiden. And since Aiden had supplied the initial financing for her business, she and Smith now saw each other at least three or four times a year. Each time their paths crossed, she was always polite to him. Excruciatingly so.

In return, he was generally mocking to her. But Smith tended to be mocking with everyone, so it wasn't as if Madelyn received special treatment from him.

"I'm in charge of security," he murmured as she crept into the elevator. "Just wouldn't be doing my due diligence if I didn't make sure you got down to the parking garage safely. You never know when someone dangerous might be lurking around."

Madelyn stared pointedly at him. "You don't say."

A sharp bark of laughter burst from him. "Still think I'm the bad guy, do you? That hurts." Smith removed his hand from the elevator door and put it over his heart. "Right here. Just feels like a knife plunging into my heart."

"Don't you need to have a heart in order for it to hurt?" The response just shot from her. Not her normal, cautious self at all. She didn't say things like that and— "I'm sorry."

More laughter came from him.

But then her apology seemed to register. His eyes—a deep, intense brown—widened. "Aw, Maddie, are you worried you hurt my feelings?"

She had been worried. For a fleeting moment. Ever so fleeting. Then she'd realized he probably didn't care at all what she thought of him. "Madelyn. No one calls me Maddie."

"I do."

She leaned around him to push the button on the control panel. The button that would get them from the twentieth floor of the Miami high-rise down to the parking garage. Then she'd escape. Madelyn thought he'd do the proper thing and scoot back so she could easily access the panel.

But she'd forgotten Smith was hardly ever proper.

He didn't move back. Instead, she wound up practically having to wrap her arm around him as she twisted to punch the button.

He inhaled. "Is that jasmine? Switched body lotions, have you? I think you used to prefer a vanilla scent."

Her head jerked up, and she gaped at him. "How would you know that?"

"Got a good nose." He tapped the bridge of his nose and winked.

She jerked her hand—and her whole body— back a good foot. "Yes, if you must know, I do use jasmine body lotion." *His* scent was all around her. Warm and masculine and the man was taking up entirely too much space. He always did that. Seemed to dominate whatever space he occupied.

Her gaze lit on the gleaming floor numbers as the elevator descended. *Nineteen, eighteen...*

"Are you ever going to tell me?" Smith wondered.

From the corner of her eye, she saw him prop one shoulder against the wall of the elevator. "Tell you what?"

"What I did to piss you off?"

Sixteen, fifteen. "I have no idea what you're talking about. I'm not angry with you for any reason."

"Really? You just hate me for shits and giggles? Interesting."

Twelve, eleven. "I don't hate you at all."

"No? You could have fooled—"

The elevator jolted. She stumbled, but Smith's hands immediately grabbed Madelyn and steadied her. "Thank you," she replied automatically, a bit breathless as—

Darkness. The elevator plunged into complete and total darkness. And it *stopped*. She could feel the sudden stillness around her. Thick, complete darkness, and stillness.

No, no, no, no. This could not be happening. Her breath stuttered out.

"Madelyn."

"Why did we stop?" A grating whisper.

"Probably just some glitch. Don't worry. I'm sure it will start again any moment." His hands remained wrapped around her shoulders.

Normally, she didn't like being touched. Went out of her way to avoid it, in fact. But this wasn't a normal situation, and his slightly rough, callused fingers pressingly lightly against her bare skin didn't make her afraid. They reassured her. She wasn't alone in this darkness.

Not like before.

"The elevator's lights are all out, but I'm going to let you go and take out my phone. We can use the flashlight on it to look around." A pause. "I'm *telling* you that I'm letting go because you seem scared."

Completely and utterly terrified. But she replied, "I have no idea what you mean."

He let her go.

She immediately grabbed for him. Her nails dug into the fabric of his suit coat.

"*Maddie.* I'm right here. Not like I can leave you. We're trapped in this thing together." Mild. So calm.

She still didn't let him go.

A light flashed on. The light poured from the small circle near the top of his phone and shot up toward his face. The illumination both concealed and revealed, making the normally handsome lines of his face appear more sinister. Dangerous.

He smiled and even his smile seemed to hold a dark edge. "See? Right here."

Her breath panted in and out. She *hated* her reaction. Usually, she was only in an elevator for a few moments. There was plenty of light. She didn't mind the small space for such a limited amount of time. Okay, fine, she still minded, but she'd learned to deal, just as she'd learned to deal with so many things in her life.

But...

But it was the darkness making her terror grow. The thickness that seemed to be all around her.

"You're okay. I'm not going to let anything happen to you."

Oddly soft and tender words from Smith when she'd never thought of him as a tender guy. Quite the opposite. Smith did have a reputation for being...well, an asshole.

And he probably thinks I'm having a breakdown on him just because the elevator stopped for a bit. She snatched her hands back. "Of course, nothing is going to happen." Her chin rose. "Just a glitch. I, um, heard something similar happened last week." She'd even seen the elevator repairman in the lobby. And she'd been grateful at the time, thinking...*So glad I wasn't trapped.*

Smith stepped away from her. His light aimed at the control panel. She saw him hit the button to open the doors.

Nothing happened.

Then he pressed the button that had a little image of a phone on it. "The call button will alert the maintenance staff," Smith told her in his calm and controlled voice. "They'll get help up here fast."

When he hit the button, it didn't light up. Didn't seem to do anything. "Are you sure it's working?" Madelyn inched closer to him.

"Do you want me to lie or tell the truth?"

She inched even closer. She also pulled her own phone out of her tiny black bag, and her shaking fingers turned on the flashlight option. "Truth, please."

"I have no fucking clue."

He hit another button. A red one this time. The alarm button?

"Can't hurt to try, though, am I right?" Smith drawled.

Her light swung around the elevator. Then up to the ceiling. "Is there a hatch we can crawl out of?" Didn't that happen in movies? People crawled through the hatches in the tops of the elevators. Or they pried open the doors or—

"Yeah, how about we try *not* to do dangerous things and instead call for help? Seem cool to you?"

Her attention flew back to him.

He had his phone pressed to his ear. "This is Smith." His voice was more grim than calm as he spoke to whoever was on the other end of the line. "I'm stuck in the elevator at the Bringam building, and I'm gonna need someone to get me out." His gaze locked on her. "No, I'm not alone. Madelyn Lake is with me. Um, yes. That Madelyn."

She nibbled on her lower lip.

"Tell them to haul ass, would you? Because I don't think the lady is enjoying her current situation. Not at all." He ended the call. But kept the flashlight on. He pointed it at the wall, and she realized that—whoops, her phone had been shining right into his eyes.

Hurriedly, Madelyn lowered her phone's light.

"That was Aiden. He's on the case. We'll be out before you know it."

Before you know it wasn't exactly a quantifiable time. "He'll get maintenance to the building." That would take some time, though because, surely, the maintenance staff was at home now. Had to be at this crazy hour. And if maintenance couldn't fix the problem, then Aiden would need to get an elevator repairman in and, oh, God, the repairman might not arrive for hours. *Hours.*

"Try taking a deep breath. A long, slow, deep breath," Smith advised.

Madelyn became aware of the heaving sound of her own breaths. *Dammit.*

"Don't like closed spaces, huh? Never knew that about you." He turned off the light.

"No! Turn it back on!" An immediate cry from her as her hand instinctively lifted, and she shone her light back on his face again.

His eyes squinted against the illumination. "Not sure how long we'll be here. Thought maybe we'd conserve the battery on the phones. How about I keep mine on for a while, and you turn yours off? We can alternate. That good for you?"

Oh, no. "You think we're going to be here for a...long time."

"Do you want me to lie or tell the truth?"

Her heart raced far too fast in her chest. "That's the second time you've asked me that question. Do you lie to people a great deal?"

"Sometimes lies can make things better. If it makes you feel better, I can tell you that we'll be rescued very, very quickly."

That's the lie.

"But I think you already realized how long it will take to get a repair going. And even if firefighters rush to the scene and beat down the doors, it will take some time to get out." Her light still hit him. "So I'm not sure my lie would make you feel better. Not when you've figured out the truth yourself."

No, his lie wouldn't help. "Turn on your light," she muttered. "I'll turn off my phone." Because they did need to conserve the battery and a glance down at her phone's screen showed she only had twenty-five percent power remaining as it was. "Aiden will probably call you with updates." It made sense to keep Smith's phone on and ready.

He tapped his phone screen. His light illuminated more of the elevator, and Smith bent to put the phone in the corner, positioning it so the light would shine upward.

With fingers that trembled, she turned her phone off. Put it in her purse. Tried for some deep breaths.

"Want to tell me about it?" Smith asked.

"About what?" Was she inching closer to him in the dark? She was, but surely that was only because he stood beside the light.

He lifted a hand. "We have air blowing in. You feel that?"

Yes, thankfully, she did.

"No lights, but the air conditioning is still working, so that's a plus for us." His tone was still all mild and easy. "We're safe. Help is on the way. And we've got light. More pluses."

Deep breath.

"But you're terrified, and that fear isn't just because you're trapped with me, is it?" A little more careful. "I certainly hope you know that I would never hurt you."

Her head snapped up. She'd been staring down at the light, and now she looked at him. "I—of course, I'm not scared of you."

"Well, there's no 'of course' about it. You've been avoiding me since we were sixteen years old. Thought maybe you'd grow out of it, but...nope. Even as adults, you run when you see me coming." His powerful arms crossed over his chest. "Guess all the stories about me got to you, huh?"

"I never listened to stories." Not back then. Not now. "I ran from you because..."

He waited.

She stopped talking.

Soft laughter. "We can pass the time by standing in silence. Or we could try talking. Nestled together in this dark elevator like we are—seems like the perfect opportunity to share some secrets."

Nestled? Uh, the word he should have used was *trapped.* Madelyn gaped at him. "You have got to be kidding."

"Oh, I'm sorry. Was there something else you were planning to do? Maybe pace around in tiny circles? Curl up on the floor and sleep? Am I keeping you from some super engaging activity?"

Deep breath.

"Didn't think so," he murmured. "Talking will make you feel better. It will help distract you from the absolute terror that you are feeling right now."

"What makes you think I feel absolute terror?" She did. *Absolute.* The ghosts from her past were grabbing her and trying to haul her under. Madelyn felt like she was drowning when she wasn't even near the water. *Help me. Help!* A frantic scream that she couldn't voice. Not now. But she had screamed like that, a long time ago. Over and over again.

He stepped toward her. A big, powerful shadow. His hand reached out, and his fingers curled around her fist. "This. This is one sign." He stroked her clenched fist. "Did you even realize that you'd clenched your hands into fists? And your spine is so stiff and straight. Tension is pouring off you, and, though I do normally think your voice is all sultry and sexy—"

What?

"Your words sound brittle. And you're still breathing far too quickly. You're either absolutely terrified of the dark and small spaces or it's me. You're terrified of me."

"It's...not you."

He turned her hand over. Feathered his fingertips over her wrist. "Glad to know." A pause. "Your pulse is racing like crazy. Baby, what made you fear the dark?"

I can't tell you. "I'm not your baby."

"Alas, you are right." He did not let her go. "Despite the fantasies I've had."

What? No, impossible. There was no way in this world that Smith Sanders had ever fantasized about her. "That's not funny."

"Good. It wasn't supposed to be a joke." He hadn't let her go. His fingers were doing a weird stroking thing over her wrist. Maybe the strokes were supposed to calm her down. They didn't.

They did make her feel...

Warm. Sensitive. *Aware*.

"You starred in my high school fantasies, then when you sashayed back into my adult life, well, guess those memories came storming back."

"I didn't sashay anywhere."

"No? My mistake. Pretty sure I remember you *sashaying* into Aiden's office, wearing a blue pencil skirt, heels that made me hard, and the sexiest white blouse I'd seen in my life. Fucking gorgeous."

She had zero idea what she'd worn to the meeting he referenced. How on earth could he remember?

"Your breathing is getting easier. More relaxed," he noted. "See, when we talk and share our secrets, you can relax more. You stop thinking about where you are, and you just think about *who* you're with."

He was deliberately distracting her. Realization dawned. "You're helping me."

"Well, if you faint on me in the elevator, then I won't have anyone to talk with, will I?"

She tried to figure him out. "So you were lying?" He hadn't actually fantasized about her. She'd known that, though. Someone like Smith would never have fantasies about her.

"I asked you if you wanted a lie or the truth. Thought you went with truth, so that's what I've been giving you."

Her mind just wasn't processing properly. "You want me."

"Have for years. Yep." No hesitation in that reply. And...

He stroked her wrist once more.

Her heartbeat kicked up.

"Don't get scared again," he soothed. "You're safe."

But the acceleration of her pulse that he'd felt beneath his fingers hadn't come because she was scared. It had come because... "I've had fantasies about you, too."

"Madelyn Lake. I am shocked."

Heat poured into her cheeks. Luckily, he wouldn't be able to see that heat and—

"And utterly delighted." He bent toward her. "The untouchable Maddie has fantasies? About *moi*? Do tell me more."

His head was close to hers. So very close. His lips were inches away. She *had* fantasized about him. Maybe because he was just something else that she couldn't have.

"Or maybe..." Smith's already deep voice rumbled even more. "You want to show me? Because it's just us here. No one else to see. No one else who ever has to know just what you did with the bad guy in the dark."

Her breath shuddered out. Her heart was back to racing, and the tension that had always been between them seemed to thicken the air. All she had to do was press up on her toes. Pull his head down a little bit more. She could kiss him so easily.

Dangerous. Don't do it. You're not supposed to get close to anyone.

But they were alone. In the dark. As he'd just said, no one else ever had to know.

"I want to kiss you," he growled. "If you don't want me close, tell me to get the hell back. You're a dream I've had for a long time, but I know how to keep my control. Especially with you."

She could barely make out his words over the crazy drumming of her heart. What Madelyn knew—she wasn't afraid. Memories from the past weren't swamping her. Smith had thrown her a life preserver. He'd pulled her up, and now she was shockingly, vividly, in the present with him. Her own personal temptation. Right there.

No one else ever has to know.

He let go of her wrist. Swore and took a step back. "I'll stay on one side of the elevator, and you can stay on the other."

She spun away from him. Found herself just staring at the darkness of the wall. *What would one kiss hurt?* He was keeping her past at bay. And she...*Confession.* "I've wanted you for years, Smith." Easier to say when she wasn't looking at him. "I've always been curious..." Her voice had gone husky. Wait, how had he described it before? *Sultry.* She'd never felt sultry or even particularly sexy, until now. "Always been curious about how you'd taste."

Silence from behind her. Thick and heavy. She wet her lips and felt his hand curl around her shoulder. Madelyn thought he'd turn her toward him, but he didn't. He eased closer to her, so close that she could feel him pressed along the back of her body. His strong chest. His powerful muscles. His...

Oh. Damn.

Smith was aroused.

Only fair, because so was she.

The elevator had been terrifying and gut-wrenching to her moments before. But now, with Smith, with the soft light spilling from his phone, it almost seemed...

Safe. Like they were hidden from the world. Like what happened here would be secret. Just for the two of them. Wouldn't it be wonderful to exchange one horrific memory for something different? Something good?

His left hand curled around her waist. The weight was warm, reassuring, sensual. Not scary at all. Nothing about Smith seemed scary.

Seductive? Yes...

His right hand eased over her right shoulder. Slid down and his fingers curled over her chest, his hand just above the quick rise and fall of her breasts. If he moved his fingers just a little bit, he could slide under the lace. It would be easy to dip those fingers of his past the fabric of her dress and under the black bra she wore.

Her nipples were tight, aching peaks, and she wanted him to touch them. She wanted to let go of the control she'd held so tightly for years.

No one has to know.

It was almost as if...as if this moment wasn't real. A dream. A fantasy. Something else. A moment forgotten in the dark.

His breath whispered over her ear, and a shiver skated down her body when he rasped, "I've wondered what you would taste like for years, Madelyn."

Her left hand rose, and her fingers curled around his. Not to push his hand away, but to press it closer, harder against her. Her head turned just a little, angling back toward him. "Wonder no more," she whispered. Her lips fluttered against his. Soft. Light. Tentative.

A growl built in his throat. The sound was animalistic, primitive, and a primal part of her—a part Madelyn had never known even existed inside of herself—responded. She could feel her panties getting wet. *From barely a kiss*. His hands seemed to brand her body where he touched her, and her mouth opened more because she desperately did want to taste him. Every single bit of him.

The hand on her hip grabbed her dress. He began to pull up the fabric. She could feel the fabric sliding up her bare legs. Air seemed to whisper over her skin, but she didn't care. He was behind her. Her head had angled toward him. His mouth had teased her with a light kiss when she *needed* more. "More." A stark cry that broke from her, when she wasn't even sure what that *more* really was.

"All you had to do was ask," he replied. Then he yanked up her dress even more.

And his fingers moved from her hip. They went right between her thighs.

***

She had to be terrified. Poor little Madelyn. All grown up, but still with the fears that had haunted her since childhood.

She'd be in the elevator. The last to leave. That was always Madelyn. She wouldn't have stayed at the party. At the first chance, she would have snuck out and rushed up to work. Time would have gotten away from her.

He'd watched from across the street as she turned off the lights. Headed out of her office.

She was trapped. Utterly terrified. Was the dark closing in on her? Was fear making her sweat and shake?

He would let her out soon. But only after he was sure the fear had consumed her.

Madelyn didn't get to hide from him any longer. No, after all of this time...

I've found you.

CHAPTER TWO

This wasn't happening. This *couldn't* be happening. No fucking way did he have Madelyn Lake in his arms. No fucking way was his hand sliding between Madelyn Lake's gorgeous, make-me-beg legs.

No fucking way was she...

Moaning softly.

And wet. *For him.*

Fuck, *yes.* If this was a dream, Smith seriously did not want to wake up. Ever. His fingers slid over the silk of her panties, stroking her carefully. A gasp broke from her. He had only kissed her lightly before. He wanted to spin her in his arms and thrust his tongue deep into her mouth. Taste her like the desperate, starving man that he was. But first...

First...

His fingers eased under the edge of her panties. He touched *her.* Soft, hot. Wet. His thumb rubbed over her clit, and that sexy moan came again. He loved that sound. His fingers crept between her delicate folds, and he pushed one finger up inside of her. Damn. She was *tight.*

And if he got his cock inside of her, he would go completely insane. No doubt.

But her hand flew down and curled around his wrist. He froze, aware of sweat trickling down his back. When had the elevator gotten so freaking hot? Oh, right. As soon as he'd started touching her. Only now she was stopping him. The best damn seven minutes in heaven of his life. *Had it been seven minutes?* Smith had no clue but wasn't that the name of the game and...*Dammit.* "You want me to stop?"

"No." She pushed his hand against her *harder*.

This wasn't a dream. This was better than any dream he'd ever had in his twisted life. He pushed a second finger into her, having to work her and stretch her because she was so unbelievably tight.

A little gasp came from her, and Smith cursed himself. "I don't want to hurt you."

"It's just...been a while."

He pulled his fingers out, only to thrust them in again. And he made sure his thumb rubbed over her clit. Again and again. Slow rubs. Then faster. And his fingers kept dipping in and out of the hottest paradise he'd ever felt.

Get her ready. Get her to come for you. Right the hell now.

His mouth began to trail down her neck. Her jasmine scent was making him damn near drunk. His lips feathered over her throat even as his fingers kept stroking her. Over and over, and he could feel the tightening of her delicate inner muscles around him.

Madelyn *would* be coming for him. But not this way.

He pulled his hand away and spun her toward him.

"Smith—"

He *loved* the way she said his name. Her voice had always been the huskiest, sexiest thing in the entire world. Her lips were open. His mouth locked to hers. Not softly this time. But with all of the lust and need he'd always felt. His tongue thrust into her mouth, and when he tasted her...*Waited forever on her*. She was sweet. Sultry. Addictive.

Her hands locked around his shoulders, and she urged him closer. Closer was exactly where he wanted to be. His mouth took hers frantically, and he never wanted to let go. He'd pinned her between his body and the wall of the elevator. It would be so easy to lift her up. To rip those wet panties away and sink into her.

If this is a dream, I will kill the asshole who wakes me up.

He'd thought Madelyn hated him. Her hate sure was as hot as hell.

Her mouth pulled from his. "I was almost coming."

It took one desperate moment for her words to register. And when they did, his poor dick— already freaking huge for her—stretched even more.

"Just from you touching me." She seemed...surprised.

Oh, baby, you have been with the wrong dumbasses.

"I ache," Madelyn told him.

He couldn't have that. No way could Madelyn be aching on his watch. So he lowered to his knees before her.

"Wait—Smith! What are you doing?"

Yep, she'd seriously been with dumbasses. "Making sure there is no *almost* to the equation." He hiked up her dress. Pushed her panties to the side and put his mouth on her.

And if he'd thought her mouth tasted good...

Fucking delicious. His tongue lapped at her, and she shuddered against him. Afraid that she might fall, his hands flew up to lock around her waist, and that was better because he could lift her up, hold her easily against his mouth, and taste and taste and *taste*.

"Smith!" A wild cry of his name that held shock and so much pleasure.

She was coming against his mouth. Hell, yes. Hell—

The elevator jolted.

The lights flashed on. He eased back, with her taste still on his lips, and stared up at her. Smith could see the pleasure on her face. The wide eyes. The red, plump, parted lips. Her chest rose and fell quickly as she stared down at him and then...

The elevator dinged.

Sonofabitch.

The doors were about to open. He was between her legs.

"Smith," she said with horror, not pleasure in her voice.

He let her go and surged for the doors. They were opening and—

"Everything okay in there?" A man in a security uniform threw up a hand to make sure the doors *stayed* open. Palmer Macuso. Smith had hired the guy about a month ago. Frowning, Palmer continued, "Mr. Warner called, said help was on the way, but then the elevator started going down on its own."

There was a choked cry from behind Smith. He didn't look back. *I was going down and having the time of my life.* Only that time seemed over. "We're good. Thank you."

Palmer craned to see around Smith. "That you, Ms. Lake?"

"Y-yes. I'm fine."

"Maybe you should come out and take the stairs down to the parking garage. Let's not do any elevator riding until we get a crew to check this thing out," Palmer advised.

Probably very good advice. Smith looked back at Madelyn. Her dress had fallen back around her legs. She stood with her spine super straight again and her chin up. Her hair slid over her shoulders, and she'd clearly tried to school her expression. Maybe most people would have bought the mask she wore.

Smith wasn't most people.

He could see right through her.

Her gorgeous, emerald eyes gleamed a little too brightly. Her lips were still swollen from his mouth. A light dusting of color slid over her high cheeks, color that he knew had come from her release. *Against my mouth.*

She stared straight at him.

Beautiful Madelyn. Oval face. Wide, mysterious eyes. Thick, dark hair.

Star of his dreams.

The woman who'd just come against his mouth.

"The stairs seem like an excellent plan." Madelyn nodded. She also hurried past Smith. Her shoulder brushed over him, and he felt singed. Before Smith could reach out to her, she practically jumped off the elevator. "I think maybe I'll be taking the stairs a whole lot from now on."

Palmer blinked. "Your office is on the twentieth floor."

"Yes, it is." She blew out a breath. "Probably great cardio. I need to get home. I, uh..." Her stare darted from Smith to Palmer. "Good night."

Oh, seriously? She thought that was it? Just a good night? Obviously so, because Madelyn made a beeline for the stairwell.

"You sure everything is okay?" Palmer wanted to know.

Smith took a step after Madelyn. He could still taste her. She didn't get to run away when he could taste her on his mouth. But before he could give chase or respond to Palmer, Smith's phone rang.

"Uh, Ms. Lake? Want me to escort you down?" Palmer called out.

"I've got her," Smith assured him. He also answered his phone, even as he kept his gaze on Madelyn. Her heels clicked across the floor. Those heels were slowing her down. His stride was much longer and stronger.

"Smith!" Aiden's voice rang in his ear. "Help is on the way. Firefighters will be arriving any moment, and I want you to—"

"Might want to cancel the nine-one-one. I'm out of the elevator and currently making sure Madelyn has an escort for the night. Call you soon."

"Uh, okay?" Aiden sighed. "Glad that's fucking over."

Smith hung up on him. *It's not over*.

Madelyn reached the stairwell. Before she could open the door, he did it for her. Her head whipped toward him. Memories flashed between them.

His aching dick wanted *more*.

"Think I promised to see you safely to the parking garage. I always keep my promises."

Her delicate jaw hardened. She moved her head in a jerky nod. Then she bolted into the stairwell. He went right after her and caught her arm.

"Smith..."

"Just making sure you don't stumble in those heels. Would hate for you to take a header down the stairs. Not the best way to end the night. Better to end on a...high note, am I right?"

Her glare could have burned him.

The stairwell door clanged shut.

He smiled at her.

Her gaze dropped to his smile, and for a moment, he could have sworn that Madelyn looked a little lost. Maybe even afraid. That just would not do. "You don't ever need to fear me."

"You have no idea what I fear. But rest assured, you are not on the list." She began walking down the stairs.

Smith kept his grip on her because he really didn't want her taking a header. "Why don't you tell me what scares you? Other than being trapped in the dark. Or was it the small space that bothered you?" Maybe it had been the darkness and the tight confinement.

"You wanted to distract me. That's why you— you did what you did."

Laughter sputtered from him as they kept descending the stairs. He'd never realized she was so funny. "I can promise you, I didn't make you come as a method of distraction."

Madelyn paused with one hand around the stair railing. Her gaze cut toward him.

"I did that because I wanted you coming against my mouth. You were close with my hand, but I wanted to push you over the edge."

Her gaze immediately jumped upward, as if she feared Palmer had followed them.

"Just you and me," he murmured.

"No one has to know." Soft. So low.

His brows pulled together.

But she shook her head and began the descent once more. Madelyn didn't speak again, not until they were in the parking garage. He'd had to use his keycard to get them access. Smith sent a wave to the security guard who waited in the nearby shed area.

Madelyn headed straight for her car, a black Audi that waited under a very bright light.

"Good choice on parking spots," he remarked.

"I believe in playing it safe."

Tell me something I don't know. But... "Felt more like you were walking on the wild side in that elevator."

She hit a button on her key ring, and the lights from her car flashed as the vehicle unlocked. Madelyn reached for the car door but stopped and spun toward him. "I wasn't myself."

His brows rose. "Really? Then who were you?"

"You probably think I led you on." Those incredible green eyes darted down his body.

Oh, sweetheart, I am still very much aroused.

Her stare shot right back up.

Noticed that bulge, did you?

Madelyn cleared her throat. "I...you're uncomfortable."

"Nope." His dick was saluting, but he'd deal with the situation. "I am curious. Very, very curious about you."

Her tongue slid over her lower lip. "I was afraid."

Now they were getting somewhere. But she needed to tell him something that Smith didn't already know.

"But when you touched me, I stopped being so scared."

Well, damn. That was some brutal honesty. Smith edged toward her.

Her hand flew up. "It can't happen again."

"It?"

That hand of hers motioned between them.

His head tilted. "You mean me going down on you in an elevator? That can't happen?" Smith pretended to consider the matter. "Fine. Next time, we can just fuck in a bed. That will work for me."

"That's what can't happen. You said—in the elevator—you told me no one had to know."

Ah. Had he? "Things were a little intense back then." So he didn't exactly remember every word but...

But she wants me to be a secret?

"I don't do things like that." Hushed. "In fact, that's the first time that I've ever..." Her words trailed away.

He wanted to touch her. But she didn't want his touch. So his hand fisted and he decided to finish Madelyn's sentence for her. "The first time you've ever had a guy go down on you in an elevator?"

Her long lashes swept down to conceal her gaze. He saw her throat move as she swallowed.

Look at me.

As if hearing his thought, her lashes lifted. "That's the first time I've ever had someone go down on me."

His whole body stiffened.

"I'm not teasing you. I'm not leading you on. I am way, way out of my element with you."

Holy fuck. He'd been her *first?* The savage flare of possession Smith felt unnerved him. So did her honesty. She wasn't holding anything back. And all he wanted to do was pull her into his arms.

And finish what I started.

"I'm sure it was, ah, probably the intensity of emotions from the night. I was afraid, you were right on that. I had—" She broke off but kept holding his stare. Smith had the feeling she was trying to gather her nerve.

What happened, baby? Tell me.

"I had a bad experience a very long time ago."

His fists tightened.

"Dark place. Tight place. I was trapped, and I didn't think I would ever escape."

He could not move.

"The elevator brought that back to me. If you hadn't been there, if I'd been alone..." A sad smile twisted her lips.

His chest ached.

"I think I might have broken apart in there."

"No." A hard jerk of his head. "Not you. You would have been just fine."

"When your nightmare swallows you up, how can you ever be fine?"

He had to hold her. His hands unclenched and lifted as if to reach for her.

"Good night, Smith." She arched up toward him. Her lips skimmed his jaw. "Thanks for giving me a bit of heaven in the middle of my hell."

He couldn't move.

She opened her door. Slid into the driver's seat and started the engine. Madelyn reached out to haul the door closed, but he finally broke from his stupor and grabbed the door. "What about me?"

Her head turned toward him.

"I got to taste heaven, now I'm going back to hell?"

She licked her lips. "I'm really not who you think."

"Then who the hell are you?"

"I'm not a woman who fucks in the dark with strangers."

"Excellent to know." *I don't want you fucking anyone else.* "Because I'm not a stranger. I'm a man you've known since you were sixteen years old."

"I can't give you what you want."

Bull. "You have no idea what I want."

"What you want isn't me. It can't be." An exhale. "Goodbye, Smith." She tugged on the door.

He let her go. The door slammed, and he backed away. "Good night, Madelyn." *Good night, not goodbye.* Because they weren't done.

She drove away. He watched her go, aware of a deep, simmering tension in his body. Sexual desire? Sexual frustration? Oh, sure. Hell, yes, *sure.* But more. So much more.

Rage. Not at Madelyn. Never her. But at the sonofabitch in her past who'd hurt her. *I was trapped, and I didn't think I would ever escape.* Some bastard had terrorized Madelyn. *And he made her run from me.* That just wouldn't do.

She'd left the parking garage.

Madelyn probably thought she'd escaped him.

She was very, very wrong on that score. He'd gotten a taste of her that night. A bit of heaven. No way was he in the mood to return to hell.

CHAPTER THREE

"It's an invasion of her privacy." Aiden Warner leaned forward, with his hands flattening on the desk in front of them. Sure, it was a Saturday, and the building should have been closed. But sometimes, it was like the song said and there was truly no damn rest for the wicked. "You get that, don't you?" Aiden pushed. "You can't just go ripping into someone's life—"

Smith winced. "It's not ripping. It's more a case of carefully examining. Or maybe investigating a wee bit." His fingers snapped together as inspiration struck. "Nope. Got it. It's helping an old friend."

"Bullshit," Aiden called immediately. "You and Madelyn Lake were never friends. You were obsessed with getting into her pants back in high school."

Still am.

"She wasn't interested. Figured you'd moved the hell on by now."

"Okay, first, no need to be insulting. You know everyone is interested in me."

Aiden rolled his eyes heavenward. "Not this again. Smith, you are not God's gift. Thought you'd come to terms with that deal."

Smith rolled back his shoulders. "I think Madelyn finds me attractive." *Attractive enough to come against my mouth.* But that wasn't a story for Aiden. "She's scared."

Aiden stopped looking at the ceiling. His gaze snapped to Smith.

"There's something in her past. It's still dragging her down like a chain. I want to know what happened to her." And when. Then he wanted to sever that chain.

"It's *her* past. Hers." But Aiden tapped his index finger against the desk. "Did she *ask* for your help? When you were trapped with her in the elevator?"

More. He could hear that husky whisper so easily. "She did ask for my involvement, in a manner of speaking."

"What the hell does that mean?"

Smith shot from his chair. He paced to the window as he thought about Madelyn and her authentication business—the business that had brought her back into his life. You wanted to collect a rare piece of art? Wanted to add a museum quality artifact to your too rich and pretentious collection? Then you needed to see Madelyn. She'd make sure you didn't get conned. Her gig was verification authenticity. When it came to seeing between the real deal and pretenders, Madelyn was a pro.

He knew she'd worked at the Smithsonian in D.C. for a while, doing the same type of work for the museum. For whatever reason, she'd left about a year ago. Decided to hang up her own shingle. But she'd needed some financing.

So she'd gone to her old friend Aiden.

And, yes, that might be faint jealousy stirring inside of Smith. It would have been far more the hardcore variety of jealousy if he'd thought that Aiden and Madelyn had ever had anything romantic actually occur in their relationship. They hadn't, though, because Madelyn had frozen out pretty much every guy who tried to hit on her.

Including me.

And these days, Aiden was quite busy with his gorgeous new obsession, Dr. Antonia "Tony" Rossi. Or, rather, Dr. Antonia Rossi-Warner.

In certain circles, she was also known as the doctor of the dead.

"Smith?" Aiden prompted. "Just how did Madelyn ask for your involvement?"

Time for a slight conversational turn. "Remember when your beloved Tony mentioned to me that I would make for a fabulous Ice Breaker?"

"Uh, yes, but—"

"The conversation happened a while ago." Smith stared out at the city below. "I think she's right, of course. I'd be fabulous."

"The Ice Breakers solve cold cases."

"Um, yes, they solved *your* cold case, so I'm quite aware of what they do."

Behind him, Aiden growled.

Smith smiled. He loved giving his buddy a hard time. Payback for when Aiden had briefly thought Smith might be, oh, you know, *a murderer*. Not that Aiden was one hundred percent wrong. The truth was, Smith had killed. His hands would always have blood on them.

But I wasn't guilty when it came to Aiden's past.

The Ice Breakers were a group of cold case solvers. They all came from various backgrounds, and it was that variety that made them so adept at cracking mysteries. Tony was the one who found the bodies. The woman was absolutely eerie when it came to digging up the dead. Working side by side with her dog, Banshee, she could find the victims that had been missing for so long.

The other members of the team were eclectic. A former bounty hunter named Memphis who could be one hell of a lot of fun under the right circumstances. A reporter. A guy who'd been a suspected murderer—Saint. Actually, Saint wasn't such a bad guy, once you got past the murder rumors. Smith had been chatting with him and Memphis a few times and—

"What cold case do you want to solve?" Aiden asked, dragging him back to the present.

"The mystery of Madelyn Lake."

"Oh, for fuck's sake."

Smith glanced back at him. "That did not sound like friendly encouragement."

Aiden rose. "It didn't sound like encouragement because I just think you want to fuck her, and you can't do that by screwing with her life. If she has secrets, she wants to keep them." He marched from behind the desk and pointed at Smith. "She doesn't want you digging them up because you think you are doing some kind of knight-in-shining-armor routine with her."

"How dare you." Smith sucked in a deep breath. "I can't believe you said that shit to me." He turned fully toward his best friend. "You know I don't play knight for anyone."

Aiden stared back at him.

And...

Wait. Hold up. Smith took a quick step toward Aiden. There was something about Aiden's eyes. "What the hell are you holding back on me?"

Aiden dropped the hand that had been pointing at Smith. "You're not going to lose your shit?"

"Aiden. This is me. I don't lose my shit." He made other people lose their shit all the time. "Talk to me."

"You're not going to like what I have to say."

"What I don't like is you stonewalling me."

"That's fair." His lips thinned. "We found something in the elevator's control panel."

Smith's spine immediately snapped to attention. "What does that mean? Define 'something' for me. Explicitly."

"When the elevator repairmen went to work, they opened up the control panel and found some sort of remote device. One of them said it looked like it might be an override mechanism, a smart bit of tech he'd never actually seen before but had heard a few whispers about in the industry."

Smith's eyes narrowed. "You're telling me the elevator was sabotaged?"

"It looks that way, yes." A pause. "There's more."

"Seriously? Just spit it out already."

But Aiden didn't. "I'm trying to make sure you will respond in a rational way."

"What the hell?" Talk about insulting. "I am rational. I'm also your head of security. If someone is sabotaging the elevator in one of your buildings, I'd think you would brief me immediately about it. This is a serious safety concern."

"Yes, absolutely. This is the brief. But, you also have a history with Madelyn Lake."

He took another step toward Aiden. "So do you. We've both been friends with her forever."

"Really? That's what you're selling to me? That you were *friends* with her back in the day? Because I'm the one who caught your fool ass stalking her when we were kids."

"I wasn't stalking her. I was making sure she got home safely one day. Clearly, there is a difference with those two things." Dammit. What Smith didn't add was that day in particular, he'd seen Madelyn crying after school. She'd always been so quiet and withdrawn, but when he'd busted out of the gym after a long football practice, he'd nearly run straight over her. And he'd seen her tears.

Then Smith hadn't been able to get them out of his head.

He'd trailed her. Maybe because he'd wanted to know who the hell had made Madelyn cry. So he could then kick the jerk's ass. But Madelyn hadn't ever told him.

Because Madelyn loved her secrets.

"Supposedly, a repairman from the elevator company came here about a week ago. I had the front desk security guard send up the sign-in sheet. Right company name was listed, but when I spoke to the reps this morning..." An exhale from Aiden. "They said no one from their business had been scheduled here in months. The guy appears bogus. Probably the one who planted the device."

"*What. The. Fuck.*" Every alarm bell he had was ringing. "I want to see the device."

"I've sent it off for examination. Got some friends at Wilde who excel at studying tech like that."

"You didn't call the cops?"

"Not yet. I want to know what we're facing first." His gaze held Smith's. "I figured you would be able to learn more than a beat cop. And that you'd be particularly motivated seeing as how—"

"Seeing as how Madelyn was clearly the target?" He did not buy for one moment that anyone else had been the target.

"We can't make that assumption yet."

His instincts had already damn well made it.

"I was going to say," Aiden continued grimly, "seeing as how you were a victim last night, I thought you'd be particularly motivated."

"I'm always motivated." *And this is about Madelyn.* "It was for her. Bet when your tech buddies get done, they're going to see the bastard had a way to remotely control the elevator's movements. He could stop the elevator whenever he wanted." *He stopped the elevator with her on it.* Smith played through the events of last night.

"I never stepped off when the doors opened on her floor. The sonofabitch probably thought she was in there alone." He remembered her fear. "Fucking put her in her worst nightmare." He spun and bounded for the door.

"Ah, Smith? What are you talking about?"

His hand hovered over the doorknob. "She's afraid of the dark and of small spaces. And she was just trapped in her own hell." He threw a look over his shoulder. "Everything in me is screaming that Madelyn was the target, but I think you already suspected that, too. Isn't that why you told me to be *rational?*"

A muscle flexed along Aiden's jaw. "I also told you that she might not want you digging into her life."

More alarm bells chimed. "What do you know?"

Aiden shrugged. "I know what you see on the surface isn't always the full picture. Not with me. Not with you." A pause. "Not with Madelyn."

You know more. Cagey bastard.

"Don't dig into her past without her permission." Definitely a warning from Aiden. "It could be dangerous."

What. The. Hell? "We have security cameras all over this building. I'm going to get the guards to pull up the footage from the so-called repairman's visit. I want to see his face. I want every detail I can get on him." *Think this through.* "And if the prick was controlling things remotely last night, then we need your techs to figure out the range on the device. It's possible he had to be in this building." He could have even been schmoozing at the damn party. Could have been *right there*. "If not here, then he had to be close." Smith's head turned so he could stare out the windows. More high-rises stared back at him.

You could have been watching the whole time.

Watching Madelyn? Trying to terrorize Madelyn?

Why, dammit?

Why?

"Smith! You can't just rush to Madelyn with your suspicions right now! You need facts. Evidence!"

He wanted to rush to her. He'd barely slept any because she'd been haunting him. When you finally had your fantasy in your arms—only for her to slip away—you didn't exactly get to drift off in an easy sleep. He'd tossed and turned and reached for her.

Madelyn had haunted him for years. He'd stayed away, mostly because he had truly thought she couldn't stand him.

Things had changed. *She wants me.*

And, if some prick was targeting her...

She needs me.

He exhaled and once more faced Aiden. "I'm getting the security footage. I'm also increasing security at this place." Particularly on Madelyn's floor. She already had her own security up there, a necessary requirement with so many valuable items coming in and out each day. Hell, he'd overseen a lot of that installation himself. Her office was like Fort Knox.

And maybe the SOB knew that. Since he couldn't get to Madelyn in her actual office, he'd terrorized her in the elevator.

"We could be wrong on this, you know. Doesn't have to be linked to Madelyn." Aiden, trying to be the voice of reason.

That was fun and all but... "You didn't see her last night." She'd been in her own hell. "The elevator was sabotaged and being trapped like that was her worst fear."

Not the elevator itself. But being trapped. The darkness. Only... "We didn't do anything to get the elevator moving again. It just started on its own." *She'd been trapped for about ten minutes. Long enough for terror to rip through her.* But...

Almost like a taunt. A tease. A dark message of what's to come? "What the fuck happened in her past?"

Aiden's lips pressed together.

"What do you know, Aiden?"

"I know she didn't want her stepfather's help when she started her company. He's got just as much money as I do."

Yeah, he knew all about Reginald Guyer.

"She wanted to be away from him, but Reginald contacted me. Tried to get me to refuse her."

Smith's head cocked at that news. "Why?"

"Because he told me it was safer for her to stay where she was. *Safer,*" he emphasized. "And that one word has stayed with me for the last year."

Smith wanted to get to Madelyn. The urge to see her burned through him.

Get the footage first. See what you can discover. "Anything else?"

Aiden looked away.

"Aiden..."

"I always run security checks on anyone who does business with me. Just to make sure there are no big, red flags. Even on people I've known a long time."

"Yeah, because you're an untrusting asshole."

"Right. I am." No denial at all. "Madelyn could have gone to any bank for financing. She didn't need me. That alone made me curious."

Smith was curious, too.

"On the surface, everything looked fine," Aiden continued. "But you know I like to look beyond the surface."

"Time is ticking, Aiden. Can you move this story along *any* faster?"

"Her credit reports were great. Everything turned up clean as a whistle. The woman had all her plans in brilliant order. But..." The faint lines near his mouth deepened. "Everything in her life is picture perfect all the way back to her sixteenth birthday. That was right when she moved and joined our school."

"Sixteen? Seriously? You went back that far? Don't you think that's overkill?"

"I don't know." His intense gaze didn't blink. "It depends, because turns out, I couldn't find a damn thing on Madelyn *before* she moved to our town and enrolled at our school. It was almost as if she was born on that day."

Oh, shit. No wonder you told me not to dig. "Did you ask her about that interesting anomaly?"

"No, because her business files were in order, and I had learned nothing to make me think Madelyn wouldn't be a great investment. I figured what secrets she was keeping—I'd pried enough. Do you get what I'm saying? *Her secrets should be hers.*"

They both knew something dark waited in her past. *Fucking fuck.*

"Don't dig more unless she wants you to do it," Aiden urged him. "Because some bodies are meant to stay buried."

"Really? That's the line you're gonna use? Hate to remind you, but your wife makes a living out of digging up the dead. You of all people should know that, sometimes, those bodies need to be dragged to the surface." He yanked open the door and marched out.

***

She shouldn't still be thinking about Smith Sanders.

She should not have tossed and turned in her bed for hours, getting tangled in the sheets, because she kept remembering how it felt to have his hands on her. His mouth.

How it felt to come with his lips pressed between her legs.

Madelyn dipped her head beneath the spray of the shower. In the grand scheme of things, she supposed it was far better to have spent a sleepless night because she'd been all hot and bothered by Smith and not because terror had kept her awake. Especially after the dark confines of the elevator, she'd expected the nightmares to hit.

Instead, she'd dreamed about him.

And woken with his name on her lips.

Madness. She should have gotten over that teenage crush long ago. But the truth was that grown-up Smith was quite unforgettable.

Her hand reached out and twisted, shutting off the flow of water. The tide turned into a light drip, drip, drip as steam continued to drift in the air around her. Even with the shower, she could swear that she still felt his hands on her. Almost like he'd branded her.

Because that's what it's like when you have an orgasm with a man and not just your handy vibrator.

Not like she had a whole lot of real-world experience. When it was second nature to always keep people at arm's length, you didn't exactly get involved in a lot of steamy relationships.

Or, in *any* relationships.

She shoved back the shower curtain. Maybe that had just been normal for Smith, though, and—

A man in a mask.

A man in a hoodie and a ski mask stood two feet away.

A scream tore from Madelyn even as his gloved hands flew toward her.

CHAPTER FOUR

He grabbed for her shoulder, and she jerked back. There wasn't anywhere to go, though, not in that shower, and she hit the tiled wall behind her.

He laughed. *Laughed.*

And his second hand surged for her, too. She shoved up with the palm of her hand, because that was exactly what she'd been taught to do in her self-defense class. The palm was hard. A weapon when you didn't have anything else. Her fingers curled down, claw-like, and she rammed her palm right toward his nose.

He screamed and clutched his face.

Madelyn used that moment to jump out of the shower. She tried to race past him, but her wet feet slipped on the floor. She went down, hard, landing on her knees, but she scrambled up and—

He locked a fist in her hair. Wrenched her back.

"Bitch, you aren't supposed to fight so hard."

What? Like she was just going to stand there? Her hand flew out, and she grabbed the only thing she could. Her toothbrush. Armed with the toothbrush, she drove her hand back over her shoulder and toward what she thought would be the area of his eyes. Since he was yanking on her hair, she couldn't see clearly enough to be sure, but she still figured she'd do some damage.

Madelyn drove that toothbrush back as hard as she could.

"*Fucking whore!*"

He let go of her. The bathroom door was open, and she bolted through it. Madelyn opened her mouth to scream again but...

Who would hear her?

Her neighbors were gone this weekend. Mrs. Rhonda and her seventy-nine-year-old husband—both retirees—had flown to Wisconsin to visit their daughter. And even if they had been home, they weren't close enough to hear her cries.

The scream broke from Madelyn anyway when she was tackled near her bed. A terror-filled cry that erupted even as he slammed her into the hardwood floor and then flipped her over.

"*You want me.*"

The hell she did.

Madelyn tried to knee him in the groin, but he shoved his legs between hers.

Her fingers flew toward his face.

"I got the key, I'm doing everything you—"

She caught the ski mask. Wrenched it up.

Shock made her go momentarily still.

The person above her—he was so young. Barely looked eighteen. Still had acne. A scraggly beard. Blood poured from his nose and one of his blue eyes was bursting with red because of her toothbrush attack.

"Why are you making this so hard?" he snarled at her. "I'm doing everything right!" He caught her hands and pinned them.

"Let me go!"

He smiled. "But I'm not supposed to..."

She tried to head butt him. He jerked back, out of her range, and even though she knew there was no one to hear her, Madelyn screamed as loudly as she could.

***

Smith's hand lifted to knock on Madelyn's door. Getting her address hadn't been hard—it hadn't been a thing at all because he already had it. *Stalker, much?* But they'd deal with that situation later. Right now, he needed to let Madelyn know that she was—

A scream. He could hear it, even through the door. Muffled, but identifiable, and his blood boiled. He didn't knock. Smith lifted his foot and slammed his boot into the doorknob and lock. Two kicks, and that door swung open.

"Stop! Help!" Madelyn's voice. Madelyn's scared, frantic voice.

Smith raced toward the sound of her cries and burst into her bedroom. With one fast look, he took in everything.

The sonofabitch who had Madelyn pinned to the floor.

Her naked body.

Her terrified expression as her head whipped toward Smith. Terror—then desperate hope.

Smith launched across the room. He grabbed the bastard and wrenched him off Madelyn. With a fierce toss, he threw the sonofabitch into the nearest wall. The creep bobbed up to his feet, weaving, and gaped at Smith.

"You shouldn't be here!"

"You're dead," Smith said, meaning those words with every fiber of his being. He threw a quick glance back at Madelyn, just to make sure she was all right. She'd grabbed the blue cover from her bed and had wrapped it around her body. All of the blood seemed to have drained from her face as she shuddered.

Shuddered.

The bastard slammed into Smith. Smith didn't even stagger. He locked one arm around the freak's waist, the better to hold him in place, then Smith drove his right fist into the fool's face. Over and over again. He heard bones crunch and didn't care.

The jerk tried to swing back at him. Pitiful, weak hits.

"I need the police!" Madelyn's voice registered vaguely. "Someone broke into my home and attacked me!" She rushed out an address. "Hurry, *hurry!*"

The attacker slumped against Smith, so he let the piece of shit drop to the floor.

The man's eyes were closed. His face battered to hell and back.

"Smith?" Madelyn's choked voice.

He didn't take his eyes off the bastard on the floor. "Did he hurt you?"

"Just...some bruises where I hit the floor. I'm okay."

No, she wasn't okay. The woman had just been attacked in her own home. There was no part of her that could possibly be *okay*.

He bent to one knee and began patting down the unconscious SOB. When Smith's fingers slid into the left pocket in the front of the guy's pants, he felt the plastic ties immediately. Swearing, he pulled them out. Zip ties.

Fucking sonofabitch.

"Smith?"

He searched the other pocket. Found a wallet. A freaking wallet. *You brought your ID to a break-in and assault?* Smith flipped it open and scanned the details. Andrew Bryson. Twenty-one. Organ donor.

Sonofabitch.

"Smith, th-the cops are coming."

Andrew groaned and his eyes fluttered open. "Wh...what the hell?" He squinted at Smith. "You...you aren't supposed to be here." Blood from his busted lips reddened his teeth.

"No shit. And *you* aren't supposed to attack a woman."

Andrew's eyes flared. "She wanted it."

"No!" A strangled cry from Madelyn. "He was—was waiting in my bathroom when I got out of the shower!"

"Just like she wanted." Andrew's gaze darted to her. "She wanted—"

Smith grabbed the guy's jaw and wrenched his head so that the creep wasn't looking at Madelyn. "You don't look at her. You don't talk to her. You don't even *think* about her again. You understand?"

"But she wanted—"

Sirens. Smith could hear them in the distance.

The attacker heard them too because he started swearing. Feverishly. And he tried to punch Smith. Fucking fool.

The blow barely landed. Smith didn't have that problem. His fist plowed into Andrew's face once, twice, and the man's head jerked around like one of those bobble toys. Smith punched again.

"Smith!" Madelyn grabbed him. "You're going to kill him!"

Andrew's eyes cracked open.

"Yes," Smith said, wanting the man to understand this. "I am."

The cops had arrived. Smith could hear them rushing around inside.

"I am," Smith promised softly.

***

"Ms. Lake?" A dip of the female detective's head as she neared Madelyn. "I need to ask you a few more questions."

Chaos. That was what had happened to her home. Cops were everywhere. Some in uniforms. Some—like the detective—dressed in plain clothes.

There was so much noise. And tension. And fear.

The fear is all coming from me.

She'd dressed. But the cops had frowned at that. As if she should have stayed naked. The detective—*What was her name? Why can't I remember?*—had said that Madelyn would need to be examined. Her bruises photographed. DNA samples taken from beneath her nails. The cops wanted Madelyn to leave with them.

But she could barely manage to stand. Every time she tried, her knees just shook.

"Did you take the sonofabitch to jail?" Smith demanded.

Smith. He had stayed right beside Madelyn, and she was so grateful for his presence. It was strange, but she felt like he was a shield, standing between her and everyone else. He kept a hand on her at all times. A touch on her shoulder. A skim of his fingers down her back.

She should have hated the touch, but, once again, she'd found that she didn't mind it when Smith touched her. If anything, he eased some of the stifling fear she felt.

Not again. This can't happen again.

"He's been transported, but I have to tell you...he's, ah, saying that you invited him here, Ms. Lake." The detective's gaze slid to Smith. "He thinks you're playing some game where you set him up so that your boyfriend could kick his ass."

Madelyn could only shake her head.

"Damn right I kicked his ass," Smith said. "I came in to find him *attacking* her. She was screaming for help, and he had her pinned to the floor of her bedroom. The bastard is lucky to still be breathing."

The detective nodded. "Yes, well, he's gonna have to stop for medical attention before we can book him." Her stare returned to Madelyn. "So, for the record, you did *not* invite him into your home?"

The woman couldn't be serious. "Absolutely not."

"And you didn't put a key under the gnome near your back door so that he could get inside easier?"

"*What?*" No, no, she had *not* left that creep a key.

"Did you or did you not put the key under the gnome and tell him how to get inside?"

Madelyn's lips parted, but she found she couldn't speak.

"What the fuck are you doing?" Smith seemed to have no trouble talking as his low, lethal words emerged. "She's been through hell, and you're grilling *her?*"

The detective's nostrils flared. "Andrew Bryson says she contacted him online. That she had a fantasy she wanted played out."

Madelyn couldn't speak, but she could shake her head. And she did. Over and over again.

"She told him where the key would be waiting. Told him that he *had* to come this morning because she was ready for him. So he did. Now he's crying and bleeding and saying he doesn't understand what the hell he did wrong."

A jolt of electricity seemed to surge through Madelyn. She found herself leaping off the couch. She could feel tears trailing down her cheeks. "I don't know that man. I have never contacted him before. I didn't leave a key outside. I would *never* leave a key outside. It's too dangerous. Anyone could find it and come in—"

Anyone had come in.

"The bastard is lying." Smith rose. His arm brushed against Madelyn. "She was screaming for help. She didn't want him anywhere near her—"

"That was, apparently, part of the fantasy."

"There is no fantasy!" Madelyn's own snarl. "I have never contacted that man before. Search my phone records. Search my house. Search *everything*. If he's saying I did, he is lying like Smith said or—"

"We found a key under the gnome."

She couldn't process that. Madelyn just blinked.

"Just where Bryson said it would be," the detective continued.

Madelyn's chest ached.

"Then the fucker put it there," Smith snapped, not seeming to miss a beat. "Because Madelyn has just told you what happened, and now, Detective Campbell, I want you to back the hell off. How about you go check *his* phone records? His social media? If messages and instructions were sent to him, you'll find them. But I'm telling you right now, they did *not* come from Madelyn."

No, no, they had not.

The detective—*Audrey Campbell, that was her name*—inclined her head. "I can assure you that I will be checking his phone records." She waved toward Madelyn. "We'd like for you to come with us so that we can...collect some evidence."

Take pictures of the marks on me.

Scrape under my nails.

Or had they already scraped? Everything seemed to be such a blur to her, and all she could really think was...

Not again. Not again. Not again.

A thunderous voice blasted, "Get out of my damn way! This is my daughter's house, and I am coming inside!"

Her eyes closed. Of course. Certainly. Why *not* have this happen? Reginald Guyer had made it to the scene, and she had zero clue how her stepfather had been notified about what had happened. Not like he'd just randomly dropped by. They didn't do random visits. They barely did *any* visits since her mother had died last year.

She waited, knowing the next thing he'd probably say would be—

"I am Reginald Guyer, and if you do not get out of my way *immediately,* my lawyers will have a field day with—"

"Please." A soft request from Madelyn. "Just let him in." Her eyes opened.

Reginald—still fit and handsome as he pushed seventy and with a thick head of white hair—marched straight toward her. He wore a Polo, his golf pants, and even the golfing shoes that she knew he adored. Clearly, the man had been called away from the greens.

His eyes widened as he drew closer to her.

But then he vanished from her line of sight because Smith had just stepped in front of her.

"Been a real eventful morning," Smith drawled in a voice laced with danger and warning "so you're gonna want to go real easy here."

Easy was not in her stepdad's vocabulary.

"Smith Sanders." Her stepfather had recognized Smith and his tone indicated he was far from pleased. "What the hell are you doing here?"

She tugged on Smith's arm. Got him to step to the side. "Saving my life." She felt her shoulders sagging. Madelyn knew she should probably straighten them up. Eventually, she would. For the moment, she locked her hand with Smith's. "That's what he's doing here. Saving me."

CHAPTER FIVE

"You are not a fucking hero."

Smith lifted his brows at Reginald's low announcement. They were in the lobby of the police station. Smith didn't like being there, he'd wanted to stay with Madelyn every single moment, but she'd shaken her head when he tried to accompany her into the back.

The cops were collecting more evidence from her. Probably asking more questions of her, too. Though if Reginald and his lawyer—yep, the lawyer had already arrived and was chatting with a nearby cop—found out, they'd go ballistic.

"You were never a hero. I don't care how many medals you might have from your time in service."

Oh, wonderful. Reginald was talking again.

"You trick people and you lie, and you enjoy your chaos." A pause. "Just like your father."

Smith turned his head toward the other man. "I'm going to be a problem for you." He felt like it was only fair to put the truth out there.

Reginald's bright blue eyes narrowed. "Excuse me?"

"You're going to try kicking me out of Madelyn's life, but that's not going to happen. You don't control her any longer." *And I bet you hate that.* "She left the job you'd handpicked for her in D.C. She flew down here. Started a new life—then you, of course, had to buy a house down in Miami, too."

"Nothing wrong with being close to your daughter."

"She's not really your daughter, though, is she?"

Reginald surged toward him. "The hell she isn't. I would do *anything* for Madelyn."

"Right and that's why I'm going to be a problem. You're not going to be able to buy me out of her life. You won't be able to keep me away from her no matter how hard you try. And you will try because we both know you hate me." For numerous reasons. Probably reason number one would be...

A long time ago, Smith's father had cost Reginald quite a substantial amount of money. But then, his father had cost a number of people a great deal of money. That tended to happen when you built a life on lies.

"You've always sniffed around her."

True enough.

"Told you before to stay the hell away from my daughter."

He stepped toe-to-toe with the older man. Smith had never been intimidated by the guy. Never had, never would. "And I told you back then, I'll stay away as long as that is what she wants."

A door opened behind him. Smith swung around, and Madelyn stood there. With shadows under her eyes. With skin that was too pale. With lips that trembled.

"Smith?"

Just like that, with her soft voice, she had him bounding toward her. He took her hand in his. Held tight.

The image from her bedroom flashed in his head. Madelyn, fighting. Madelyn, terrified.

I want to fucking kill that sonofabitch.

"Will you get me out of here?" she asked.

He'd take her any place she wanted to go.

"The detective drove me here."

Yeah, something else that he hadn't liked. Smith had tailed them to the station.

"I don't have a ride, and I really need to get out of this place." Her words broke around the edges.

"I'll take you," Reginald immediately announced. "Got my car and driver waiting outside. Of course, you won't be staying at your house again. Warned you against buying it in the first place. You can stay with me, and I will make sure you are protected."

Her hand jerked in Smith's grasp. Going with his instincts, he lifted her hand to his mouth and pressed a light kiss to her knuckles. "She won't be staying at her house," he agreed. Not an option. "Because she's staying with me." Smith stared into her deep emerald eyes. "Aren't you?"

Her lips parted.

"Madelyn." Shock filled Reginald's voice. And a good mix of anger. "Tell me you are *not* involved with this—this—"

"Fine, upstanding, former special ops hero?" Smith sent her stepdad a cold grin. "A man who can handle shit when times get scary and who isn't afraid to fight hard and dirty to keep her safe? I'd actually think that you might want her around someone like me. A guy who would tear her enemies apart before he so much as lets them ever touch her again."

Reginald held his gaze.

Smith kept his cold grin in place.

"I want to go with you, Smith," Madelyn said. "Please, let's get out of here."

Her "please" seemed to break something loose in his chest. "On it." He tugged her closer, but, before they left, he told Reginald, "We're not involved." *Yet.* "I have a spare room, and Madelyn can stay there as long as she wants. And rest assured, I will make certain she's safe."

Reginald stepped into Madelyn's path. His hands lifted as if he'd touch her, but he seemed to catch himself. His stare raked her. "You *are* okay?" Gruff.

"Yes."

A jerky nod. "*I* will make certain the bastard never troubles you again. Count on it." He pointed a thick, stubby finger at Smith. "Make damn sure you guard her. If anything happens, I'll bury you."

Was he supposed to be intimidated? "Threats? In a police station? I'm shocked. Shocked, I say."

A muscle flexed along Reginald's jaw.

Smith leaned toward him. "Don't worry." Low. Just for Reginald. "The only people who are getting buried are the ones who try to hurt her."

With that, he led Madelyn toward the door. He'd already given his statement to the cops— twice. Time to get the hell out of there. Tension pounded in his temples, and he knew that tension wasn't going to ease until he got Madelyn alone with him.

Far away from the cops and prying eyes.

And as soon as they were settled, he intended to find out what the hell was happening.

He secured Madelyn in the passenger side of his vehicle. When she just sat there, seemingly dazed, he reached around her and snapped the seat belt into place. At the little click, she flinched.

"I have you," he told her.

Her head turned. Her gaze clashed with his. "What if you hadn't been there?"

I will always be there from now on. Instead of telling her that, he rasped, "I was. Forget the 'what if' bullshit. Does nothing but give you nightmares." He slammed the passenger door shut and hurried around to the driver's side. Reginald hadn't come out of the station. Probably still in there, giving the cops hell.

Smith jumped into the driver's seat. When he turned on the ignition, the doors locked automatically. He'd planned to save his questions until he had her safely at his home, but...

Screw it.

"Baby, what the hell is happening?"

Her hands flattened on her thighs. "A freak broke into my house and attacked me. You saved the day when I was sure no one could hear my screams." A ragged breath.

"And last night? When someone threw you into your own personal hell in that elevator? That took some tech skill, and I'm not so sure that jackass currently in a holding cell has that kind of talent."

Another ragged breath broke from her.

His fingers tightened around the wheel. "I want to help you."

"You already did."

No, he hadn't. Smith checked for traffic, then pulled away from the curb. "In order to help you, you're going to need to tell me the truth."

"I didn't invite that creep to my house! I never wanted—"

"Baby, I know you didn't." He needed to ease his hold on the wheel before he ripped the damn thing straight out of the dashboard. "I'm talking about whatever ghosts from the past are haunting you. I want to know about them."

"I-I don't know what you mean."

"It's cute when you lie. Hell, it's cute when you do most things. But lies aren't going to help you. I was serious when I told your stepfather that I was the kind of man you needed. I'm very concerned that you have danger stalking you." He braked at the light. "Luckily, I know exactly how to deal with a dangerous situation."

***

"It's a corporate rental." Smith tossed his keys onto the gleaming, white granite countertop. He motioned toward the condo's floor-to-ceiling windows that overlooked the beach. "Killer view, am I right?"

She inched inside, still feeling chilled to the bone. Chilled, aching, scared. A trifecta that she detested. During the car ride to the condo, she'd been quiet, despite Smith's attempts to pull her into conversation. The day had been one from hell, and Madelyn kept wishing that she could wake up and discover that this had all been a bad dream.

"Guest room is that way. Actually, two guest rooms are down the hall." He pointed to the left. "And the master bedroom is off to the right." A wave of his hand toward the doorway near the fireplace.

Her attention locked on his hand. "You have bruises on your knuckles."

"Huh. Do I?" He lifted his hand. Then shrugged, as if they didn't matter. "Must have gotten them when my hand pounded into that jackass's face."

Her lips pressed together. A shiver slid over her.

"He's not here." Flat. "He won't ever hurt you again, I promise you."

She swallowed.

"I said that because it looked like I lost you there for a moment, and I don't want to ever lose you." He crossed to stand in front of her. "We need to talk. The kind of don't-hold-shit-back, no-lying chat that will rip a soul wide open."

Her tongue slid out to quickly lick her dry lips. "I don't think I like that kind of chat."

"Yeah, most people don't. But we need to have it anyway." He studied her in silence. Then, "You get that Andrew Bryson could be telling the truth."

There was a hard whistle as she sucked in a breath. "I thought you believed—"

"Oh, I believe you, one hundred percent, but I have a bad twist in my gut, and that twist is telling me there is a lot more going on here than meets the eye. You were terrorized last night in the elevator."

"A glitch. Power failure. It happens. I-I saw the repairmen there about a week ago—"

"Not the repairmen, baby. Aiden and I found out this morning that no repairman had been scheduled at our building recently."

The floor seemed to be opening up beneath her. Something like that had to be happening because her legs suddenly felt incredibly unstable. "What?"

"There was some sort of device wired into the control panel. Aiden has his tech buddies at a place called Wilde analyzing it, but the current suspicion is that someone remotely controlled the elevator via that device. Made it stop on command. I think the person deliberately stopped it when *you* were inside. Think he even might have believed you were in there alone because I didn't step out when it arrived on your floor. If someone was watching you—say, from one of the nearby buildings—that watcher would have just seen you step onto the elevator."

This can't be happening.

"First the elevator, and we both *know* you were terrified in there. It brought back memories you haven't shared with me."

Because I'm not supposed to talk about them. Not with anyone. Not ever.

If you didn't talk about it, you got to pretend it had never happened to you. Another bad dream.

Wake up, wake up, wake up.

"Then today, that sonofabitch breaks into your home." Smith's voice deepened with anger. "What if—yeah, screw it, I know I said I hated the 'what if' game, but go with me here—what if he really did get messages telling him to come to your place? Telling him that you wanted everything that he was planning?"

Her head shook frantically.

"The key to your house was waiting out back. Someone could have put it there for him to find. Someone could have pretended to be you. *Someone could have set you up.* Slammed you right into the middle of another nightmare."

She took a step back. But the floor wasn't opening up or even shaking. She was the one doing that. Shaking so hard.

"I'm not a nice guy, Madelyn."

What? *What* was he saying now?

"I wasn't nice when you met me years ago, and the truth is, I've turned into even more of a bastard as I've aged."

Was that supposed to reassure her?

"I've done things that would give you nightmares."

Oh, he had no clue about her nightmares—

"I was carefully trained by the government. I spent years working special ops, and the things I saw, the things I did..." A twisted smile. "I was good at my job. Still am, and that's why Aiden hired me to watch his ass. The world thinks he's some spoiled billionaire, but Aiden has side hustles you can't even imagine. We go to some very dark places and face some very dangerous people." A shrug. "And I don't flinch. I don't back down. I don't stop until my enemy is on the ground."

She couldn't move at all. Every part of Madelyn seemed to have turned into stone.

"Do you understand what I'm saying?"

Not really. "I think you're trying to tell me that you're...the boogeyman?"

A rough laugh. "Close." His hand lifted. The back of his knuckles skimmed down her cheek, and for some crazy reason, she found herself tilting her head into his touch. "I'm saying that I can protect you. Better than any guard your stepfather will hire. Better than any cop. I can do it because I play by my own rules. I don't get afraid. I just get the job done."

A lump rose in her throat. On the second attempt, Madelyn swallowed it down. "Why would you want to help me?"

"Guessing you don't believe it's out of the amazing goodness of my heart?"

She shook her head. "You just told me you weren't a good guy." He'd specifically said that he'd turned into even more of a bastard as he aged.

Smith's hand fell to his side. "What about the idea that I'd be helping for old times' sake? Do you buy that one?"

She did not. "We didn't have a lot of old times together."

"No?"

"No." They'd hardly run in the same crowd. Actually, she hadn't run in any crowd, at all. She'd kept to herself. Never went to the parties or the sports games. *Been so lonely.*

"Then how about this one? How about I just don't like the idea of some sick sonofabitch out there trying to hurt you?"

"That...makes you seem like a good guy." Again, something he'd just told her he wasn't.

"I'm not. That's why you need me. *You* are the good girl. The one who always had the answers in class. The one who didn't go to the parties. Who never stayed out past curfew. The one who played by all the rules."

A tear streaked down her cheek.

"The one who had the good sense not to go out with the asshole who let the snake out during biology lab."

He was trying to stop her tears. To tease her. But another tear slid down her cheek.

His hand flew up and caught the tear. "Why don't we just say it's my occasional good deed and call it done? Even the bad guys can do a good deed every now and then."

Her fingers curled around his wrist. "I'm not who you think I am."

He leaned in even closer. "Then tell me who you are."

"I'm not the good girl." Pain twisted around her. The icy covering that had encased her for so long.

"No?"

"I don't always have the answers." She'd spent too long running and never getting the truth.

"Want some help finding them?"

Yes. The pain twisted more, but instead of feeling the cold, she began to feel heat burning inside of herself. Anger, no, rage for all that she'd lost over the years. Every single thing that she'd had to give up because she'd been told to be careful. To never attract attention. To never get close to anyone.

Because if she got close, those people could get hurt.

Her lashes lowered. "You can protect yourself." She'd never forget seeing him pound her attacker. A brutal show of strength. Savagery. It hadn't scared her.

He hadn't.

"I'd better be able to protect myself or else Uncle Sam wasted a ton of money on my training."

Madelyn peeked up at him. "What exactly did you do during your years in the military?"

"You don't want to know." A muscle jerked along his jaw.

"I absolutely do."

His lips thinned, and Madelyn didn't think he would answer her. Time ticked past. The tension stretched and she was about to just tell Smith to forget it when—

"The dirty work. The dangerous work. I was Special Forces, and I can't give you a whole lot of specifics because most of my missions were classified." His hand pulled away from hers. "Let's just say if you knew everything, you wouldn't want me touching you."

He had no idea what she might want. "You know how to kill."

One eyebrow quirked. "In so many ways."

Her breath shuddered out.

His expression hardened. "I swear to you, I would never hurt you. You don't need to be scared of me."

Is that what he thought? "I'm not." She focused completely on him. "I think you might be exactly what I need."

His forehead crinkled. "Excuse me?"

"You can protect yourself."

"I sure as fuck hope so." His head cocked to the right. "I can also protect you." Deep. Almost rumbling. "But you need to be straight with me. I have to know what I'm facing so I can help you."

She pulled in a deep breath, then let it out slowly. "I did not invite that man to my house. I didn't leave him a key, and I-I certainly did not tell him that I wanted some kind of rough sex."

"That wasn't rough sex. That sonofabitch was there to rape you." Savage. "And I should have killed him."

Madelyn backed up a step.

His sharp gaze noted the retreat. "Sorry." His shoulders rolled back. "Should have warned you that sometimes I can be a little...primitive."

She thought that might be exactly what she needed. "I don't care what the police find on his phone or computer—I didn't send him any messages."

"I believe you."

That simple? How? Why? "I didn't," Madelyn insisted, needing to get this out so she could be completely honest with someone. "Because I sure as hell would not want my first time to be that way."

He was the one to back up. Or, to stagger back. Several steps. *"What?"*

"I think you heard me." She'd spoken very clearly on purpose.

"I think I must be hallucinating right now. How the fuck—why the fuck—*how the fuck—*" Smith sputtered to a stop, seemingly at a loss.

"I don't get close to people." Another truth. "I can't. My mother always warned me again and again that getting close to people would be dangerous."

His dark and stormy eyes narrowed. "Why? Did she think they would hurt you?"

"No, quite the contrary." Madelyn licked dry lips. "She thought I would put them in danger."

"What?" Smith surged toward her. "Why the hell would she think that?"

"Because when I was thirteen years old, I killed my best friend."

CHAPTER SIX

"I don't believe it." Smith couldn't. Wouldn't.
He was staring into her tear-filled, green eyes, and
he knew it was impossible. Not Madelyn. "An
accident," he decided at once. "Those happen,
baby, and you can't blame yourself."

"You don't accidentally get stabbed fifteen
times. That's just not possible." Her words were
wooden, and her expression could only be
described as...*heartbroken*.

Still, he shook his head. "You didn't do it." He
knew evil. He'd seen it up close and personal too
many times. "Explain. Tell me everything."

"I wasn't ever supposed to do that, either.
Don't talk about it. If you don't talk, it didn't
happen. It was someone else. Not you. No one
ever has to know."

The way she said those words...it was as if
Madelyn was repeating instructions or rules.
Things she'd been told before? "I want to know
exactly what happened when you were thirteen
years old."

Madelyn blinked. "I'm really tired.
Maybe...maybe this isn't a good idea."

She was probably crashing from adrenaline and fear. There were bruises on her skin—fucking bruises—and whenever he saw them, Smith just wanted to run back down to the police station and destroy that sonofabitch who'd hurt her.

Stay in control. Stay calm. For her. Because something important was happening here. "You can tell me as little or as much as you like." *But I will get the full story.* He had connections, and she was in danger. So, him, intending to be a bastard and go around her if she didn't tell him all the details herself?

Yep, guilty as charged. But he'd warned her, hadn't he?

She was in danger, something horribly sinister was all around her, and him being his usual bastard self was the best way to keep her safe.

"I got away."

Madelyn's words were so low that he barely heard them. "What?" His arms ached because he wanted to wrap them around her, but he couldn't. Not yet.

"I got away. He took me. I went to sleep in my bedroom a little after eight. With my things all around me. And I woke up someplace else."

Fucking hell.

"My mother was at work. She always worked nights. But, the apartment door was locked. Our dog Molly was down the hall. I went to bed in my room, and I woke up somewhere else."

No, no, no. "Baby..." Gentle, when he was so rarely gentle. "Did he hurt you?"

She blinked, but Smith didn't think Madelyn saw him. "It was dark when I woke up. Pitch black."

Like the freaking elevator?

"That was weird because I had this window in my bedroom, and sunlight always poured through the blinds in the morning. I kept wondering— where's the window? *Why don't I see the light?* And I didn't move at all for a while because I was so confused and scared."

He could hear the echo of fear in her voice.

"After a while, I realized something was wrong with my hands. My fingers felt funny, and I—something was around my wrists. I was trying to figure out why my hands were stuck together when a light turned on. It just flashed on above me. A little light in the ceiling. And I saw that I was in a bed that had a comforter just like mine. And the posters on the walls were just like the ones I'd had but...the room was so small. Tight. No other furniture, just the bed. No windows at all. Just a door. And my hands—my hands felt funny because my wrists had been zip tied together."

Her rasping words broke his heart. Yeah, he had one. For her.

"I tried to open the door, but it was locked. And that was when I noticed a video camera on the wall. Up high, in the corner. I-I pounded on the door, and I screamed and screamed for my mom, but no one came. Not until later. Then *he* came."

Smith had known her for years and had never suspected she carried this horror.

"He brought food to me at some point, and I thought he was a monster." A shake of her head. "He wore a mask and bulky clothes, and I wanted to scream but I'd lost my voice."

Because you'd already screamed so much?

"He told me that he'd watched me for a while. That I was special. That he wanted to take care of me. I just had to be good." Her eyes squeezed closed. "Do you know how tired I am of being good?"

"Then be fucking bad."

Her eyelids flew open.

"I excel at it," Smith assured her, voice gruff. "I can teach you everything you need to know."

She swallowed, the little click of sound almost painful. "Please do," Madelyn whispered. "Because I would like that very much."

His chest ached. No, every part of him ached for her.

"I'd been crying for so long. I was huddled on the bed and crying, I just wanted to get away. I didn't know what had happened, but I didn't want to die in that little room."

How did I not know this? How had he never suspected that she carried this heartache?

"It was soup. That's what he brought to me. Soup. A spoon. I guess he thought that was okay? That a spoon wasn't much of a weapon. But I was thirteen, young but not stupid, and I was afraid that he'd drugged the food. I *had* to have been drugged before. Somehow, at my house, because I should have woken up when he took me—when he moved me." Her gaze hardened. "I should have woken up. I stared at the soup as he told me to eat, as he said that I needed it to *feel better*, and I was afraid if I took even one sip, I wouldn't wake up ever again. I'd stay in that nightmare forever."

Smith had *never* expected this.

"I took the spoon from him. I can still remember how cold it felt in my hand." A ragged breath. "He was telling me how good I was, and I-I jumped at him. I flipped the spoon around, and instead of the rounded end, I drove the sharper edge at the back right toward his eye. I shoved it as hard as I could through the fabric of that mask, and he started screaming. He'd left the door open, and I ran out."

You are my fucking hero.

"That's why I used the toothbrush on that man in my house." She wet her lips. "I knew what kind of damage an attack like that could do to an eye because I'd done it before. I got away once like that, and I thought I could again."

"You *did* get away again."

"Only because you were there. Did I—did I say thank you?"

"You don't need to thank me for any damn thing." *Take her into your arms. Hold her tight. Never let go.*

"I'm glad you were there, Smith. In my house. My bedroom." Her head leaned forward. "I don't want to be a victim again."

"You're not. You're a survivor."

Her lower lip trembled.

"But there's not a damn thing wrong with being a victim." She needed to understand this. "You didn't do anything wrong. The predator is the one who needs to pay." *I will make sure anyone who hurt you pays.* From here on out, Madelyn had her own attack dog at the ready. "Finish your story, baby," he urged her because he could tell she was nearly dead on her feet. "Get it all out." Maybe talking would help her feel better.

It would sure as hell help him to learn more about the bastard he intended to utterly destroy.

Madelyn blinked away her tears.

"You stabbed him in the eye with the spoon." Smith smiled at her. He hoped the sight was reassuring and not scary. He felt scary. Like he wanted to rip and tear and annihilate. "What happened then?"

"He was yelling behind me, telling me to stop, that I'd be sorry. That he'd punish me..."

She lived with this? For years? Damn. Smith didn't have words to comfort her. He *wasn't* the comforting type, but he wished in that moment that he could be, for her.

"I didn't care what he threatened. I ran and ran. It was dark outside, and I just kept running. I ran until my feet bled. Until I didn't think that I had any breath left. I ran and ran, and the headlights of a car hit me. That was when I froze." A shudder. "I can still see those lights sometimes. I thought the car was going to hit me, but it was okay because getting hit by that car had to be better than whatever waited for me in that little room."

He couldn't hold back any longer. Smith grabbed her. Held tight. And knew in that instance that he would never be able to let her go.

Whatever I have to do, I'll do it. She'd never be alone again.

Fuck it.

She was so stiff in his embrace. No, stiff was the wrong description. More like brittle. Fragile. If he held her too tightly, he was afraid she'd shatter apart. With something precious, you always, always had to use care. He would use the utmost care with her. "Baby, you are so amazing."

Her head shook against him. "I'm not. I was terrified. And I couldn't lead the police back to him because I didn't even know where I'd been. And I-I don't think they believed me. My wrists were still zip tied, *but I don't think they believed me*. My mother...she hadn't called the cops yet. It felt like I was with him for forever, but when I got to the police station, dawn hadn't even come yet." A ragged exhale. "I found out my mom believed I'd run away. When she got home and I wasn't there, that was what she thought."

What. The. Hell?

"We'd argued earlier that night. I'd forgotten about that." Even softer. "And she thought I was mad at her."

He stroked her back. "What did you argue about?"

She shivered. "My friend Heather—I wanted to spend the night with her that upcoming weekend, but my mom said no. It was Heather's birthday, and my mom told me that we didn't have enough money for a present, and I couldn't go to the party without a present and I—" Her head angled up so that she stared into his eyes. "I killed Heather. Did I tell you that?"

His heart seemed to be in a million pieces, all tossed down near her feet. "Baby, you need to rest." The remainder of her walk back through hell could wait. Shadows were under her eyes, deepening more with every moment. Her words had started to slur. They'd talked to the police forever. The day had stretched and stretched. And now she was reliving her own nightmare, for him.

Enough.

"It can wait." He scooped her into his arms, all of his plans forgotten. The only thing that mattered was taking care of her.

One of her arms automatically looped behind his neck. "Why don't you care what I did?"

He started for the guest room. Stopped. Turned instead to go to his room. The bed was bigger, more comfortable, and his room offered the best view of the ocean.

"Is it because you've killed, too?" Barely a breath.

Smith tightened his arms around her. "I don't believe you killed her."

"I did." Her head snuggled against him. "And I regret it every single day."

His nostrils flared as he inhaled the jasmine scent that clung to her. She was soft and warm against him, and all he wanted to do was slay every single monster that wanted to hurt her.

"I can walk," Madelyn said, her words slurring a little more.

"I don't care," he returned as he headed into his bedroom. The French doors that led to the balcony were closed and locked, but their floor was so high up that he didn't worry about some threat. No one would be bursting inside. This was the penthouse. You'd have to be freaking

Spiderman to get access to their level from the exterior of the building.

He took her to the bed. Lowered her carefully until her feet touched the floor. Then Smith reached around Madelyn and tugged back the covers. It was a king bed, so there would be plenty of room.

You're not getting in there with her, jackass. You are being a gentleman. Or, pretending to be one, anyway.

"I'm not getting undressed."

He sent her a faint smile. "You don't have to. How about you just take off the heels?"

She kicked them aside.

His hands closed around her waist and lifted her up. He tucked her beneath the covers, then pulled the comforter up to her chest. He had never—not once in his entire life—tucked someone into bed before.

Sure, he'd fantasized about getting Madelyn into bed a million times, but that fantasy had never gone quite like this.

Smith reached over and turned out the light on the nightstand. Then he just had to brush back a lock of hair that had fallen over her cheek.

"He took Heather. When I was still trying to convince the cops and my mother that everything was real, that I hadn't run away, he took her. And he called the police station. And he told everyone that because I was bad, he had to hurt me."

Smith could not look away from her gaze.

"I heard her screaming. We all did." Madelyn licked her lips. "Did I tell you that she was my best friend? My best friend in the whole world. I tried to make my mom understand—Heather wouldn't have cared that I didn't bring her a present. She just wanted me at her party, and I wanted to be there." A tear leaked down her cheek. "But I was bad, and I ran, and he took her because of me. He took the person I loved most. My very best friend, and we all heard her die."

Smith curled protectively over her, hurting so much for his Madelyn. "That wasn't your fault."

"If I'd been good, she wouldn't have died." Soft. Another tear. "I've spent all the years since then trying to be good. He's been out there, I know he's been out there..."

In an instant, Smith jerked upright. "You're telling me they never caught the sonofabitch?" *I will rip him apart.*

Her lashes swept down. The sun was setting outside, so faint rays poured through the glass of the French doors.

"He's always been out there, and I had to be good. And I couldn't get close..." Slurred. Soft.

But Smith had a very bad feeling that he knew what she'd been trying to say. *I couldn't get close to anyone.* Because her best friend had been killed. Because in high school, he'd never seen Madelyn mixing and hanging out on the weekends with anyone. Because she was a *virgin.* Fucking fuck.

Madelyn had been too afraid someone else would get hurt because of her. She'd stopped living and that shit was not going to last on his watch.

Bending over her once more, Smith brushed a kiss over her cheek. "Sleep, Madelyn. You're safe, and you're going to stay safe." He had to clear his throat because his voice had come out too gruff.

They never caught him.

Smith wanted to stay right there. To sit on the bed and watch over Madelyn in case she had a bad dream. She needed to know that she was safe. Would be safe, always, under his watch.

But he also had work to do—*I need to find this bastard.* Because Smith didn't like the growing fear that Madelyn's past had come back with a vengeance. He rose. Headed for the door. That door would be staying open in case she called out for him. Smith wanted to be able to hear her and—

"It's not my name."

His shoulders stiffened.

"Madelyn. I'm not her." Rasped.

He spun around, but her eyes were closed. Her chest rose and fell.

I'm not her.

CHAPTER SEVEN

"It wasn't her."

Andrew Bryson shifted in the God-awful chair. The wooden seat was uncomfortable as fuck. "Look, I think I need to go back to the hospital. That big bastard really messed me up." His face hurt like a mother. He'd looked at himself in the mirror. Black and blue. Bloody. And his eye—his eye looked bright red, the vessels busted or some shit. "I'm pretty sure I should be in an ER right now." He jerked a hand to indicate the small, tight interrogation room. "Not here."

"We looked through your social media records. Your texts. Your life. We know that you're a convicted sex predator."

"No!" Andrew surged forward, sending the chair tipping toward the table on its front legs. "That's just because Brooke was fourteen. I was eighteen. Like, I didn't know, okay? She looked so much older. That shit isn't on me."

"It actually *is* on you. On your records." Detective Campbell sat before him, and her dark eyes never wavered from his face. "Just as the break-in at Madelyn Lake's house will be on you.

Just as the attack will be *on you*. Her attempted rape. The—"

"She *asked* me to do all that—"

"And I say to you again, it wasn't her. Our PD actually has some very good cyber guys. In fact, we're top in the state. That wasn't her you were talking with online. Madelyn Lake—the real Madelyn Lake—doesn't have a personal social media presence. Her company has a few profiles, but her assistant runs them. They are all only about her authentication business. The person you were communicating with—the account was literally created the day first contact was made with you."

"I...No." He shook his head. "She reached out to me. Left the key for *me*."

"We understand that you are involved in some very specifically geared sexual fetish groups."

He flushed. Even beneath the bruises, he could feel the burn on his skin. "She was in there, too. She reached out to—"

"We were able to determine that the person who set up Madelyn's fake accounts was actually based in Chicago."

He blinked.

"Did you know that you can track things like that? No? You can. Easy enough to do. Especially when you have the cooperation of the site or group's owner. We had cooperation. Complete, eager cooperation."

"Is that shit legal? I thought—thought that was all private." He hoped like hell it was because he'd shared some crazy-ass pics on some of those groups.

"Nothing on the Internet is ever truly private. You should know that."

Fuck me.

"When you broke into her house, Madelyn fought you."

"Yes." A hiss.

"She kept telling you to stop. Screaming for help."

"Yes." Oh, God. *God.* Shit. Shit. His hand raked through his hair. "But she told me in her messages, said to ignore whatever she..." *Ignore whatever I say. Don't stop.* His eyes widened. *"Fuck me."*

"Yes. Indeed." Detective Campbell pursed her lips. "Maybe you're not aware of exactly who Madelyn's family is, but I am. Her stepfather has incredible reach. Such reach that he can get *anyone* to cooperate with him."

Wait...was she saying that was how they'd gotten the info on the groups he used? That wasn't legal, was it? He didn't know. He didn't *know.* He—

Breaking into a house isn't legal. If she didn't send me those notes, then what I did—

Andrew could see his whole life rotting away. "I need a lawyer!" He should have asked for one sooner. Isn't that what always happened in TV shows? You got a lawyer. The lawyer helped you. When he'd had that trouble with Brooke, his lawyer had cut a deal, so he hadn't served any time. Just gotten on some registry. *I need a lawyer*. "I'm being set up! I need a lawyer, right now! I'm not saying another word without one."

Nodding, she rose. Her short nails tapped against the top of the table. "Asking for a lawyer *now* doesn't magically delete the confession you just made. Your rights were fully read to you. You confessed to breaking into Madelyn's house and ignoring her cries to stop." The detective sent him a cold smile. "Thanks for the chat." She turned and made her way to the door.

"No!" Andrew leapt to his feet. "No, I didn't—" He lunged forward.

But he'd forgotten the uniformed cop who stood behind him. The cop grabbed him and slammed him onto the table. His already bruised face screamed at the contact.

"Taking you back to holding," the cop grunted. Then, his face came close to Andrew's ear. "And Madelyn's dad sends his regards..."

What? *What?* "No!" Andrew screamed.

But he was already being hauled away.

And my life is rotting away. Falling apart before my eyes...

***

"Memphis, I have a case." Smith stood on the balcony and watched the waters churn below as he held his phone to his ear.

"Well, well. Someone does a little side work for the group and suddenly wants to go all-in," Memphis Camden rumbled back to him. "Told you it was addictive, didn't I? Once you're in, you don't turn back."

"It's personal."

"Your dad. Right. I wondered when you would want to focus on—"

"No, nothing about him." He had revealed way too much to Memphis during their last chat. They'd been at a speakeasy in Savannah, and Smith knew he'd been too chatty. The bourbon had just been too damn good, and as for Memphis—hell, the former bounty hunter was just someone Smith had instantly connected with. Maybe because he saw the same old hell in Memphis's eyes that Smith knew inhabited his own gaze. "I have a..." He looked over his shoulder. He needed to get back inside. If Madelyn woke, he had to be close. "I have a friend who needs our help."

"Okay, look, you know we have a whole back log of cases. Enough cases to last for *years*. We're not supposed to play favorites. That's not how we work—"

"She was attacked today. And I think last night, too. I'm worried it's all tied up to her past, and I need your resources. *I need* the Ice Breakers on this one." One hand grasped the top of the railing in a steely grip. "The bastard who kidnapped her when she was thirteen years old was never caught. I need to know if he's still out there. I need to know if he's gunning for her."

Silence.

The waves crashed below.

"Thirteen?" Memphis repeated.

"Yes. The freak kidnapped her, then killed her best friend when she got away."

"*We're taking the case.*"

He'd thought that might be the response.

"Give me her name. Give me the town. Give me some starting point, and I will get every piece of evidence the cops had on the case, and the team will pour over it."

"Yeah, that might be a little tricky." He had to get back inside. Smith turned away from the waves and headed into the condo. Carefully, he closed the doors behind him, the faint snick of the lock seeming too loud. "She changed her name."

"Witness protection." A fast response from Memphis. "I've worked those cases before. I have a few friends who are US Marshals. I will reach out to them and see what shakes loose."

"I'm not sure she is in witness protection." It made sense for her to be but... "She's sleeping. I'll find out when she wakes up."

More silence.

"I can practically *hear* your thoughts," Smith groused. "You got something to say, spit shout out."

"It's harder when you care." A careful response. "You led by saying this one is personal. And, man, I get it. I do. *I have been there.* How the hell do you think I met my Eliza? But when it's personal, that means you will lose control. That's dangerous. For her and for you."

"If you think I'm just gonna step back and let someone else take over her protection—"

"Is that what you're doing right now? Protecting her?"

He cast a look around his condo. "Her home wasn't safe. Someone made a copy of her backdoor key. She's staying with me for the foreseeable future because my place has state of the art security. It's on the top level of the building, and security patrols the full facility on a reliable rotation. Surveillance cameras are everywhere, and no one will be getting in without my knowledge."

"So, that means you *are* protecting her?"

"I want to find the bastard from her past."

"Sometimes, we don't find them. No matter how badly we may want to."

"Yeah, but the Ice Breakers have better odds than anyone else." He'd bet on them any day of the week.

"For this to work, we need her cooperation. That means her real name. The city where this happened, and her sharing every single detail that she remembers about what happened to her."

Sure. Nothing like a walk into her own hell again. "I will talk to her. But with her cooperation or without it, I want to find this bastard."

A whistle from Memphis. "Damn, man, see, this is what I was warning you about. When it's personal, you go off book. I did this same shit. It is *dangerous*."

"No, I'm dangerous. And anyone coming for Madelyn needs to realize that." He sucked in a breath. "Can I count on the team?"

"You can."

Hell, yes. "Then we will be talking again soon." He hung up. Paced back to his bedroom to check on Madelyn.

Still asleep. Still looking far too vulnerable and delicate. He found himself edging closer to the bed. To her. His hand lifted, and his fingers skimmed lightly over her cheek.

After all these years, he'd finally gotten Madelyn Lake in his bed. And all he wanted to do? *Protect her. Eliminate every threat.*

He pulled his hand from her.

She rolled on the bed, and her right arm rose to tuck under her chin. There were faint bruises on her arm. Little blue and blackish spots that resembled fingertips. Smith's jaw clenched as he stared at them.

Slowly, quietly, he backed out of the bedroom. Then, when he was clear, Smith pulled out his phone once more. He tapped the screen and a moment later, he heard a ringtone in his ear. He knew Aiden would pick up. His buddy always did. *Aiden will have my back.* More importantly, *Aiden will have hers.*

"What in the hell is going on?" Aiden demanded by way of greeting. "I'm hearing that Madelyn was attacked in her home? Who attacked her? Why? What is going on?"

Vaguely, he'd wondered who had tipped off Aidan. *And who the hell tipped off her stepdad?* Smith had never gotten to the bottom of that mystery. He would, though. "She's safe. Got her in my place."

"Figured as much. Dammit, Smith, who is after her?"

"The guy who attacked her is sitting in a jail cell right now." But Smith didn't know how long he'd be there. If some fool judge set a low bond, the man could be in the wind. "I need to have a one-on-one talk with him. *Now.*"

"Uh, you get that's not going to happen, right? If the jerk is in jail—"

"He's in holding at the station, and some cops there owe me favors."

"Of course, everyone tends to owe you favors."

Not always. Sometimes, he pissed off a whole lot of people, and they just held grudges against him. For now, he'd focus on those who owed him. "I need someone I can trust staying at my place with Madelyn. She's exhausted, so she crashed. Can you come over here and stay with her until I get back?" Yes, he'd just asked his freaking billionaire buddy to babysit, and he knew even before Aiden replied that his friend would say—

"On the way. I'll bring Tony with me. That way, if Madelyn wakes up, she'll have another woman in the house, too. Might make her feel better, you know?"

Probably would. Aiden's obsession in life was his Tony. He'd fallen hard and fast for the so-called doctor of the dead. Tony was another member of the Ice Breakers, and Aiden had first met her when he'd wanted to unravel the mystery of his twin brother's disappearance.

Tony had helped Aiden get the truth he so desperately needed, but along the way, Aiden had fallen hard for his doc.

"I'm gonna want the Ice Breakers on this one," Smith told his friend. "So, hell, yes, bring Tony."

"The Ice Breakers?" Surprise rippled through Aiden's voice. "But I thought you just said her attacker was in custody."

"There's one hell of a lot more involved in this."

"Smith, I *warned* you. You can't go digging up her past—"

"Madelyn wants my help. More than that, she needs it. Me and the Ice Breakers. I already talked to Memphis. This is happening. Madelyn will not be looking over her shoulder for the rest of her life. She's not going to be terrified every single day."

A swift inhalation of air. "Like that, is it?"

"It won't be like that for much longer." A guarantee. "And step one is for me to get down to that police station and have a one-on-one chat with the perp in lockup. How fast can you get here?"

"Buddy, I'm already in the car..."

***

"This didn't happen," the grizzled cop told Smith as the guy unlocked the heavy door that led back to holding. "You didn't see me. I didn't see you."

"I know the drill," Smith assured him.

"No cameras are back here. Going through an upgrade right now, and the new tech won't be installed for another week." But sweat still slickened the man's forehead. "So no video will exist. You get, though, that this prick can tell the world about you? He goes shouting to some public defender, and you could get his case tossed. You want that?" His body shifted so that he blocked the entrance to the long corridor. "I heard

Campbell got a confession already. We don't want anything screwing this up. I don't need shit like that on my conscience."

Smith tried his harmless smile. "Your conscience will be clear. This conversation will have never happened."

The cop didn't look convinced, but he did move out of Smith's way. Without another word, Smith marched down the narrow corridor. He already knew that Andrew Bryson was the only prisoner in this area. He headed past the first two empty cells and locked his eyes on the one at the end of the hallway. But as Smith drew closer...

He caught sight of Andrew in the cell. Only—

"Get help in here!" Smith bellowed. *"Now!"* He ran for the cell door and his fingers closed around the bars. "Andrew! *Andrew Bryson!"*

The prisoner didn't stir. He remained slumped partially on his knees near the edge of the bunkbeds, with a sheet wrapped around his neck and tied to the top rung on the upper bunk. His body sagged toward the floor, a seemingly dead weight as his head hung forward.

"Fuck! Andrew!" The door was locked tightly.

The cop who'd let Smith inside sounded an alarm. The blaring echoed around Smith as more cops came running. Smith was shoved to the side as the cops unlocked the door and filed inside the cell. They grabbed for Andrew, yanking the bedsheet loose, and lowering him to the floor.

The man didn't move.

There were yells for a medic. One cop was feeling for a pulse on Andrew's wrist. But Smith could tell by the unnatural color of Andrew's skin that it was too late. Andrew's limbs flopped around, and even as the cops tried to help the bastard, Smith knew they were working in vain.

"What in the hell are you doing here?" A snarl from behind Smith.

He turned to see Detective Audrey Campbell glaring at him.

"Finding a dead man," Smith returned. "That's what the hell I'm doing." A dead man, and a dead end. *Because the dead can't give me any leads.*

A dead man could tell him nothing.

Sonofabitch. "Better questions," Smith snapped. "Where in the hell were you? Where were the guards? Why is he *dead?*"

CHAPTER EIGHT

"She's still dead to the world," Aiden announced when Smith walked through the doorway at the condo hours later. "But, damn, man, that took you one hell of a long time. I was starting to think I needed to send in the cavalry."

"He's dead."

Aiden rose from the couch. Tony still lingered on the cushions, her dark hair in a long braid, though several strands had come loose to tease the sides of her face.

"Who's dead?" Aiden demanded. He took a hard step toward Smith. "What have you done?"

A mocking laugh slid from Smith. Damn but he was tired. Bone tired. Soul-deep tired. "Funny. That's what the detective asked me, too. During our lovely interrogation session that never seemed to end. Don't really see how I could be responsible, though, considering that I had a cop at my back from the moment I entered the holding area. So at least I had that alibi going for me. Though why you need an alibi on a suicide is beyond me."

Aiden looked back at Tony. A little furrow appeared between her brows. After a moment, they both turned their heads and peered at Smith. "I don't follow," Aiden said.

"I could use a drink." A very, very strong one. He marched for the bar. Reached for the whiskey, but stopped when he caught sight of his reflection in the mirror above the bar. Jeez, he looked like the grim reaper. Dark stubble covered his jaw. Dark shadows lined his eyes. His expression was cold and sinister, and, sure, fine, maybe he did look like someone who was ready to kill.

Campbell knows I wanted Andrew Bryson dead. "Guy beat me to the punch." He grabbed the whiskey. Poured the amber liquid into a shot glass, then drank it, feeling the burn all the way down his throat. "Went in to see the SOB and found Andrew Bryson with a sheet wrapped around his throat. He'd tied one end to the top of the bunk bed and shoved himself forward until it was tight around his neck. The bastard strangled himself, and I was the one to find the body."

A sharp inhale came from the right. The doorway that led to his bedroom. For a moment, Smith's eyes squeezed shut. *Fuck.* Way to break the news. Slowly, he lowered the glass until it clinked when it hit the top of the bar. Squaring his shoulders, he turned to the right.

Madelyn stared back at him, with her eyes wide and her lips slightly parted.

"Probably could have said all of that with a great deal more tact," Smith decided. "If I'd known you were there, I would have."

"I heard your voice."

"Sorry to wake you." That felt like a dumb thing to say.

She shook her head. Her gaze remained locked on him. "The man who attacked me—*he's dead?*"

"Yes. Knew it as soon as I saw him. Skin had lost all color. The cops tried to help him, but there wasn't anything to be done."

Tony cleared her throat.

His gaze dipped toward her.

She rose to her feet and stood beside Aiden. "Pallor mortis," Tony explained softly. "Typically, that's the first thing you notice with the dead. Within fifteen to twenty minutes of dying, the body starts to pale." A roll of one shoulder. "Pallor mortis," she said again. "It's because the blood stops traveling its way through the body. Blood isn't going through the capillaries any longer, and it's a change that you notice fast." Biting her lower lip, she glanced toward a seemingly frozen Madelyn. "We've met in passing a few times," Tony reminded her. "And I know you were at the recent party." A wince. "The party *before* the unfortunate situation in the elevator."

"The elevator situation is why she's here," Smith rumbled as he crossed to stand in front of Madelyn. "The elevator, the attack at Madelyn's house..."

"He's *dead?*" Madelyn shook her head. "But...I don't understand." Her hair was tousled. A beautiful tangle around her shoulders. She still had her shoes off, so she appeared even smaller than normal. And still seemed heartbreakingly fragile to him.

"The cops are saying it's a suicide." He wasn't going to keep anything from her. "Detective

Campbell said Bryson confessed to breaking into your house and attacking you, but the jerk still swore that you had told him to do everything."

She shook her head—

"Baby, I know," he assured her, voice gruff. "The cops know, too. The accounts were fake. Set up the day the guy first received contact. Detective Campbell told Bryson that news, too, and she thinks the guilt must have gotten to him. Bryson realized he was facing serious jail time, realized what he'd done to an innocent woman, and he just couldn't live with his actions."

Pain flashed in her eyes. "How am I supposed to feel about that?"

He had no fucking clue.

"I hated him. I didn't know him. I *hated* him," she said again, voice fierce, "but he was used. I was used. Someone else set it up, and now that—that Andrew Bryson person is dead. *How am I supposed to feel?*"

"Feel any way you want," Tony said as she strode closer to them. "There isn't a wrong or right way to be."

Madelyn's head whipped toward her.

"You want to feel glad that he's dead? Then feel glad. Someone hurt you. Someone tried to do something very bad to you. You can feel glad that he won't ever hurt you again." Tony's tone remained calm. Careful. "You want to feel sorry for him? Because his life is lost now? Fine. Feel sorry for him. You don't have to just feel one thing. You can feel a million things all at once, and *every* feeling is okay."

Smith heard the swift inhale of Madelyn's breath. "I thought you were a forensic anthropologist. You sound like a psychiatrist."

"I've done my share of psych classes over the years, but I'm not speaking as any kind of professional. I'm just speaking as someone who has walked through hell before herself." Tony's dark gaze held Madelyn's. "We can feel anything we want."

Madelyn's shoulders shuddered, then squared. "Thank you."

Smith hadn't known how to comfort Madelyn, but Tony had. He turned his head toward Tony and mouthed, "*I owe you.*"

She shook her head. But her gaze had turned pensive. "You're saying this guy committed suicide in holding? No other prisoners tried to call out for help when they saw what was happening?"

"He was alone," Smith replied. He needed to reach out to Madelyn. The urge to touch her was too strong. He caught her hand in his. Threaded his fingers with hers. A big part of him expected her to immediately pull her hand away. She didn't. Instead, Madelyn slowly exhaled.

"No other prisoners were in that holding area." Smith turned his body a bit so that he could see everyone clearly. "And the security cameras had been taken offline for a system upgrade. No cops were back there at the time, so no one even realized what had happened until I went in for my, ah, chat with him."

"Why were you chatting with him?" Madelyn wanted to know.

He was about to get to that part. Actually, Smith would have launched right to that part, but he'd just caught the hooded look exchanged between Aiden and Tony. "What?"

Aiden scratched his jaw. "Convenient, isn't it?"

Smith didn't find much to be convenient about any of this mess.

"I'd really like to see that body." Tony cocked her head to the right. "I know you think that he's a dead end now—literally—but this is where I shine. I know the police chief down here. I've worked with her a few times before. I can give her a call and see if I can get access."

Smith's gut tightened. "The cops said it's a suicide."

"Very fast conclusion, one they shouldn't have made already. They need to know the exact time of death. They need an expert to look at the body." Tony's tone remained calm and steady. "You said he was pale, but was his body stiff? Had rigor mortis set in?"

"No. I remember..." Jeez, he hated saying this right in front of Madelyn. "His arms flopped when the cops cut the sheet from the top bunk. There wasn't a whole lot of stiffness at all."

"Did you touch the body?" Tony pressed. "Was it cool? Usually, we'll have a temp decrease of about 1.5 degrees Fahrenheit each hour after death."

"Ahem." Aiden curled his arm around Tony's shoulders. He also nudged his head toward Madelyn.

Smith looked at Madelyn, too. Hell, she had gone nearly as pale as a ghost herself. "I didn't touch the body." He wanted to wrap his arm around her like Aiden had just done with Tony. Pull Madelyn close. Warm her. "The cops didn't let me inside the cage. Campbell had me escorted out, then she grilled me forever before admitting what she'd already learned about Bryson. She was pissed that I'd ever been let back into the holding area."

"I want to see that body." Tony tucked a stray lock of hair behind her ear. "And I want to know what else the Ice Breakers can do to help." Her focus remained on Madelyn. "I've been to hell, too," she said again. "And you have to remember that you got out. That's what matters."

Madelyn's eyelashes flickered. "The Ice Breakers?"

"We should have this conversation at a time that isn't 3 a.m.," Smith announced. There had already been more than enough sprung on Madelyn. He wanted her back in bed, and he wanted to be in that bed with her.

Not happening.

But...this wasn't the time. Not the time at all to tell Madelyn that he'd already called in people to rip her life apart. In the morning, after a big breakfast and a giant cup of coffee, then he could ease into the news with her.

"I know who the Ice Breakers are." There was nothing sleepy about Madelyn's voice. "I know you're one of them," she said to Tony. "That's how you and Aiden met." Her brows lowered as her head swung toward Smith. "You're getting the Ice Breakers to take my case?"

This was not gonna be a good three a.m. talk. He'd already started with the suicide announcement, and now he was jumping into how he was about to rip open her life. He'd be lucky if she didn't take a swing at him. "Don't be mad..." *Right. Fuck.* "Ah, I have the best intentions..." *Double fuck.* "I want to help." *Screw it.* "I don't want you pretending to be someone else for the rest of your life. I don't want you looking over your shoulder. I want to know what happened to that bastard who took you when you were a kid because you need some peace. Please, baby, let me—let us all—try to give you that. Let us help you. Let us find him and let us stop—"

Madelyn threw her arms around him. Her body smashed to his, and she held him as if she never, ever wanted to let go.

His own arms hung in the air, just for a moment. Then he curled them around her. And he held her as if he never, ever wanted to let go. *Because I don't.*

"Everyone else wanted me to act like it didn't happen." Mumbled from Madelyn. Almost feverish. "It had to be forgotten. '*Move on. Don't get close. Don't talk about it.*'"

"I want to find him." There was danger around her, and his gut said that danger was tied to her past. She wasn't ever going to be truly free, not until the nightmare was over for her. "You're not mad?" Because, yep, he could be an overstepping and dominating asshole some days. Most days. This day in particular.

But Madelyn eased away so that she could peer up at him. "You're the first person to help me. Smith, I'm not mad. I could absolutely kiss you right now."

"*Okay*." An oddly loud throat clearing came from Aiden. "I think that's our cue to leave, sweetheart," he said to Tony. "How about we pick things up at a normal hour? Maybe after everyone has gotten a good night's sleep and we can all focus better?"

Smith stared into Madelyn's green gaze and felt completely and utterly focused.

"Talk soon, Smith. *Soon*," Aiden emphasized.

Yes, soon. Sure.

"But I want to hear more about the body," Tony protested.

"Yes, love of my life, I know you do, but that can wait until morning. I think those two need some time alone." Aiden ushered her toward the door. After throwing a wave at Smith, he left with Tony and pulled the door shut behind them.

Madelyn was still hugging him. She seemed to realize that fact at the same moment he did. "I—" Flushing, Madelyn eased back.

Expected, but still damn disappointing. "I'll lock up and make sure the alarm is set again." Smith headed across the room, aware of the uncomfortable bulge in his pants. As close as she'd been to him, she must have felt it, too. After her day, was there any wonder she'd jerked away?

He punched in the alarm code. Stared at the small screen. "Two things. One, you never said anything to the cops about the alarm going off at your place. I know you have a system, I saw it. Did you not have it on?" Wouldn't be odd if she hadn't. Most people didn't keep their alarms on during the day. But Madelyn wasn't most people.

"It was on. I always turn it on when I'm sleeping or in the shower or when I might be doing something that would allow a person to catch me off guard."

He turned toward her. Propped one shoulder against the wall. "So he must have disarmed it. Didn't just have a key to your house. Bryson had the alarm codes, too."

She wrapped her arms around her stomach. "You really saw his body? He's not going to come after me again?"

"Bryson won't." *But the SOB who fed him all the info? Maybe. Probably.* Dammit. "We need to know who gave Bryson intel on you."

Madelyn rocked forward. "You think it's the person from my past because—what? Because even I couldn't have the horrible luck of getting two psychos locked on me?"

"Because I think the elevator was a deliberate play into your fears. You told me that when you were a kid, you were locked in a small room and trapped in the dark."

A jerky nod.

"When you were trapped in the elevator, it made you remember that time."

"All the fear came flooding back," Madelyn admitted. "But, you distracted me. You helped to keep the fear at bay."

I will always keep that fear at bay. "You said he had zip ties around your hands when you were a kid."

Another jerky nod from Madelyn.

"I don't know if you saw them, but when I was patting Bryson down at your place, the bastard had zip ties on him."

Her lower lip quivered, just a moment, before she pressed both of her lips together.

"Two recent attacks on you. Both that link to your past. Potentially to the sonofabitch who took you so long ago. It's a possibility we can't overlook. The Ice Breakers typically investigate cold cases, but I'm afraid yours is very much heating up."

"Why?" The question seemed torn from her. "After all of this time, why now?"

"Maybe he just found you again." *Or maybe he's been watching you for a long time.* Smith didn't want to get into all of the reasons and dark suspicions right now. "Talking in the morning is the best idea. We're both dead on our feet. We should—"

Her eyes widened in something like horror. "You didn't get to sleep." Madelyn bounded forward. Reached out to him, but jerked her hand back before making contact. "I took your bed. I'm sorry. I don't even remember going in there. I was just suddenly so tired and I..." Her hand pushed back a thick tangle of her hair. "I must have gone to the wrong room. I'm sorry."

He didn't like her apologies. At all. "I carried you in there. You don't need to tell me that you're sorry. That bed is more comfortable, and I wanted you to rest in there." He had no clue if the bed was more comfortable. *I wanted you in my bed.*

"You—oh. Ahem, thank you."

His teeth snapped together. He wanted her gratitude even less than he wanted her apologies. Maybe he should be clear on that. "You don't need to kiss me because you're grateful to me," he gritted out. He could still hear her saying... *I could kiss you...*

Her amazing eyes widened.

"You don't need to thank me in any way," Smith clarified.

"But you're helping me. I would think that some gratitude would be expected."

"I don't expect it. I don't want it."

She flinched.

Damn. That had sounded harsh. "We should get to point two."

"I don't follow. Like, at all."

He'd originally said he had two points to cover. The first had been that he wanted to know about her alarm. But yeah, he'd definitely strayed from his list. Time to get back to his second point. It was best to just get it out of the way now. "What happened in the elevator won't happen again." There. Done. She should feel better. Safer.

Madelyn blinked.

Silence stretched.

He should say more. Smith struggled desperately to fill the awkward quiet in the room. "I didn't know about your situation."

"My situation," Madelyn repeated. Her hands were loose at her sides.

"If I had, you can rest assured, I would never have touched you."

Her chest heaved with her fast breaths. "Just what every woman wants to hear."

He actually *had* thought she might want to hear those words. Helpless, he stalked toward her.

Madelyn didn't back up. She did glare at him. "You think I'm damaged goods?"

"What?" Shocked, Smith shook his head. "That's the exact opposite of what I think." He thought she might be the most precious thing in his world, and he was trying his best to handle her with kid gloves. Only he'd never used kid gloves in his life until this very moment. "You're a virgin."

"Yes. Not like it's some virus you're going to catch from me. You won't touch me and automatically become one yourself. I'm pretty sure you're way past that point."

His eyes narrowed. "What the hell is that supposed to mean?"

She stepped toward him and stabbed him in the chest with her index finger. "It means you don't need to put up warning signs for me to stay away from you. I *get* that I come with baggage. I knew it would probably scare you if you found out the truth. Smith, the one-night-stand king, would hardly want to get tangled up with someone like me."

"I'm not a freaking one-night-stand king." His brows climbed. "I thought you didn't listen to gossip about me." Because that shit had been circulated in high school. It had been wrong then, and it was even more wrong now.

Her nose popped higher into the air. "I won't try to seduce you, don't worry." She snatched her hand back. "When I said that bit about kissing you a few moments ago, I was—I was just—"

"Feeling grateful, I know, but when you felt my dick shoving against you during that enthusiastic hug, I wasn't feeling grateful." Just so they were extra clear. He very much felt they weren't on the same page. Time to get there.

Her lips parted. Her little tongue darted out to lick quickly over her lower lip. "Excuse me?"

"You had to feel it. I want you. *That's* the point I was trying to make. I wanted you when we were teens. I want you now. I don't think you're damaged." *He* was the damaged one. In so many ways. Which was why he shouldn't have ever touched her. "You need someone who knows kindness and patience. Someone who doesn't make you come in a dark elevator."

Her hand lifted, and she...wait, was she fanning herself?

"Warm in here," Madelyn muttered.

"You went through an attack in your home. In a place where you should have been completely safe. The last thing you need is me getting turned on when you just give me a freaking *gratitude* hug. See, that's a problem I have."

She fanned a little faster.

"I want you, but I am not the lover you need. Hell, not that you *need* a lover. After your attack, you probably do *not* want someone's hands on you." He was completely mucking this up. Maybe he should blame that on lack of sleep? Finding a dead man? An adrenaline crash? "I'm not easy and slow. I'm rough. Demanding. Virgins need care. Just know...I will keep my hands the fuck off you."

She blinked.

"You don't have to worry about any sexual pressure from me. I'm sorry for what you went through today." Oh, wait, shit, technically it had been yesterday since it was three a.m., right? "But you can rest easy with me. I'll keep you safe, and I'll be sure to keep my damn dick away from you."

Madelyn's expression was completely unreadable.

"We should go to bed." Rumbly. He had no idea what else to say. "Separately. You take any room you want. Just know you're safe, and I'll be close if you need me."

Madelyn made no move toward any of the bedrooms, but her left foot did start tapping against the floor.

He looked at the tapping foot—freaking adorable toes—then back up at her face.

"Is it my turn?" Madelyn asked sweetly.

She wanted a turn? She could have whatever she wanted. "Knock yourself out."

"Great. Fabulous. Point one. What occurred between us in the elevator was the best thing to happen to me in *months*. You're not the first man to touch me. This may shock you to your bad-boy bones, but I have tried being intimate with others."

Fucking sonsofbitches.

"They've touched me. I've touched them."

Sonsof—

"I didn't get off with them. I got off with you. I was finally able to let go with *you*. And maybe it's because you weren't all gentle and patient. Maybe you didn't treat me like I was too delicate to touch. Maybe it's because you touched me like

I was the one thing that you wanted most in the world, and I responded back to you that way—like you were the one person I wanted most, too."

His dick was about to bust out of his pants. *Like you were the one person I wanted most, too.* This conversational reveal was not going to help his body settle the hell down. "Ah, Maddie..."

"*Madelyn.* And on point two, I don't remember telling you to keep your dick away from me."

Smith could not breathe. He realized that she'd also been right. It was oddly hot in that condo. Stuffy. Maybe the air conditioning had shut off.

"Do I want to jump your bones and have sex right now? No, I don't because you were right—I am shaken by that attack. More than shaken. It scared the hell out of me." She swung away from him. Took two fast steps toward *his* bedroom. Then stopped. "Want to know one crazy thought that kept rushing through my head when it was happening?"

He wanted to know every single thought in her head. Madelyn had been a mystery to him for far too long.

"*I don't want my first time to be like this.*" She looked back at him. "I kept thinking that because I was afraid of what he was going to do to me. I'd been so careful and followed all the rules. I didn't let anyone get close because getting close to me is *dangerous.*"

"No, baby, it's—"

"I followed the rules," Madelyn continued doggedly. "And I did *not* want pain and terror for my first time. I wanted you. I wanted to only care about pleasure and to feel safe with my partner. I was afraid I would never have that. I was afraid that would be taken away from me."

He surged toward her, helpless.

"Someone is playing a game with me."

Yes, he knew it.

"That person is going to keep playing."

"I'll stop the sonofabitch." A guttural vow. "Let me and the Ice Breakers loose. Let us hunt him." She needed this. "Yes, we will dig up the past, but it needs to come to the surface. You don't have closure. For years, you've just been running and hiding, and it's time to stop."

She turned to fully face him. "Being close to me will be dangerous for you."

"Told you before, *you* aren't the danger." But if she wanted to keep holding onto that twisted illusion... "Want the truth? I don't give a shit either way. I like danger." He sent her a reckless smile. "Makes me feel alive. If a former special forces guy can't handle some piece of shit who likes to hurt and scare the innocent, then who the hell can?"

Her gaze searched his. Time stretched. And then... "If you're in, so am I. All the way. I *want* this over. And like I told you before..." Her hands fisted. "No one else offered to help me find him. Just you."

I want to be the first on so many things with you. Nope, no, no way. Not saying that. And not saying...*Baby, no one should have a first time that is about pain and fear. You should only know pleasure*. Even though that was exactly what he thought.

"If it's okay with you, I'd like to go back to your bedroom. I, just, ah…" Her hands unclenched. Then fisted. "You were right. The bed is really comfortable."

"Have at it."

She swung toward the door. Took another step, then stopped once again. "I feel like a total bitch for taking your bed."

"That's one thing you could never be."

"It's big enough for two. More than big enough. You can stay on one side, and I could sleep on the other."

Smith wished he could see her face. "You think that's a good idea?"

Her head tipped forward. "I lied."

About what?

"I didn't wake up because I heard voices. I woke up because I had a nightmare. I was terrified, and the first thing I did—I reached for you."

And I wasn't there. "That bed is plenty big enough for two. You're right. And it's the most comfortable one in the condo. Doesn't make sense for either of us to use anything else."

Her shoulders sagged as she headed into the darkened bedroom. He followed her and saw that the room wasn't completely dark, because the bedside lamp was on. She slid onto the right side of the bed and pulled the covers up to her chin.

She hadn't taken off her clothes and if that was the way Madelyn wanted to sleep, fine by him. But, was he supposed to do the same thing?

He usually slept naked, but Smith didn't think she'd appreciate that at the moment. After a brief hesitation, he grabbed a pair of boxers and headed for the bathroom. He needed to wash off the stench of the jail.

Five minutes later, he walked back into the bedroom. Back to a deeper darkness. The lamp was off, but his eyes adjusted quickly so that he could see the soft curve that was Madelyn beneath the covers. He slid into the bed, making sure to stay as close to the edge as possible.

Her scent reached him first. Jasmine. His grandmother had grown jasmine in her backyard when he'd been a kid. He'd loved that smell.

Still did.

He couldn't hear Madelyn breathing. She was so quiet and still. Had she gone to sleep already? That quickly? He didn't think so. And maybe that was good. Because it gave him the chance to say... "Your first time isn't going to be about pain and fear." He'd made that decision in the shower while the water pounded down on him and all he could think about was her.

She'd said she wanted him, more than she'd ever wanted anyone else.

If she wanted him...*take me, baby*. For her, he would keep his control on a chokehold.

The covers rustled. He knew she'd turned toward him, so Smith rolled onto his side, too. He stared at her, wishing he could see her eyes better. "Your first time is going to be slow and tender and you're going to have so much pleasure that you scream."

"Is that an offer?"

"Yes."

"And is it also a promise?"

"Yes." It was whatever she wanted the words to be. *A vow.* That was what they were to him. But for now... "Get some sleep, sweetheart. You need to rest." They both did. They had no idea what attack might be coming next. "If you have any other nightmares and you wake up reaching for me, I'll be right here."

The covers rustled again. "You're really not as bad as the rumors used to say."

Oh, he was. Just...*Only not with you.* With her, he was completely different. But only with her. With everyone else, he was the baddest sonofabitch in town. Her enemies would learn that.

I will make you sorry you ever thought to hurt her.

"Sleep well," Smith told her tenderly. Then he shifted position, stared up at the ceiling, and considered all the ways to rip apart the bastard who was playing with his Madelyn.

I will make you beg before I'm done with you.

CHAPTER NINE

She rolled onto her side, stretched, and slowly opened her eyes.

And Madelyn found herself staring straight into Smith's deep, penetrating, and very *awake* gaze.

"Good morning," he told her with a slow, sensual smile.

Her lips parted. She had one frantic moment of confusion where she tried to remember—

Wait. I've got on my clothes. The covers are tangled around us. He's on his side of the bed.

"Don't want you to think that I was just hanging out here, watching you sleep in a truly stalkerish fashion."

"I..." She had not been thinking that. Mostly because her thoughts had not progressed that far. Instead, she'd just realized that his broad chest was bare and that the covers on his side of the bed dipped toward his waist.

Smith had a tat on his chest. Near his heart. A very, very scary looking tat. A skull with incredible definition. Such perfect, eerie detail. The skull wore a hat—a beret—and had a knife gripped between its teeth.

"My whole team got one the last day we were all together. Some things you always want to remember because they mark you."

With an effort, she made her gaze rise to lock with his.

"I wasn't watching you sleep." He pursed his lips. Looked even sexier. His thick hair slid over his high forehead. "Okay, I was. But I was doing it only because I made a promise to you."

Madelyn remembered the rumbling words that had followed her into her dreams. *Your first time is going to be slow and tender and you're going to have so much pleasure that you scream.* She felt the burn as her cheeks flushed.

He laughed softly. "Don't know what you're thinking about, but I meant I told you that if you woke up from a nightmare and reached out for me, I'd be here." A pause as his smile slipped away. "Didn't want to leave the bed until you woke up. I'm trying real hard not to break *any* of the promises I make to you."

She sat up and the covers slid to her waist. "Why are you doing this for me?"

"Doing this?" He sat up, too. The covers dipped more. Even lower on him.

Madelyn saw the top of his black boxers. She also caught sight of the most incredible abs she'd ever seen in her entire life.

"Madelyn?" He waved toward her.

Wonderful. She was staring. "Still sleepy," she muttered. "Takes me a minute to process."

"Um. Process all you like."

Her cheeks puffed out.

"No more bad dreams?"

No, not a single one. She shook her head.

"That's great." Yet the tone of his voice sounded off. He smiled at her, and a muscle jerked along his cheek. "How about you shower and get dressed, and I'll get started on breakfast for us. Then you can tell me all of your secrets over the best eggs you've ever tasted." He started to ease from the bed, then stopped. "Yeah, just so you know. My dick is huge right now."

Her eyes widened.

"Could say it's a morning wood thing. But that'd be, at best, a partial lie. It's a you thing. You're sexy as fuck when you sleep. Or when you're awake. Just whenever. So, you've been warned."

He threw the covers to the side.

Holy mother of—

Huge had not been an exaggeration. He slowly climbed from the bed, did a little adjusting, and snagged a faded pair of jeans. After dragging them on, Smith headed for the door. Just as he was about to cross the threshold—

"Smith?"

He stilled.

"I remember your other promise to me."

He glanced back at her. "This is probably not the time to bring that up. I've been in that bed, waiting for you to wake up, for a very long time. My own Sleeping Beauty. Time to see the world around you."

"If I'm Sleeping Beauty, then are you supposed to be the prince?"

"No, sweetheart, I'm the huntsman."

Her fingers twisted with the covers. "In the story, I'm pretty sure the huntsman tried to kill Sleeping Beauty."

"Really? Huh. In my version, he protects her. Hides her from threats. Then he goes out with his big ax and fucks up anyone who tries to hurt her."

That was an interesting version of the tale. "I can see the appeal of that storyline."

His grin flashed again. "Take as long as you want in the shower. Breakfast will be ready when you're done." With a little salute, he marched out of the room and pulled the door closed behind him.

***

Click. The door had closed, and Smith's grin instantly vanished. Sleeping next to Madelyn and not touching her had been a freaking *living hell.* A dream and a nightmare all wrapped up in the sweet scent of jasmine.

He raked a hand through his hair. A few times during the night, she'd snuggled close to him. Put her hands *on* him. And she'd felt like heaven.

But he'd held himself perfectly still, trapped in his own hell.

A phone rang somewhere, and his head whipped up. The peeling sound came again, and he recognized the ringtone as belonging to Aiden. Smith followed the sound and found his phone tossed on the little table in the entranceway. Scooping it up, he fired a glance back at his bedroom room. His finger slid over the screen, and he put the phone to his ear. "Someone is up early on a Sunday." It *was* Sunday, wasn't it? His days were all confused. A blur of Madelyn.

"Can't be up early if you never went to bed," Aiden grumbled back.

"Never went to bed?" Smith's grip tightened and so did his gut. "What happened?"

"Tony happened. I should have expected it. When it comes to her work, she is determined." But admiration filled his tone. Admiration and a bit of sleepiness. "She wanted to see the body at the station, and I guess I underestimated her connections—something I should *not* have done. Especially not with her working at the University of Miami now. If anything, word about her has spread even more. As soon as she walked through the doors at the police station, they were practically recruiting her and offering her a badge."

Now he was the one having trouble processing. "Slow down, man. You're saying Tony has access to view Bryson's body?"

"Not *has* access. She's *already* viewed it. And she's—hell, Tony, you just tell him, will you?" There was a rumble in the background and then, "You're on speaker now. We're in the back of the limo, heading home. *Home*, Tony," Aiden repeated, voice roughening. "You can update him, but then you need sleep, so don't give me that look."

Smith could well imagine Tony's look.

"You damn well know you need sleep considering what the doctor said," Aiden added.

Smith's spine stiffened. Alarm flared. "What doctor? What's happening?"

Silence. The sense of alarm spread.

"We *weren't* going to say anything yet, Aiden," Tony chided. "That was not the point of this phone call."

"Are you sick, Tony?" Smith demanded. Because he didn't want her trying to work on his case if something was wrong.

"Perfectly healthy. We're all perfectly healthy."

We're all... Understanding dawned. "You're not talking about you and Aiden, are you?"

"Hmmm?" A vague sound from Tony. Or maybe it had come from Aiden. Hard to tell.

But Smith knew he was on to something. "Are you pregnant, Tony?"

Silence.

Then... "Yes." There was no hiding the pleasure in Tony's voice. "Turns out that we are expecting our own Ice Breaker."

"And she's already started taking the baby to morgues." Aiden let out a very loud sigh. "Can you believe that?"

With Tony, yes, he could.

"It was a medical examiner's office, not a morgue." An instant correction from Tony. "And the baby can't *see* through my body. Though, honestly, it will probably be incredibly educational for the child to come with me later when I—"

"Congratulations," Smith cut in to say because he knew that he was rapidly losing control of this conversation. "Thrilled for you." He was. Aiden deserved some happiness. Especially after—

"Actually, I suppose we can go ahead and tell you everything. I mean, Aiden started this." Tony cleared her throat. "We're having twins. So it will do both children a world of good to come with me when I do my work."

Twins. Aiden was also a twin. Aiden and his brother, Austin, had been the best friends that Smith had ever had. For years, they'd all been tight. Until Austin had vanished. Then Aiden's life had spiraled. "Happy for you, man," Smith said to Aiden. He was happy as hell for Tony, too. But he knew Aiden got the special link of a twin. He'd seen that link between Aiden and Austin so often over the years. They could communicate so easily to each other without ever saying a word.

"Thank you." Low. From Aiden. "I've been telling Tony to take things easy. To cut out stress."

Smith swore. "And then I dragged you into my madness." So much for cutting stress.

"Not madness." Tony's instant denial. "And I can't just do *nothing* for the entire length of this pregnancy. I'm fine. The babies are fine. Aiden is having a bit of a breakdown, but otherwise, we're all fine."

"I'm not having a breakdown," he fired back, sounding affronted. "I just want to be by your side twenty-four, seven, and I don't want you lifting a damn finger. I would also prefer that you leave the bodyguards I've assigned to you alone and stop telling them that they can take *coffee breaks* all the damn time!"

Okay. Aiden did not seem so *fine*. "You two clearly need sleep. How about the update? A fast and dirty version?"

"It wasn't suicide." A crisp delivery from Tony. "I barely had to do any exam to get that info. Spent most of the time talking to the ME about other cases, then when the all-clear came from the chief for me to get eyes on Bryson's body, it took me all of five seconds to reach the conclusion that foul play was involved."

It wasn't suicide.

"Just want to double-check something you said earlier," she continued very matter-of-factly, as if she hadn't just blown up his world. "*You* found the body, yes?"

"Yes." *It wasn't suicide.* If it wasn't suicide, then—

"And you said that part of the bed sheet had been wrapped around the upper bunk? One piece tied around the bunk top and the sheet looped around his neck? I believe that is what I read in the statement you gave Detective Campbell."

His eyes closed. "Yes. Bryson had slumped forward, partially on his knees, and the bastard had been strangled by the sheet."

"So he would have been at an angle. That's the way most suicides are. The ligature marks *should* have angled up on his neck to reflect the placement of the sheet and its diagonal attachment to the top of the bunk."

Smith opened his eyes. "They didn't angle up?"

"No, the marks—the bruises—went straight back. As if someone stood behind Bryson, looped the sheet around his neck, and pulled directly back. The ME on duty agreed with my assessment, by the way. Bryson did *not* commit suicide."

Fuck. Just so they were clear... "You're telling me that the man who attacked Madelyn was murdered in a place *full* of cops?"

"Yes. That's exactly what I am telling you. But, seeing as how you were able to get to his cell so easily, I'm sure you can imagine that someone else would have been able to slip back there, too. Unless, of course, Bryson was killed by a cop. Then an outsider wouldn't have needed to sneak back to holding. Two distinct possibilities for our perpetrator."

Again...*fuck.*

"Here's another tidbit for you," Aiden said. "While I was waiting on the love of my life—"

"Thank you, darling," Tony returned.

"Like I would have freaking left you there. Ahem. Anyway, while I was *waiting*, I got a tip from a very helpful cop that Madelyn's stepfather stayed at the station for quite a while after you left with her. Thought that might be an interesting bit you wanted to file away for later."

Absolutely, he did. Smith had gotten access to Bryson by using favors that were owed to him. Reginald could have gotten back into holding by paying the right person the right amount of cash. But that raised the question, *would Reginald kill for Madelyn?* Smith thought the man just might.

He also thought that someone else might have a very strong reason for eliminating Andrew Bryson. And that someone would be *the person who set up Bryson in the first place*. Because maybe that SOB had been afraid that Bryson knew something that could lead back to his true identity.

"Watch yourself," Aiden warned him. "And keep an extra close eye on Madelyn."

"Trust me, she's not going any place without me." If he had to handcuff her to his side, he'd make sure that he stayed close to her. "Think I might need to take a bit of that vacation time coming my way, boss."

"*Buddy*, you take whatever you need. If there is anything else Tony and I can do, let us know."

There would be more, but he'd be calling in help from the other Ice Breakers. Tony had already assisted plenty, and the last thing he wanted to do was put Tony in any stressful situation that might jeopardize her and the babies.

A man was dead. Tony and Aiden would not get pulled into the crosshairs.

I want the perp's attention all on me.

Smith ended the call a few moments later, and his gaze drifted helplessly to the bedroom door. Still closed. Was Madelyn in the shower? He'd have to tell her the news about Bryson. His steps headed slowly, reluctantly, for the door. He didn't *think* that he heard the rush of water. Maybe she was already out of the shower? No, not that fast, surely. Perhaps she just hadn't gotten in yet. His hand curled around the doorknob. "Madelyn?"

No answer.

He twisted the knob. The door squeaked open. "Madelyn, are you—"

"*Smith!*" A frightened, desperate cry.

Smith flung that door open and raced toward the sound of her voice.

CHAPTER TEN

This was *madness*. Madelyn stood inside the massive shower, the water barely trickling from the spray. Each time that she tried to turn the water on fully, she froze.

Her gaze kept jumping toward the shower door. A *door*. A clear, glass door. Not a shower curtain like she'd had at her house. A door. She could see that no one was there. No one watched her.

But the instant water had hit her skin, she'd locked up. She couldn't move. She was shaking and shuddering and "*Smith!*" Madelyn yelled his name. This was crazy. She knew it. There was nothing to fear, so why was she about to rip apart? "Smith!"

He burst into the bathroom, shoving open the door she'd partially closed. His eyes looked wild as he surveyed the room for a threat. Only there was no threat. There was just a naked woman in a shower—*me*—who was unable to move.

"Baby?" He grabbed a fluffy, white towel from the shelf. "What's wrong?" He pulled open the shower door.

There were tears on her cheeks. Stupid tears. Why was this happening?

His jaw hardened.

"I-I…" Her teeth chattered. It wasn't cold. The small trickle of water was warm, so why was she shivering? "I was in the shower at my house. I pulled back the curtain, and he was there. Waiting. I don't know how long he'd been there, watching me through the curtain."

He swore. Long and viciously.

"Wh-when the water touches me here, I have to keep looking, I have to make sure—"

"There is no one in this place but me. *I will not let anyone hurt you.*"

She knew that. She *knew* only Smith was there. Her mind knew it, but her heart hadn't received the message. Her heart was shattered and scared, and she was sick to death of being scared.

Smith held the towel up for her. Not once did he look at her naked body. His gaze remained on her face. "I should have thought—before telling you to take a shower, I should have thought about how you'd react. That's on me."

No, it wasn't. A shower was a *normal* thing. She wanted to do normal things. Wasn't that the story of her whole life? She'd wanted to do normal things just like everyone else, but normal hadn't been an option for her. No dates. No sleepovers. No best friend to learn all of her secrets.

Because my best friend died, and I couldn't have another. Couldn't let anyone else be put at risk.

The person who knew more about Madelyn than anyone else?

Smith.

He kept holding the towel, but she couldn't seem to move her arms to take it. One hand was over her chest. One over the V between her legs. She didn't even remember when she'd positioned herself like that. What was she shielding? Smith wasn't looking at her.

He pitied her.

"You need to talk with someone," Smith told her in his deep, rumbling voice. "The attack has left emotional marks on you. It's normal to respond this way."

That word again. *Normal.* She managed to shake her head.

"It is, baby. You're gonna have PTSD. You're gonna be scared. You're gonna get flashbacks. I'm sure when you talked to a counselor before, you learned all of this."

Again, she shook her head.

His eyes narrowed. And he kept holding the towel. "You *didn't* learn all of this?"

Her tongue seemed awkward in her mouth. "I didn't talk to anyone."

His eyes widened.

"It didn't happen," she said, voice wooden. "Not to Madelyn Lake. I couldn't tell anyone. No one could know. He was still out there. My mother was afraid he'd find me. Don't talk about it," she repeated the old rules. "It didn't happen to you. *Don't talk—*"

"Fuck me," he stepped into the shower, still wearing the jeans he'd dragged on before leaving the bedroom. He wrapped the towel around her and pulled Madelyn against his chest. "It happened, it hurt, and you need to heal. You need to talk about this. You face it, and you move on, and, *God, baby,* you are ripping me apart."

She didn't mean to rip him apart. Madelyn never wanted to hurt Smith. Her head lifted. His hold was so strong, but it didn't hurt. He'd never hurt her before, and she knew with utter certainty that he never would. He wanted to protect her and help her.

And she...

I want him.

She wanted to exorcise her demons. To stop being so afraid all the time. She wanted to be able to take a shower. To have sex with a man. To *live.*

Fire grew inside of her. Starting in her chest. Pulsing and stretching and shoving its way out as her heart raced faster and faster and faster. So fast she felt as if it might burst from her chest at any moment. Madelyn shoved onto her toes. Her hands flew out and curled around his shoulders— those big, broad shoulders. "Kiss me."

"Madelyn," he breathed her name.

Their mouths collided. Should have been awkward. Too frantic because she was beyond control, but it wasn't. Their mouths met, and it was passionate. Intense. She felt his kiss in every fiber of her being, and it was like something within herself was being unlocked.

She wasn't afraid. No longer so petrified that she couldn't move. Her body was hot and aching, and she kissed him with a desperate, ferocious hunger. This was Smith. Smith was safety and passion and every fantasy she'd ever had. He was power and pleasure, and in that moment, he was hers.

The towel was between them. She could feel it rubbing against her as she pushed ever closer to him. The water still trickled from the shower, and she should turn it off. Get out. Move out of the bathroom with him.

Go back to the bed?

Because this was what she wanted. With one hundred percent, absolute certainty, Madelyn knew that she needed this man. She wanted her first time to be with Smith. She wanted that time to be now.

No more fear. No flashbacks. Nothing but the two of them.

"Baby..." His head lifted. His breath came out on a ragged pant. "You're...you're stressed."

Oh, sure. Definitely.

"You're not thinking clearly. This—I'm not what you need right now."

She stared into his eyes. "You are exactly what I need. More than that, you're the only man I want."

His pupils flared. "Be careful saying things like that." He started to back away.

He let go of the towel. She didn't bother to grab it.

The towel slithered down between them.

His chin lifted. His jaw hardened. His eyes stayed on hers.

"Look at me," she told him. Dared.

"I *am*."

"All of me. I want you to see all of me, and I want to see all of you. I need you, Smith. This isn't stress or PTSD or anything but—" Madelyn stopped. Her lips pressed together, and she tasted him. She was no shrink. She didn't know exactly what was happening, but one thing she was sure of... "I want my first time to be with you. I wanted you in that elevator, but I was too afraid to hold tight to what I wanted. I don't want to lose my chance again. I. Want. You."

He swallowed, and his gaze dipped down. Moved so slowly. Carefully. Over her shoulders. Down her chest. That stare of his heated when it locked on her breasts.

Her nipples were tight. Aching. Thrusting toward him.

Another swallow from Smith. Down, down his gaze went, and she could have sworn that he was touching her. Trailing his fingers over her stomach. Skimming his knuckles over her hips. Dipping his fingers between her thighs.

Her breath shuddered out. "I want you. You want me. No more waiting."

He reached down and scooped up the towel that had fallen. It was wet and dripping, and she thought that he was going to try to give it to her again. Instead, he tossed it onto the bathroom rug. "You need to replace one memory with another," he told her.

What she needed—

"You're afraid to shower because of him. I'll give you a different memory. I'll give you as many different memories as you want." His hands dropped to the front of his jeans. When his hands dropped, so did her gaze. He unhooked the button. Lowered the zipper.

Then his jeans and the boxers hit the floor.

Smith kicked them out onto the bathroom rug and tugged the shower door shut. His cock bobbed toward her. Long, thick, fully erect. "If you don't like anything I do, at any time, you say the word. We do as much or as little as you like." His hand reached out. She thought it was going to touch her. Instead... "Scoot a little to the side, sweetheart. Make more room for me."

He was staying in the shower with her? Automatically, she scooted back more, and he adjusted the spray so that a powerful rush of water poured from the showerhead. The water wasn't cold. It was warm, not steaming, somehow just right as it brushed over her skin.

Most of the water hit Smith. It slid over his powerful shoulders. Angled down his chest. He dipped his head under the water, then ran his fingers through his wet hair as he shoved it back from his forehead. Smith sent her a careful stare as she stood there, watching him, with her hands twisting in front of her.

Then he lifted his hand toward her. "Tell me if you get scared."

She took his hand. Tilted back her head.

He kissed her. Softly. Carefully. Tenderly. Her lips parted for the thrust of his tongue, and she was distantly aware of the rush of pounding water. He was her focus. Smith's mouth. His body. His touch. One hand held hers, and the other had curved around her hip. He brought her closer to him as he kissed her, taking his time with her mouth. Savoring her.

Their bodies weren't touching, not yet, but it would be so easy to eliminate that last bit of distance and press fully against him.

The hand on her hip eased down. Slid around.

Her legs parted for him. His fingers moved between her thighs. Ever so slowly. As if he feared she'd pull back, and he wanted to give her time to retreat.

Madelyn had no intention of pulling back.

She caught his lower lip with her teeth. Nibbled.

Loved the sound of his groan.

His fingers teased her clit. A light touch. Soft. Not enough. Not nearly. "Smith." A demand.

"Tell me what you want."

Her breath stuttered out. "You. In me."

His fingers dipped inside of her. Madelyn immediately pushed up on her toes as a gasp tore from her lips.

His mouth had lifted from hers. His eyes held hers. "Good?" His fingers flexed. His thumb rubbed over her clit.

This was better than good. This was—

"Let see if we can make things better." He pulled his hand away from her core.

That was *not* better. That was way worse. She was aching and on edge, and he was putting soap on his fingers. What? Why was he doing that? "*Smith.*" Her body felt tight and too tense.

His soapy fingers didn't go back to her sex. His fingers covered her breasts. Stroked her nipples. Squeezed and caressed, and a sensual current surged through her.

"You've got gorgeous breasts," he told her, voice rough. "Actually, every single inch of you is gorgeous."

The touch of his callused fingertips on her sensitive nipples had her biting her lip. Pleasure. Everything with him was all about pleasure.

His left hand kept teasing her nipple. His right—he slid his fingers back to her sex. Dipped them into her.

"Ride my hand, baby."

Her hips arched.

"Put your hand on mine, Madelyn. Show me how much you want."

Her hand flew down. Locked around his wrist. She pushed him against her, *harder*.

"God, you are so fucking sexy." Two of his fingers were inside of her. They stretched her even as his thumb pushed and rubbed her clit over and over.

Her hips rocked against his hand. She held tightly to his wrist. She rode him, and he watched her and those fingers stretched wickedly again inside of her.

"You're gonna feel fucking fantastic around my dick."

His fingers felt fantastic inside of her, but she needed more. She wanted *him*. She wanted—

His thumb pushed hard on her clit. His fingers strummed inside of her.

The climax hit her before she could have another thought. Fast. Surging. It ripped through her, and her head tipped back. Her breath shuddered as her sex tightened greedily around his fingers. Fingers that still stroked and thrust.

Steam drifted in the air. The shower door had fogged over. She couldn't see beyond it.

But she didn't care. Madelyn wasn't afraid.

The pleasure kept coming. A wave that spilled throughout her whole body. And when he pulled his hand away, she tightened her grip on his wrist in protest.

"Your first time isn't gonna be against the shower wall, baby. Or, at least, that's the goal. But I need to get you to a bed, *now,* in order to make that goal happen." His voice had gone ragged around the edges.

Her stare flew back to him. She saw the lust burning in his gaze. The savage need that had to be a reflection of what she felt, too. The orgasm still had aftershocks slipping through her, but she wanted him pounding in her. No more holding back.

Smith kept giving her pleasure. She wanted to do the same to him. So why wait? Madelyn let go of his wrist, and, even as his fingers slid out of her, she reached for his cock.

"*Fuck me,*" Smith growled.

Her hand curled around him. Not completely, he was far too big for that. And she had a moment's thought that—oh, yes, this was going to hurt. No way could it not the first time. He was huge and thick, but she didn't care about the pain.

She wanted all of him.

She pumped him. Stroked from base to head. Loved the way he felt beneath her touch. Heat and power. So hard. Madelyn stroked him again.

"Baby..."

He'd used his fingers on her. But he'd also used his mouth in the elevator. It was time for her to do the same to him. Her knees started to lower.

"Nope. No way." He yanked off the water.

Drip. Drip. Drip.

"You put my dick in your mouth, and all my plans for your fantastic, unforgettable first time go out the window. My control will *not* last, and I am trying my best not to screw up with you." Again, ragged. Each word seemed bitten off.

He scooped her into his arms and stepped out of the shower. She was soaked. So was he, but Smith made no move to stop for a towel. Instead, he stormed for the bedroom. Madelyn wrapped an arm around him and held on as best she could.

They crashed onto the bed together.

"Sorry," he grunted. "Need to be more careful." They were a tangle of limbs. He started to rise.

One of her arms was still around his neck. She used her grip to pull his head toward her. "Be sorry for nothing." She kissed him. Hot. Passionate. Fiercely.

Her legs were spread, and he was between them. The head of his cock nudged at her, and it would be so easy to take him inside. She wanted him in her. All the way.

"No." Smith pulled back.

Madelyn blinked up at him.

"You think I'm gonna let you know anything but pleasure? It's not gonna be fast and hard. You aren't ready."

"I feel plenty ready." The readiest. She wanted him. *Now*. "Smith—"

He pushed her legs apart even more. Then he put his mouth on her.

Already sensitive from her previous orgasm, the touch of his mouth on her had Madelyn's hips leaping off the bed. But his hands clamped around them and held her in place. When his tongue thrust into her, she grabbed for the covers and fisted them in her hands.

He licked. Thrust that amazing tongue. Then withdrew it to swirl his tongue around her clit.

"Smith!"

He devoured her.

Tongue. Lips. Tasting. Licking. Kissing. And making her come. This orgasm was even stronger than the first, and it didn't hit her like some wave. It took over her body so that she couldn't do anything but shake and quake beneath him.

"Now, you're ready." He let her go and grabbed for the nightstand.

Vaguely, Madelyn saw him pull out a packet and rip it open. Her panting breaths filled the air, and her sex still quivered with aftershocks when he thrust into her.

No pain. No discomfort, or, if there was any, she didn't feel it. Because those aftershocks ignited into something else. *More pleasure. A new orgasm? Or one that just hadn't ever ended?*

Madelyn didn't know, and she really didn't care. Her legs locked around Smith. Her arms held him tight. He thrust into her. Deep, powerful thrusts that rammed the whole bed into the wall, and she loved every single second.

Her nails might have clawed along his back.
She might have bit him on the shoulder.
She *did* scream. "Smith!"
When he came, he bellowed her name.

CHAPTER ELEVEN

How the hell was he supposed to go back from *that?* From hands-down, the best orgasm of his life. Was he supposed to just go back to acting like they were friends? Partners in an investigation?

Oh, screw that. Not going to happen.

After ditching the condom, Smith marched back into the bedroom. The sheets twisted around Madelyn's beautiful legs. She'd made no move to cover up, and he had to take a moment for a serious mental self-talk about *not jumping her again.*

He didn't get back in the bed. If he got in the bed, he'd get in *her* again. She'd just had her first time. That meant she might be sore, and she didn't need him slamming deep into her over and over again. Even if all he wanted to do was slam deep.

"Smith?" Her eyebrows rose. Madelyn sat up. One hand grabbed a sheet, and she pulled it up to cover those world-class breasts. "What's wrong?"

Oh, just his whole world realigning. "Was I too rough?" He'd held back as long as he could, but at the end, his control had slipped, and he'd pounded into paradise.

A slow, satisfied smile curled her lips. "Not at all. You were perfect."

Fuck, fuck, fuck. His already hard dick jerked toward her. He needed to put on jeans. Stat. Smith marched for his closet.

"You...you came, right?" Madelyn called after him.

"Oh, hell, yes, I did." How could the woman doubt that? He hauled on a pair of boxers and came out of the closet with a fresh pair of jeans in his hand.

Her hand motioned to the front of his boxers. Or, to the tent there. "Are you sure? Maybe...look, I know inexperience isn't always sexy. I can try again. If you let me, I can make it good for you, too." Red stained her cheeks.

Smith squinted at her. "If you make it any better, I'll want to chain you to my side and never let you go." Who was he kidding? That was how he already felt with her. "Baby, I came. So hard that I nearly shoved the bed through the wall."

Her eyes widened.

"My dick is like this not because I didn't come, but because I want to get inside you again." In the interest of full disclosure... "And again. Then again. Basically, I just want to be inside you. Done."

Her tongue snaked over her lower lip.

"But it was your first time, and I'm trying not to be a total bastard. If I fuck you the way I want, you'll be sore. I don't want to hurt you."

"You didn't. No pain. Just pleasure."

He took a step toward her but caught himself before actually pouncing. "Nope. Not gonna do that. There *will* be pain." If he had her as endlessly as he wanted, she would hurt. He couldn't have that. "Giving you recovery time." *Trying to give myself time for control.* "Then when you're ready..." He blew out a breath. "I'll go easy."

Pulling the sheet with her, Madelyn rose from the bed. She wrapped it around her body, toga-style, and walked toward him.

Smith realized he was just standing there, holding his jeans, like an ass. So he hauled them on right before Madelyn stopped in front of him.

"Thank you," Madelyn told him. Her hand rose and pressed to his chest.

Right over the skull tattoo.

"For what?" *Not fucking you into oblivion? Sweetheart, the struggle is real.* Especially if she kept touching him and if that sheet of hers kept dipping...

"For giving me good memories to replace the bad ones."

He caught her hand. Lifted it to his mouth and pressed a kiss to her palm. "I'll give you as many good memories as you want."

Her lips curled in the faintest of slow, hesitant smiles, and damn if it wasn't like seeing the sun peek out from behind gray clouds.

What. The. Fuck? Had he seriously just had that thought? And he wasn't even drunk? Well, maybe he was. Drunk on her. His reaction to Madelyn was way over the top. He needed to pull things back, fast, only Smith had zero clue how to pull away from her. All he wanted was to pull her closer.

"Why are you so kind to me?" Madelyn asked him.

"Because it's you." That was the honest truth. He let her hand go and stepped back. "We need breakfast." Actually, they needed to talk because he had to tell her about Bryson, and that wasn't going to be a fun chat for her. He also had to poke into her past and pull up all of Madelyn's deep, dark secrets. Another project that wasn't going to be fun for either of them. Kind? No, it would be cruel. But they needed the truth. He turned away. "I'll get started in the kitchen. If you need me—"

"I won't scream for you again. I'm okay."

He wasn't. His whole life had just been upended by a beautiful pair of green eyes.

***

"I want to be involved as much as possible." Madelyn nodded determinedly even as she reached for a fork and tried to ignore the grumbling of her stomach. She couldn't recall the last full meal she'd had, and it took all of her restraint not to attack the food. Some of her clothes had been brought to Smith's place. She didn't even know when or how they'd arrived, but she suspected maybe Aiden and Tony had delivered them during their late-night visit, and Madelyn just hadn't realized it. When she'd woken this morning, the clothes had been waiting in a suitcase near the foot of Smith's bed. After using a washcloth to clean away the faint spots of blood between her legs, she'd snagged fresh clothing and rushed to join him for breakfast.

He'd made what had to be the fluffiest pancakes on earth. And the eggs...seriously, one bite, and she'd almost moaned with pleasure. A sound that would have been way too similar to the moans that had occurred when she'd had sex with Smith.

A good memory. No, far better than good. An outstanding memory.

Smith poured syrup over the pancakes on his plate. He lifted his brows in inquiry. "Involved? Want to clarify?"

"In the investigation. My case." She got butterflies—both from fear and anticipation—just thinking about this. But Madelyn didn't want to be afraid any longer. Smith had been right. It was time to stop looking over her shoulder. "I've lived by my mom's rules for far too long." Though it hadn't really felt like living. "I want to change." Her fork dove into the eggs, and she just had to take another bite. "I want to hunt *him*. I want him to see what it feels like to be in someone's sights."

Smith ate in silence. She tried not to notice the way the sunlight fell onto his thick hair. They weren't in the kitchen. She'd expected that, but when Madelyn had emerged from the bedroom, he'd had the food set up on the balcony. The waves crashed below. The sun shined. Madelyn felt something she hadn't experienced in a very long time. *Hope.*

"This guy has eluded capture for a very long time." He chewed slowly. She couldn't see his eyes because he wore a pair of aviator sunglasses. "Finding him isn't going to be easy. I don't want to give you false hope."

There was that word again. *Hope*. Only she didn't feel anything false about it. "I know it won't be easy. I also know we may not find him. But you're willing to help me try, and that's huge for me. Not hiding and fearing, but doing something?" *Life changing*. She reached for the syrup. "And I know where we should start. The man who attacked me at my house. I think he's important, just like you said. If his attack was tied to my past, if the man who took me when I was a kid somehow reached out to that Bryson guy, then he is a lead we can't ignore. I know Andrew Bryson is dead, but if we can access his messages, his social media accounts, maybe there is a clue that we can use—"

Smith's hand flew out and curled over her wrist. "I need to talk to you about Bryson, baby."

A little quiver of awareness went through her at his touch, but his expression had suddenly turned extra intense.

"It wasn't suicide."

The waves pounded below. She heard a sea gull crying out in the distance.

"Tony examined his body. The scene in the cell was staged as if Bryson had killed himself, but she doesn't believe that's the case. Based on the marks around his neck, it's her professional opinion that someone strangled Andrew Bryson in his cell."

The sun shone down on her, but goose bumps rose on her arms.

Slowly, Smith released her.

Her shaking fingers poured the syrup. She picked up her knife and fork and cut off a small square of the pancake.

"His death leads to some interesting questions," Smith spoke thoughtfully.

His murder, not his death.

"Could be the man just had enemies. Could be that the person who sent him after you—that individual might have been afraid that Bryson would talk. That Bryson had intel that could incriminate him. So he had Bryson eliminated."

She took a bite of the pancake. It had looked so light and fluffy, but Madelyn had to swallow twice in order to choke it down.

"Or maybe there is a third possibility. Maybe someone really didn't like what Bryson did to you and that someone had Bryson killed so you would never have to fear an attack from him again."

The fork fell from her hand and hit the plate with a clatter. "No."

"No to which possibility?"

She knew where this was going. *No.* "You think it was Reginald, and it wasn't. He's many things, but my stepfather isn't a killer."

"You seem very certain of that." A pause. "He stayed at the police station long after we left. He's a man of substantial means. It wouldn't have been hard for him to bribe his way into Bryson's cell."

A rough bark of laughter came from her, but there was nothing funny about this situation. "Reginald wouldn't get his hands dirty by actually killing someone. That's not what he does. He likes to use his money to get his way, yes. He's an absolute control freak, but he would not wrap a bedsheet around a man's throat and strangle him to death."

Smith inclined his head. "Not even to protect his daughter?"

"I'm not his daughter. I'm his stepdaughter."

"You are his only heir. I've known that for quite some time. No blood relation, but when Reginald dies, everything he owns will go to you."

Her gaze jerked away from him. Her head turned and Madelyn focused on the distance, on the small boat that she saw bobbing in the middle of the waves. "He can't have biological children of his own. He doesn't have any other close family, so he just directed in the will for things to go to my mother and me. It was all supposed to go to my mom, but then..." A swallow. "Then she had a sudden heart attack. She was so young, and we didn't see it coming and it changed everything."

"With your mother gone, you quit your job in D.C."

"Yes."

"Because working there, staying behind the scenes and hiding in the museum so you would never attract attention or headlines, that was part of *her* plan, wasn't it?"

She nodded. The boat looked so small surrounded by those waves. Pushing forward even as the waves surged to send it back.

"You opened your own business. Stepped into the light."

Her head swung toward him once more. "I authenticate art and antiques. That's hardly a spotlighted career."

"You work with the rich and famous, Madelyn. I've seen articles on you in several high-profile magazines."

Her fingers fluttered around the plate. "You think I drew his attention again?" Before Smith could answer, Madelyn shook her head. "I made it into a few scholarly magazines while I was working at the Smithsonian, too. I'm older now, though. I hardly look like the same thirteen-year-old girl. It's doubtful anyone would recognize me from that time. And my name is different. Everything is different."

He lifted his orange juice and took a long drink. She suspected that—behind his glasses—his eyes never left her face. After putting the glass down, he asked her, "What's your real name?"

"Margaret." A name she hadn't said in years. "But back then, everyone called me Maggie."

"Maggie." Rasped. "Maddie." A shake of his head. "No wonder you didn't like it when I called you that. Too similar, wasn't it?"

Yes, it had been too similar. Anytime Smith—or anyone else—had ever shortened her name, it had been like a ghost from her past came calling. "Maggie is gone. I'm Madelyn now."

"You are, but Maggie is the key to this. I need to know everything about *her*. About you. About what happened so long ago." He pointed to her plate. "You really should eat more."

She should. Right. Madelyn forced herself to pick up the fork and knife and to cut another piece of pancake. This time, it didn't feel so heavy.

Or maybe it did. But she ate it anyway. That bite. And more until the pancake was nearly gone.

"What was your last name back then?"

"Edgewood." *Maggie Edgewood*.

"And where did you live?"

She reached for her orange juice. Her fingers curled around the cold glass. "Vegas. I told you that my mom worked nights—she was a showgirl. Not on one of the big productions or anything. She, um..." *No. Stop. Give him the truth.* "My mom was a stripper." A shrug. "The job paid the bills, and it made sure we had a roof over our heads. She wanted to be a showgirl. That was the plan." Her mom's big dream. "But Vegas is hard. Even harder when you're young and you're a single mom."

"Your dad was never in the picture?"

She had no memory of her dad. "I don't even know his name. My mom just said he left when he found out about me." The glass trembled. No, dammit, her fingers were doing the trembling.

"I'm sorry."

"For what?"

"Because the dumbass never got to realize how special you are."

The glass stopped trembling. "What happened to your dad, Smith?"

His jaw hardened. "You know the story. I'm sure most of the people in high school knew it. He lost everything."

"But—" No, she stopped. Just because she was digging up her hell, it didn't mean Smith had to do the same. Clearly, he didn't want to talk about his father. He was helping her. *Respect his wishes. Don't push him.* "My mom wanted to be a showgirl. That was her dream. Only you can't live on a dream, and she had to get money." But her mother had always lied to everyone. Lifted up her chin and smiled and said she was a showgirl when she'd introduce herself to people. And then her mom would name a lavish casino and say no one ever recognized her without her costume.

But that hadn't been true. So much hadn't been true.

"My mom met Reginald at one of the clubs. I know the story was that they'd met on a ski trip, but that wasn't true. They met at her job. They actually..." She let go of the glass. "Reginald has always felt guilty where I'm concerned."

"Why would he feel guilty?"

Madelyn wadded up the napkin that had been in her lap. "The night I was taken? My mom was with him. I found out later that they'd met about two weeks before. She stopped going to the club for work and just went to his place. They were together there when I..." *When I was taken. When I screamed for help that didn't come.* "She didn't tell him that she had a kid. He didn't know about me until the news broke on TV. Not my story, not at first. Heather's. Heather led to me, and he figured out what had happened and then...then he took me and my mom away." For a moment, the past swirled in her mind.

"Where are we going?"

Her mother tightened her grip on Maggie's hand. "Far away from here."

They ran down the stairs. Maggie almost fell, but her mom pulled her up. They burst outside, and there was a limo waiting. A long, black car. Just like the kind you saw at funerals.

A funeral. Heather had just had a funeral.

"Am I going to die, Mom?" A shaking question because part of her already felt dead.

Her mom let out a gasp and spun toward her. "No, of course you—" Her mom broke off, then nodded. "Yes, yes, we're both going to die." Her hands moved to Maggie's shoulders. "And we're going to be born as brand-new people. We're going to get in that car and become somebody new, and you will never, ever have to be scared again, do you understand me?"

The limo's door opened. A tall man in a black suit rose from the back. He was dressed just like one of the men who'd carried Heather's casket.

"I don't want to go in the ground," Maggie cried.

The man's face tightened. "I swear, you won't."

"Baby?" Smith leaned forward. "You with me?"

Madelyn forced a smile. "Of course. Where else would I be?"

His lips thinned. "I don't know. One minute you're telling me how Reginald spirited you and your mom away, and the next, you phased out on me."

"I'm here."

"You think Reginald felt guilty because of what happened to you, so the guy gave you a new life." His voice was doubting.

"No." She shook her head. The breeze caught a lock of her hair and sent it teasing across her cheek. "Reginald loved my mother. He wanted to marry her. I was part of the package deal."

Smith drummed his fingers on the edge of the table. "This isn't going to work if you're not honest with me."

"I am being honest." Excruciatingly so. "He wanted to marry my mom. He loved her." Her voice hardened. "He gave her everything that she ever wanted. And he gave me protection. They both did."

"They gave you a prison."

She flinched. "Sometimes a prison and protection can be one and the same." She tossed down her balled-up napkin. "For the first three years, we lived in Europe. Reginald had his house and business in the US, but he flew to us every few weeks. Mom thought it was safer there. She wanted to be as far away from Vegas as she could." *So did I.* Europe had felt like another world. "I actually thought we'd stay there forever, but then one day, Reginald came, and he said they were getting married. He had a whole new identity for me. Social security card. Even a driver's license." It had been on her sixteenth birthday. Her mom had baked a cake, and Reginald had given her a card. When she opened it... "He told me I had a new life waiting. That it was safe now. I was someone new."

"Madelyn Lake."

"And my mother became Stephanie Lake. She got a new identity, too. Only she didn't stay Stephanie Lake for long. She and Reginald got married, she became Stephanie Guyer, and we moved into his house. And then I met you."

"That's a fast summary."

She rolled one shoulder in a shrug. "Life was quiet in Europe. Quiet was good."

"And what was life like when you moved in with Reginald?"

"Not so quiet." A big part of her had just wanted to keep hiding in Europe. But Reginald had wanted her mother to move in with him. "No matter what, I was grateful to him and my mother. Yes, there were a whole lot of rules, but I'd been terrified in Vegas. I was back in the US, and I had a new home. His house was *huge*. But there were always guards there, so I knew that no one would get to me."

"And when you weren't inside the huge home with all the guards, you were scared?"

Yes. "When I wasn't there, I followed the rules we had. It worked. Everything worked until—"

"Now? A year after you stopped following the rules?"

She stood and strode toward the edge of the balcony. The wind hit stronger there, and she turned her face into it. "I thought he was dead." The absolute truth. "My mother had died. It had been *years*. And I would scan the news. I did it without her or Reginald knowing. I would always look to see if there were any other cases like mine out there. Guys like him—they're not normal predators." Something she'd learned. "After Heather's body was recovered, FBI agents were brought in to investigate. They talked to me for hours." She'd been terrified. Madelyn remembered telling them...*I'm sorry. I'm so sorry. I should have stayed with him. I'm so sorry.* "I got the impression back then that the authorities were sure there would be more crimes." From conversations she'd overheard. From files that had been left open right in front of her because she guessed they hadn't thought a kid was paying much attention. "I heard them say they had to stop this guy before he left a trail of bodies. But no one ever did. No one stopped him."

"And you didn't see any cases that matched, so you thought you were safe."

No, she'd *hoped* that she was. "My mother didn't report me missing. If I hadn't gotten away, I think she might have believed I was a runaway. I don't—I'm not sure she would have gone to the police." This was the part that gnawed at her. That had made her think...

He could still be hunting. So easily. And no one would know. "I think he knew that she wouldn't report me missing, at least not right away. I think he knew a whole lot about me. Enough that he *could* get in and out of my home without disturbing anything." *Not even the dog.* Molly had been left at her apartment. "I think he knew my mom's schedule." *And mine.* "I never saw other stories like mine in the news." She turned toward him. "But maybe that's because those victims weren't ever reported. If I hadn't escaped, I could have gone down as a runaway. It's different when you have a runaway versus a child who is abducted. It's all so different." Her nails bit into her palm. Madelyn glanced down, surprised at the small stab of pain. "I don't want there to be other victims. I don't want him to have taken someone since me, and I don't want him to ever take anyone else again."

When he rose, his chair legs groaned as they raked over the tiled balcony floor. "Did you ever find the location where he took you?"

"No. The cops didn't, either. It was night when I escaped, and I ran and I ran and I—everything was a blur."

"Have you thought about trying hypnosis? Talking to—"

"The rule was to forget. Not to remember."

He closed the distance between them. His hands reached out and curled around the railing on either side of her body. "We're making new rules."

Her hair blew toward him.

"Rule one is that you aren't going to be afraid."

That was a pretty hard rule to follow. "You don't just stop fear." It came no matter what. You couldn't turn it off at will. Fear was one of those basic responses. Like anger. Sadness.

Lust.

Smith was teaching her plenty about lust, but she didn't think he could magically teach her how not to be afraid.

"You can learn to channel your fear. Learn how to pull it inside and turn it into anger so that you can fight back. Or if the fear gets to be too much, instead of letting it eat you up, you can come to me. We'll turn that fear into something one hell of a lot more pleasurable."

He was so close. The heat of his body reached out to her. "What's the next rule?"

"That you trust me completely. Hold nothing back from me, and I'll hold nothing back from you. We will be in this together."

Madelyn nodded. "I can do that." With him. When she hadn't with others.

"You might not like what the Ice Breakers dig up. Hell, you might not like what *I* do. The Ice Breakers—they're more like a surgeon cutting in with a scalpel to find the truth." Her reflection stared back at her from his sunglasses. "I'm more like the guy who busts in with the big ass axe. Huntsman, remember? I will wreck the place, but I will get the job done."

"I could use a big axe," she whispered.

"Then consider me your weapon of choice." Before she could respond to that, Smith leaned forward, and his lips brushed over hers. "You will be safe."

Her hand rose and pressed to his chest. Right over that tattoo that drew her so oddly. A fierce, scary tattoo. But something about that skull gave her the oddest sense of security. "Tell me more about your tat." Her fingers stroked him lightly.

He looked down. Then back up at her. "Tats like this one are common with special forces."

His military time. A period in his life that was a total mystery to you.

"Why don't you just think of him as your guardian angel?" Smith murmured. "Might look a little scary on the outside, but you don't need to fear him."

She got lost in Smith's eyes.

"Because he'll face any threat for you."

The tat wasn't her guardian angel. But she was starting to think that Smith was. She wanted to kiss him again.

But he eased back. He let go of the railing and stepped away from her. "Our first stop will be your stepdad's place. Then I think we may need to fly out to Vegas."

Her stomach twisted. "I haven't been to Vegas in years."

"Then I'd say you're overdue for a visit."

"Nothing is going to be out there. It's been too long. The little apartment I lived in back then— someone else has to be there now, if the building hasn't been torn down. And I could never remember where he took me. I told you that before. We can't just go there and expect for my memories of that night to miraculously come flooding back."

He just watched her.

Her arms wrapped around her stomach.

"Scared to go back?" Smith asked.

"Yes," she gritted out.

"We're channeling that fear, remember? Don't worry about what you might find. Be pissed as hell that the bastard out there *made* you have to run in the first place. Be pissed. Fight. Fight with me."

A jerky nod.

"I have contacts at the FBI. You said agents worked your case, so I'll pull in some favors and see if I can get access to the old intel."

Madelyn blinked in surprise. "They can do that? Just turn over case files that way?" It didn't quite seem legal.

Smith's shoulders rolled. "It's not exactly an on-the-books deal. But rest assured, I'll get what I want."

Madelyn didn't doubt it.

"I'll also want to see what the investigating officers from the Vegas PD had. When we go to Vegas, we'll pay a visit to their station."

So his tricks might work with his Fed contacts, but the local cops in Vegas weren't just going to play nicely with him. "They are not just going to hand us over case files."

"You'd be surprised at what I can accomplish when I put my mind to it."

Smith kept surprising her.

"The visit will be more to talk with the officers on your case, if any of them are still there. And to actually get our eyes on the evidence that was collected. They should still have it. You'll go with me. We'll talk to them, and we'll see what shakes loose."

The wind sent her hair dancing again. "I feel like this is us returning to the scene of the crime."

"That's exactly what we're doing." He turned toward the table.

The wind seemed to carry a chill. "He's not just going to be waiting there."

"Oh, I don't think he's in Vegas at all."

Her shoulders stiffened.

"I think he's here. I think he's been watching you." He looked back at her. "And I have a feeling he just might follow you wherever you go."

Jesus. "That is *not* reassuring, Smith."

"Wasn't supposed to be. I'm not lying to you. You're not lying to me, remember? The truth can be uncomfortable, but we're not just doing the easy parts."

She didn't have easy parts in her life.

"I think he's been watching you, and I think your dear stepfather is aware of that fact."

Her mouth dropped open. No, that just wasn't possible.

"Don't believe me?" His lips twisted. "Let's go have a little chat with Reginald and find out." His hand extended toward her. "Bet you a night of screaming orgasms that I'm right."

Her mouth snapped closed as she surged toward him. She grabbed his hand and squeezed his fingers. "*Smith.*"

"That mean you're taking the bet?"

Madelyn wasn't sure how to respond.

He winked at her. "Relax, baby, I was just trying to lighten the mood for you. You looked scared as hell, and I hated that."

There he went again. Throwing her off. Being *good.* She tipped back her head. "One night of screaming orgasms. *Done.*"

His mouth was the one to drop open.

"But you're going to be the one owing me. My stepfather has no clue about what has been happening to me. He's not going to be able to help us."

"We'll just see about that."

Yes, they would.

CHAPTER TWELVE

"Glad you came to your senses and decided to come stay with me." Reginald Guyer jerked his hand toward the open doors of his study. "If you hadn't come yourself this morning, I was going to send my driver after you. Madelyn, go inside and get settled so we can talk about the plans we need to make." He then made a shooing motion toward Smith. "Thanks for dropping her off. I'm sure you can see yourself out."

The guy was such a prick. Smith sent him a broad grin. "Sure, I can see myself out." They were in the foyer, after all. The exit was like five feet away. "But I think I'll just see myself into the study instead." His fingers twined with Madelyn's, and when he headed forward, she moved in perfect time with him.

Reginald's face reddened. He hurried into Smith's path. "I didn't extend an invitation for you to stay."

"Madelyn and I are a package deal," Smith murmured. "Didn't you realize that? Wherever she goes, I follow." *Gladly will I follow.*

If anything, the flush deepened on Reginald's face. That shade of red wasn't flattering on anyone. Reginald swept a fuming glance Madelyn's way, but whatever he saw in her expression convinced him to get out of the way. Reginald swung around and loped angrily into the study. "Shut the door," he barked over his shoulder.

After he and Madelyn had entered, Smith pulled the door closed. He didn't want this little chat overheard, either.

Reginald threw himself into the leather chair behind the big, mahogany desk. Giant antlers hung on the wall behind him. Smith's stare lingered on the antlers.

"I'm a bit of a hunter," Reginald declared, obviously following Smith's gaze. "That's one of my smaller prizes."

Smith made sure Madelyn was settled in the chair across from Reginald's desk. Then he took up a position behind her. His fingers curled around her shoulders. The spot and stance were deliberate. He was showing exactly where he belonged. *With her*. "I'm a hunter, too," Smith told the other man. He sent a smile to Reginald. One that would show a whole lot of teeth. "And I always catch what I'm after."

"Got mounts on your walls, huh?"

"No, just bodies in the basement."

Reginald blinked and jerked forward. "What? What in the hell kind of response is that?"

Before Smith could taunt the man more, Madelyn asked, "Did you hear about what happened at the jail?"

Her stepfather settled back against his chair. "Suicide." His lip curled. "Guess the guy couldn't live with that he'd done." His eyes narrowed on her. "But at least you don't ever have to worry about him again. And when you move in here, you'll have the best protection that I can buy. You won't have to ever worry about *anything* again."

"It wasn't suicide." Her voice was flat. "And I'm not moving in here."

No surprise showed in Reginald's expression at her revelation about the death not being suicide. Instead, Reginald's face took on a determined glare. "You *need* protection. I can provide that for you. Didn't I protect you when you were growing up? Didn't I always make sure that you didn't have to fear an attack? That you didn't have to look over your shoulder? I kept you safe. Now you're away from me and look what's happened!"

Yes, indeed, Smith was looking. "You already knew Bryson's death wasn't a suicide." So why the initial subterfuge? Had Reginald thought Smith and Madelyn didn't know?

Reginald pursed his lips. "This is a family matter. I don't get why you're still here."

"He's here because I want him here. Where I go, he goes," Madelyn responded in an emotionless voice. "Thought we covered that."

Smith could have kissed her. Oh, hell, why not? Smith leaned down and brushed a light kiss over her temple. "Thanks, sweetheart. Love it when you have my back."

"Sweetheart?" Reginald seemed to be choking. "You're not actually involved?"

"Actually, we are," Smith assured him.

"No, impossible. She hasn't been dating anyone. Madelyn doesn't get involved with—"

"And you'd know, because you've had her under surveillance?" Smith cut in silkily. "You've had eyes on her, so you know exactly what she has and has not been doing? Or rather, who she has or has not been seeing?"

Reginald flattened his hands on the desk. "That was a terrible tragedy about your father, Smith. How awful you must have felt all of those years ago."

Smith just shook his head. Was he supposed to take that obvious bait?

"One minute, you were at school with my Madelyn, and the next, well, you vanished, didn't you? Ran away from everyone."

The fuck he had.

But Reginald sent a sympathetic glance toward Madelyn. "I remember you were quite distraught about his disappearance."

Wait, hold up. Now Smith was vaguely interested in the shit Reginald was spewing. She'd been upset about his departure?

"Smith left you without a word, Madelyn. Slipped away for years because he wanted to go out and have adventures."

That was hardly what had happened. Someone was sure enjoying a rewrite of history.

"Now you're thinking you can rely on someone like him?" A sad shake of Reginald's head. "I was there for you and your mother. I never left. I wouldn't. I'm someone you can count on." His stare rose to pin Smith. "Not some hired gun who is just sniffing around because he wants a payday."

Smith couldn't help it. He laughed.

Reginald's jaw tightened. "Everything is a joke to you, isn't it? Including Madelyn's safety."

He let the laughter linger, then slowly fade away. His hands were still around Madelyn's shoulders, and Smith hated the stiffness that had settled into her body. "You don't know anything about me."

Reginald's smirk told him that Smith had just walked into trouble. "Don't I?" Reginald hauled open the top, left-hand drawer of his desk. The drawer didn't squeak or groan. It just slid open soundlessly. Then Reginald pulled out a manila file and dramatically dropped it on top of his desk. Bam. "Background report on you. Hits all the high points, I can assure you. Oh, do let me give you credit for being a decorated soldier, but my, those were some vicious kills, weren't they?"

The smug bastard. Reginald clearly thought he'd just nailed Smith, but the opposite was true. *You just proved yourself guilty as hell.* "Even with your cash, there's no way you could have dug up a file on me this fast. You would have needed to request the investigation months ago." He cocked his head to the right. "Let me guess, I bet you did it shortly after Madelyn moved into Aiden's building and you realized I worked for him. Or maybe it was when my path and Madelyn's began to cross a few too many times for you. The guy you had tailing her—does he report to you on everyone who comes within her radar? Or was I special? Was I a red flag waving at you, so you decided to see what dirt you could discover on me?"

"Wasn't hard to find dirt."

Smith let go of Madelyn and strolled around her chair. He picked up the file, flipped it open, and scanned the contents. His lips pulled down. "I think it probably was hard to find, considering that a lot of this is supposed to be classified intel."

"Meaning you wanted your dirty secrets to stay buried?" Reginald fired.

Smith shut the file. "Meaning national security is at play, and I'm sure there are some government officials who would be very interested in learning how a civilian like you managed to get his hands on this kind of information."

Reginald rose and lunged across the desk to snatch the file from him. "Please. You're going to pretend that you never access classified files for your buddy Aiden? That you don't circumvent the law when necessary?"

"I'm not going to pretend anything." He looked over at Madelyn. "She knows exactly what I am."

"Madelyn knows about the people you took out for Uncle Sam? She knows how you are a trained killer?" Doubt dripped from every word. "She knows—"

"*Enough.*" Madelyn shot to her feet. Her small hands fisted. "I don't want to hear another negative word about Smith, do you understand? You're not going to make me turn on him. I want him with me. I trust him completely."

A little hum came from Reginald. "You shouldn't."

"Maybe it's you I shouldn't trust." Her hair slid over her shoulder. Her eyes were stark. "How did you know that Bryson's death wasn't a suicide?"

Reginald's fingers skimmed over the closed file. "I got a tip from one of the officers at the station. I have a very positive relationship with local law enforcement." A shrug. "I play golf each week with the former police chief and mayor. If you came to visit me more often, you'd know that."

Of course, he had a positive relationship with them. Smith barely contained an eye roll.

"I wasn't aware that Bryson's actual cause of death was public knowledge yet," Reginald continued carefully. "And I didn't want to drop a big bombshell on you. Your nerves are very delicate, Madelyn—"

Smith snorted. "Bullshit. The woman has nerves of steel."

Madelyn's throat moved as she swallowed. Her gaze didn't leave her stepfather. "How did you know to come to my house after the attack? I didn't call you."

"You should call me more often." He crossed his arms over his chest. "Perhaps you would be a great deal safer if you did."

"How did you know to come to my house?" Madelyn pushed.

Reginald's eyelids flickered. "Like I said before, I enjoy a good relationship with local law enforcement. I received notice about your attack from a concerned acquaintance, and I immediately rushed to make certain you were all right."

So he'd been tipped off? That was his story? "Not sure I buy that," Smith drawled. "But, sure, what the hell? Let's say it's true."

Reginald's already tight jaw seemed to harden even more.

"Let's say it's true," Smith repeated with a nod. "And let's say that you also have some sort of surveillance going on where Madelyn is concerned. You must, right? Since you've been digging into my life—your fancy report proves that you've got surveillance happening on her. You knew I was circulating in Madelyn's orbit again, so you started your research on me. Probably thought you'd find enough dirty deeds that you could use it to get me out of her world, didn't you?"

No answer from Reginald. But, silence *was* actually an answer, wasn't it? Did Madelyn realize that? *Such a dick.* "You're not going to keep me away from her. You just don't have that kind of power," Smith told him bluntly. *No one does.*

"It's not always safe to be around Madelyn." Reginald's tone had turned smooth. A bit sad. "Unfortunate, isn't it, darling?" Reginald said to her. "But you have to look out for others. I'm sure you remember all the lessons your dear mother taught you."

Smith caught one of her fisted hands with his. Tenderly, he opened her fingers. Slid his between hers. "Screw the guilt routine. I'm plenty safe with her. Just as she's gonna be safe with me." Time to get to the point. "You have a bodyguard or a PI watching her?"

Reginald's eye lashes flickered. "I don't know what you mean."

"Yeah, you do. I spoke clearly enough. You have eyes on her. Not twenty-four, seven, or the attack at her place would never have happened. But enough surveillance that you get a feel for who might be circulating in her life. I'm figuring if you don't like the people around her, you make fun little files on them." He inclined his head toward the desk and the manila file. "And you either threaten them by saying you'll reveal dirty details of their lives, or you buy them off—whatever it takes to make sure that Madelyn stays alone."

"Stays *safe*," Reginald snapped back. "I make sure that she is *safe*. She can't trust just anyone. People lie. They deceive. Without my care, she will be hurt. I promised her mother that I'd look after her, and that is exactly what I am doing."

Madelyn sucked in a sharp breath.

"Good thing she went to Aiden when she wanted to start up her own business, huh?" Smith tightened his hold on Madelyn's hand. "You couldn't buy him off, so he finally helped her to get some freedom. Oh, hey, here's a fun tip for you—you won't be able to buy me off, either. I'm with her for the long haul."

"Fuck you, Smith."

Smith just shrugged.

"Why?" Madelyn demanded. "Why have you been doing this to me?"

"Because I love you. You're my daughter. I want you *safe*."

That key word. *Safe.* It blasted in Smith's head. "You know he's been watching her."

Reginald's hard expression cracked, for just a moment.

But that moment was all Smith needed. *Bingo.* "You've been aware that he was out there, closing in. You thought he might use someone else to hurt her, so you investigated anyone who seemed like a threat in your mind. You kept a guard in the background because you were afraid the attack on her could come at any time. You even moved down here because you were so scared."

No denial.

How about that? Looked like Smith would be winning that bet with Madelyn. But first... "I want every piece of information you have on the sonofabitch who took Madelyn so long ago." Smith raised one brow. "I'm guessing the file on him must be a whole lot thicker than the one you have on me. Give me everything you've got."

Madelyn pulled her hand from Smith's. She surged forward and slapped both her hands down on the desk. "You've known that he was watching me? This whole time?"

"No." A hard, negative shake of Reginald's head. "No, I haven't. I *don't* know."

"You suspect," Smith said. "Come on. Drop the bullshit."

"I don't—" Reginald began.

"You think he's been watching me all these years?" Pain cracked through Madelyn's voice. "You think he's been out there, waiting to hurt me again, and you didn't tell me?"

Reginald blanched and reached for her hand, but Madelyn pulled back before he made contact. "I was...I was just trying to take care of you," he explained, voice gruff. "You were safe in D.C. You were anonymous there."

Bull. She'd never been anonymous as Reginald Guyer's stepdaughter.

He kept her locked away, like a princess in a castle.

"Then you came down here." Reginald added after a thick swallow. "You put your name in the press so much. You were taking clients left and right. People with contacts, and I-I just was afraid that the past might get stirred up." Reginald ran a shaking hand over his face.

"Stirred up?" Madelyn questioned. "What does that even mean?"

Reginald grimaced. He did not speak.

"We're going back to Vegas," Madelyn told her stepfather.

Another fast, negative shake of his head. "There is nothing in Vegas—"

"Then we'll find nothing, but we're going there. Smith thinks it's a good idea. Before we came here today, Smith told me that you knew the bastard had been watching me. I told Smith that he was wrong. That you wouldn't keep something like that from me."

"I would do anything to protect you," Reginald told her. *"Anything.* I swore to your mother—"

"She's not here. I am. I am in front of you, asking for your help. If you do have files on what happened to me, if you have a suspicion about who took me all of those years ago, *tell me*. Help me. Tell me. Don't leave me in the dark."

Those last words hurt Smith's heart. She had been left in the dark before, but she'd gotten herself out.

Pain shadowed Reginald's eyes. "There isn't anything to tell. I looked for him, yes. I have considerable resources, and I used those resources. For the three years that you were in Europe, I tried to dig up every bit of information that I could. My investigators searched. They found nothing I could use. Eventually, your mother and I decided that with new identities, you should be safe enough. And you were. You were safe for years."

Her head tipped forward, and her hair slid over her shoulder once more. "Do you think what's happening to me now is tied to the past?"

His lips thinned.

"I hate bullshit," Smith announced.

Both of their heads whipped toward him.

He rolled one shoulder. "I do. It wastes my time. Pisses me off." True story. "So let's cut to the chase, shall we? Because I have a whole lot to do on my agenda today, and listening to you sputter and stall just isn't gonna work for me." Now, to get focused. "You had investigators looking for the man who took Madelyn all those years ago. You kept her out of the country for three years. That tells me you never thought Madelyn's abduction was random. You believed she was a very specific target. You believed the man who had her would track her down again. That he wasn't going to give up just because she moved away." Damn disturbing. "That's not the usual MO of a kidnapping."

"Her case was hardly usual," Reginald rasped. "In case you weren't aware, the man killed her best friend because Madelyn left him."

Madelyn jerked away from the desk.

"I'm aware," Smith assured him. "What I'm not aware of is why you think Madelyn was targeted. What was it about her that drew the perp's attention?"

Reginald looked away from Madelyn. "We were never able to determine that. The FBI believed the man felt a connection to Madelyn."

More bullshit. "It will go faster if you tell me the truth."

Reginald rushed from behind the desk and stomped toward Smith. "Just what do you think you'll be able to do? Hmm? You think you're going to ride in and solve the crime? Find the man who has been missing for *years?* I thought he was dead. I thought this was over. I thought that maybe she could have a regular life and then—" He broke off, catching himself.

"Don't stop now," Smith ordered. "You can't leave us in suspense."

But Reginald had stopped. His attention shifted to Madelyn, and his face softened. "Want to go back to Paris? You love the art there. Or maybe Rome. You can see the Sistine Chapel again. Remember how excited you were the first time? Told me it was the most beautiful thing you'd ever seen in your life."

She blinked. "You don't think he's dead any longer."

"*Let it go.* I can have you on a plane within the hour—"

"Because...what? One of your investigators finally found something? Or he—he contacted you—"

"The bastard sent me your ring."

Madelyn's brow furrowed. "I don't know what you're talking about."

"It was a little birthstone ring that your mom gave you. You never mentioned it. Never seemed to notice that it was gone after the abduction, but your mom knew. She searched your apartment, and it wasn't there, and she was so certain you'd been wearing it that night." His breath blew out. "He took it. The Feds said that—that certain types of killers do that."

"They take trophies," Smith said as his gut twisted. "Helps the bastards to relive the crimes."

Madelyn grabbed her stepfather's arm. "*He sent a trophy to you?*"

Reginald's chin lifted. "The ring was found in the back of my limo. In a little, black box. I opened the box, and I found the ring and a note."

"What did the note say?" Madelyn asked, voice tight.

His head turned so he stared into her eyes. "*Authenticate this.*"

"Fuck," Smith swore.

Madelyn let go of her stepfather and stumbled back.

"It was shortly after you opened your authentication business."

"No." Madelyn retreated one step. Then another. "No."

"That's why I moved down here. Why—yes, dammit—I *do* have a bodyguard watching you. I even had your neighbors reporting to me. I needed to protect you. I kept trying to get you to move in with me. The house here is so much more secure than your place."

"Why didn't you tell me?" Madelyn burst out. "It's my life. I needed to know!"

"You had finally stopped being so damn scared." His hand yanked through his hair. "You had your own business. Your house. You were so proud of yourself. And I just—I couldn't take it all away again. I was trying to find him. *I still am trying.* I hoped we could take him out—" Reginald stopped.

Too late.

Smith had caught the slip up. "You wanted to find him and kill him."

Madelyn retreated another step. "I need to get out of here."

Reginald rounded on Smith. "Like your plans are so different? What are you going to do? Find him and give him a long talk about how he's a terrible person?" The biting words mocked Smith. "Are you going to let the cops send him to a cushy prison for the rest of days while he lives on the dime of taxpayers? He *kidnapped* Madelyn. He murdered her best friend. He's probably killed others over the years."

"You should have told me about the ring," Madelyn blasted. "You should have told me everything!"

Reginald sent her a tortured glance. "Maybe I wanted you to be able to sleep at night. Maybe I wanted you to have a life again. If I could have found him, you never needed to know. He would have been eliminated, and you could have been happy. Really happy. Not just the pretend smiles you give so easily."

So Reginald had noticed those, too. "I want the ring."

"I don't have it any longer."

God save him from idiots. "You do." He pointed toward the antlers. "It's in the safe behind those big-ass antlers."

A hitch in Reginald's breathing. "I have no idea what you—"

"Save me some time and effort. Give me the ring. You should have turned it over to the Feds right away. You *get* that you contaminated evidence, right? Get that you could have turned it over and maybe there was a clue on the damn thing? DNA? A fingerprint? *Something?*"

"I had it examined," Reginald snapped. "By the best forensic experts that I could get. *Nothing* was on the ring or the note. If there had been something I could have used, I would have done so."

You mean you would have used it to hunt down the bastard and kill him.

"Give us the ring *and* the note," Smith demanded. "Because maybe my experts are a whole hell of a lot better than yours."

Reginald didn't move.

"I want my ring," Madelyn said.

And her stepfather deflated like a balloon. Shoulders hunching, he rushed to his hidden safe. A safe that was exactly where Smith had suspected. Moments later, he was handing a clear, zipped bag to Smith. Through the plastic, Smith could see the ring and the note.

Fury poured through him. "Anything else you haven't told us?"

But Reginald's lips clamped together.

"I want to leave," Madelyn said. "Smith, come with me?"

His head turned, and he saw that her hand reached for him. Automatically, he stepped toward her. His left hand held tightly to the bag, but his right reached for hers. As soon his fingers curled around her hand, he saw her release a long breath.

She led the way to the door. Yanked it open. Didn't look back.

"You're not just going to turn him over to the cops."

Reginald's low voice easily carried to Smith.

"But killing him won't be as easy as you think."

Smith glanced back. "I never think killing is easy." *But I still get the job done.*

"She'll hate you before this is all over," Reginald warned.

What in the hell?

"No." From Madelyn. "I could never hate Smith. Not him." A pause. "And not you, either. But right now, I am so pissed at you that I feel like I'm shaking apart. *You should have told me.*" She tugged on Smith's hand again.

He wasn't going to stand there a moment longer. She wanted out. They were getting out. He followed her through the doorway but still heard Reginald softly say—

"Sometimes, it's the truth that hurts the most. That's why people lie."

CHAPTER THIRTEEN

"Well, this is a beautiful cluster of a situation." Detective Audrey Campbell stared at the plastic bag that Smith had dropped onto the small table in the interrogation room.

Not that this scene was an interrogation. At least, Madelyn didn't think it was. Honestly, though, she didn't know exactly what was happening.

He's out there. He's been watching. He's in Miami. He's...

God, Smith had been right. The monster from her nightmares had been behind the entrapment in the elevator. Behind the attack at her house. Behind Andrew Bryson's murder?

"Chain of custody is screwed to hell and back." Audrey tilted her head as she studied the evidence bag. "And if your stepfather already had the ring examined, well, that is just like extra fuckery. A dozen hands would have touched it."

"If they were professionals, they would have handled the ring and the note with care." This response came from Tony. Because she and Aiden were also squeezed into that little room. Smith had called them on the way over and briefed them. Madelyn had heard him order Aiden to stay away from the police station.

But Aiden and Tony had already been there waiting when Madelyn and Smith arrived. Madelyn figured Aiden didn't take orders from anyone, even his best friend.

Audrey glanced at Madelyn. "You can confirm that this ring belongs to you?"

She stared at the little amethyst stone in the bag. "I-I did have a ring like that one." A lifetime ago. "I don't know what happened to it. Can't even remember the last time I wore it."

"The night you were taken?" Audrey pushed.

"I don't know." She hadn't been thinking about jewelry when she escaped. "I can't remember. I used to wear it a lot, I know that. But after the attack, I just—I didn't think about it again. We left. We boxed up everything and flew away." Her temples ached. "After we arrived in Europe, my mom decided to get rid of all our old stuff. She told me it didn't fit with our new life."

"So maybe you thought the ring had just been tossed out by her." Aiden nodded. "Only it hadn't been. Perhaps she was even ditching everything just so you wouldn't notice the ring was gone."

Audrey's red nails tapped against the tabletop. "You are a childhood abduction survivor."

Madelyn looked up and found Audrey's eyes on her.

"Didn't think this was important to mention to me during our last big chat?" Audrey asked, voice curt.

"I don't mention my past to many people."

"I'm not people. I'm a police detective. And I'm the cop investigating the *murder* of the man who attacked you in your home." She pointed at the ring. "Now I'm seeing this shit. I'm hearing that some old stalker may be terrorizing you. You get that this changes the whole course of my investigation?" Her voice rose. "How can I do my job if I'm not informed?"

Smith had been standing near a long mirror that ran the length of the wall on the right. He stepped forward and made his way to Madelyn's side. She sat in one of the chairs near the little table. Tony was beside her.

Smith put his hand on Madelyn's shoulder. "She's the one who wanted to give the evidence to you. I wanted to turn it over to my own contacts. *Madelyn* is the one doing things the right way."

"Your definition of right and mine are quite different," Audrey snapped. "After all, you're the one who snuck in to see a prisoner last night and nearly compromised my case—"

"You mean I'm the one who found the prisoner who'd been murdered under your nose?" he returned silkily. "Guilty as charged."

Audrey glared at him. Madelyn couldn't see Smith's face from her position, but she suspected he wasn't glaring back. Knowing Smith, he probably wore his devil-may-care grin.

"The Feds will be coming in on this one," Tony announced, drawing everyone's attention. She pointed to the bag. "A killer who collects trophies. And a man who has stalked his prey for this length of time?" A swift inhale. "That's a serious obsession. For whatever reason, he's escalated in the last few days. Another attack will be imminent." Her head turned toward Madelyn. "It's not safe for you."

She didn't know if anything had ever been safe.

"You should get out of town," Tony advised her. "Go off the radar for a bit."

"We are getting out of town." But it wasn't exactly off the radar. "Smith and I are heading to Vegas."

Surprise widened Tony's eyes. "You're going home?"

How did Tony know that Vegas was home for her? "Smith told you that already?" She'd only told him that morning.

"I found out myself. I knew you were young when the attack happened. Just had to get access to the FBI database—"

"I do *not* need to hear this," Audrey snarled. "If you're illegally accessing information—"

"You probably don't need to hear this," Aiden agreed. "So forget my lovely wife said that, will you? I've already forgotten. Didn't hear a word."

"Me, either," Smith added.

Tony's gaze didn't waver as she told Madelyn, "Home isn't a haven for you."

It never had been.

Tony reached out and squeezed Madelyn's hand. "Be careful there."

"I'm not going to let her out of my sight," Smith promised. "Don't worry about that. And your pal Memphis is going to fly in and meet us. I already texted him. He'll be watching our six."

"I'm investigating a murder, and you're leaving town?" Audrey straightened. "No, no, that's—"

"You can't tell them not to leave." Aiden adjusted his suit's left sleeve as he stood at Tony's side. "No cause for that. And I'm pretty sure you cleared Smith last night. At least, that's what my lawyer said. She *was* present for part of the grilling, wasn't she? So unless you are about to arrest either Smith or Madelyn, I don't see how you can stop them from doing what they want."

And what Madelyn wanted to do?

Stop this bastard. Before he comes for me again.

***

"If you want to talk, you can call me anytime."

Madelyn felt a trickle of sweat slide down her back as she turned to stare at Tony. They were outside the station. Finally. Audrey had stopped grilling them all and stormed away with the evidence bag. Madelyn and Tony stood on the sidewalk, a few feet from the station's entrance. Aiden had opened the back door of his limo for Tony, but she hadn't climbed inside.

Her gaze was on Madelyn.

"I know I'm basically a stranger." Tony grimaced. "But you and I have more in common than you might suspect." She sent a faint smile to Madelyn. "Some scars are just on the inside, you know?"

"Yes. I-I know."

Tony's stare swept toward Smith. He stood close by, talking softly on his phone. "He's not as bad as he wants the world to think." Low.

And again, Madelyn heard herself say, "Yes, I know." She didn't think Smith was bad at all.

"Tony?" Aiden called. "How about you get inside the *air conditioning* and put your feet up and relax? Can you do that for me and my poor heart? Relax for like, five minutes?"

Tony shook her head. "Some men just like to worry." She turned away. "Smith has my number. Call it anytime." She ducked into the back of the limo.

Aiden didn't immediately follow her. His worried stare darted to Madelyn. "You *sure* you want to head to Vegas?"

"That's where it all started for me. Maybe that's where it will all end."

He shut the door of the limo and walked toward her. He was as tall as Smith. But he didn't have that whole sense of raw power that she associated with Smith. Aiden was polish. Sophistication.

Smith was sex appeal. Savagery.

Strength.

"Just be sure that when things *do* end, you and Smith are the ones standing."

Yes, that was a very necessary part of her plan.

She heard the pad of steps behind her and knew that Smith had closed in. When he touched the small of her back, warmth seemed to pour through her.

"Our plane will be ready when we get to the airport," Smith said. "Thanks for letting us use the jet, Aiden."

"Anytime," Aiden murmured. His stare had drifted to Smith. Narrowed. "Buddy, you good?"

"Can't say that I am, no. Some prick is gunning for Madelyn, and she's lived her life in fear." Each word pounded with a hard intensity. "Nope, can't say that I'm good at all. Probably just the opposite."

Aiden whistled. "That worries me."

"No worries necessary. Like I said, Memphis will be meeting us."

Aiden pursed his lips. "Yeah, because you and Memphis Camden together is what I call a reassuring combo."

A second limo pulled up to the curb.

"That's our ride." Smith urged her forward. "Let's go, baby."

But Aiden still stood in their way. "Got a call from my contact at Wilde right before Tony and I arrived at the police station. That bit of tech we found in the elevator? It did allow someone to remotely control the car. My guy thinks the person pulling the strings would have needed to be within a half-mile radius. Said it was damn good tech—good and dangerous as hell. He's passing it along to Uncle Sam because he's worried about potential terroristic threats."

Her breath caught.

"Do you get what I'm saying?" Aiden stepped closer to them. "This isn't the case of some crazy guy in the woods abducting kids. Something else is happening. You're dealing with someone who either has some great tech skills or who has enough money to hire someone who can get the job done for him. This isn't amateur hour. We're talking about next-level tech." His gaze raked Madelyn. "Tony told me what she discovered about your past. Your attack from childhood doesn't track with what's happening now."

Didn't track? "You're saying it's not the same person?" She shook her head. "He sent the ring to my stepfather. It *has* to be the same person."

Aiden opened his mouth. But stopped. He shared an unreadable look with Smith, and when she turned her head, she caught the faint incline of Smith's head.

Her stomach knotted. She'd just missed something.

"Stay alert, my friend." Aiden backed up a step. "Let me know if there is any way I can help when you get to Vegas."

"Thanks. You just keep eyes on Tony."

Aiden reached for the door's handle.

Smith and Madelyn hurried toward the second limo, but she couldn't help but glance back, and when she did...

She found Aiden still standing beside his ride, watching her, with worry in his eyes.

***

Aiden hauled the door closed behind him, not waiting for the driver to shut it. "I don't trust him."

Tony—who had *not* put her feet up like he'd so nicely requested—sent him a frown. "Smith?

You don't trust *Smith?*" Surprise had her voice rising. "I thought we were past that—"

"We are past it. I meant Reginald Guyer. Madelyn's stepfather. It's him I don't trust." He lifted her feet up and put them on the seat. "The guy just magically turns up this ring, and we're supposed to take his word about how he got it? And when?"

Her beautiful brow furrowed. "You think he's involved?"

"I think you had to examine a dead body last night. I think Reginald was at the police station." Proximity and opportunity. "I think someone with money and connections needed to get the piece of tech that sabotaged the elevator." *And Reginald is loaded.*

"You're saying this man sent someone to attack his own daughter?"

He—Aiden stopped. "Maybe I'm not thinking clearly." He hadn't been thinking clearly ever since he found out about the babies. All he wanted to do was grab Tony and run away with her. Wrap the woman in freaking bubble wrap and watch her like a hawk. But Tony wasn't someone who would ever be cosseted away. He *knew* that about her. Loved that about her, too.

"I worry Smith isn't thinking clearly."

Her statement had him doing a double take.

"Did you see the way he watched her?" Tony tapped her chin. "They're involved."

"Um, so, Smith had a crush on Madelyn back in school, but—"

"This isn't a crush. You need to take a look at his eyes when they are on her." A definite nod.

"They're involved. When the mighty fall, they fall hard."

"Smith said he wasn't playing knight in shining armor." He distinctly remembered that conversation.

"Then I guess he lied to you." She didn't seem particularly concerned. Her finger tapped against her chin once more. "Or maybe, he's just not *playing*."

Smith, serious about a woman? As far as Aiden knew, his buddy had never been in a serious relationship. "Smith isn't big on ties."

"Doesn't matter if you're big on them or not. Sometimes, you still find yourself caught in them." She bit her lower lip. "You really think Reginald might be involved in this?"

Ah. She'd circled back. Tony never let a point go. "I don't know." He was running on fumes and worry. "Maybe."

"Wouldn't be the first time a father hurt a child." Sadness slid through her tone. He knew that Tony had covered too many tragic cases where the victim had been hurt by the person who was supposed to be a protector.

Helpless because he couldn't stand for her to ever be sad, Aiden leaned forward. His fingers curled under her chin. "Our kids will always be loved. Always."

She smiled at him. "I know."

His lips brushed over hers.

***

"A bag for you and a bag for me will be waiting on the jet." Smith could see Madelyn's profile as she stared out one of the limo's windows. "You can eat and rest on the plane. We'll be in Vegas before you know it." The benefit of a private flight? It was direct, and they didn't have to worry about an eternal boarding wait.

"When did you arrange all of this?" She seemed dazed. "I was with you all morning."

"Just took a few texts to set up. Not a big deal. Aiden and I travel all the time, so the pilot stays at the ready." She was sitting right across from him, but Smith felt like Madelyn was a million miles away. "Baby?"

She flinched.

"You don't have to do this." The words needed to be said. "You can stay here. I can get you the best security in the world. You'll be protected. I can go to Vegas and see what I can uncover."

"No." Her head turned toward him. There were no tears in her eyes, just a steady determination. "I do have to go. I have to do this." Her chin lifted. "I don't want any lies or secrets. I don't want you to hold back anything that you discover because you're afraid of my reaction."

"I won't. Count on it."

"We're in this together," she added. "And I—" Madelyn blew out a hard breath. "I don't know how I'm supposed to repay you."

"Repay me?" His brows shot up. "That's easy. You don't."

"Smith."

"Madelyn."

Her lush lips pressed together. "You're uprooting your life for me."

He stretched out on the leather seat. "I had vacation time coming. A few days in Sin City? Sounds like one hell of a party."

"Stop. This isn't a pleasure trip for you. You're helping me, and I need to repay you."

He crossed his arms over his chest and studied her. "I don't need your money, sweetheart. Actually, since you're asking for full disclosure, I don't need anyone's money. I have plenty of my own. Oh, sure, I'm not exactly in Aiden's category. Who is? But I more than get by." He could walk away from his position with Aiden's company right that moment and never have to work again. Smith had made plenty of profitable investments over the years. "Unlike my father, I know how to manage my money."

"You never told me what happened to him."

Because he didn't particularly enjoy taking that walk. But if Madelyn was asking, he'd share. With her. "Reginald thinks he knows everything about my dad and me. He's wrong."

She shifted a bit in her seat. "*I* know you're not a killer."

Dammit. "I am."

She sucked in a breath.

"I warned you about that before. I was trained well for the job." An area where he'd excelled. "But I'm not a criminal. At the end, my father—he got desperate. He lost everything that we ever had. My mother left him. Married someone else who didn't have, ah, financial difficulties. She didn't exactly want a pain-in-the-ass teen dodging her steps, so I didn't belong in her new life."

Madelyn leaned forward. "Yes, you did. You belong anywhere you want to belong."

The woman was fucking sweet.

"My dad got desperate." *No secrets, right?* "He misled people who counted on him. He misled me."

"You left school."

"Didn't have a choice. Found out the cops were gonna close in."

She reached out. Her hand pressed to his thigh. "I'm sorry. I didn't know. I just—there were so many stories in school."

"Ah, baby, you weren't supposed to listen to stories, remember?"

"I didn't believe them." Her stare held his.

Maybe I don't want her listening to stories because I don't want her to think I'm the villain. "My dad went to jail. You know, one of those places that's more like a country club than anything else? He still acted like it was hell. He got put in a cell, and I got a ticket into the military." It had been the option that gave Smith a second chance. A new life. "Served my time. Learned dangerous skills. Came back to find that my dad had gotten out early and had already remarried. His new wife was five years older than me, and she was seven months pregnant."

Madelyn's lips parted.

"He's happy. My mom's happy. They're doing their thing. I'm doing mine." He looked down at her hand. Such slender, delicate fingers.

"You didn't say you were happy."

Smith glanced back at her face.

"You said your father was happy. That your mother was happy. What about you?"

Interesting question. Smith wasn't sure if anyone had ever actually asked him if he was happy before. "I've got a great job. Great best friend. I'm staying in a penthouse on the beach. What's not to be happy about?"

"That's still not a real answer."

It was the only answer he had. "What about you?"

"I was...close." Her hand moved away.

Dammit. He'd liked her touching him.

"When I opened my business. Got my own place. Got my own life. I was starting to feel happy. Then with you—when I let go in that elevator—" Her nostrils flared. "Only now I find out that he's been watching me for so long. It's hard to be truly happy when you keep waiting for something bad to happen."

"Nothing else bad is going to happen to you."

Her fingers twisted in her lap. "I'd like for you to be happy, Smith."

His breath caught in his chest. "I'd like that for you, too, Madelyn." *More than anything else.*

She sent him the smallest smile, but it hit his heart with the impact of a punch. And she told him, "Maybe when this is over, we can both really be happy."

"We will be." A vow. *Or at least, you will be.*

"I'm glad you're my friend."

What the hell? The sexiest woman he'd ever met had just said she was glad they were *friends* and he—he... "I'm glad, too." He freaking meant those gruff words. He was so screwed.

She jumped out of her seat and moved beside him. In a flash, Madelyn had caught his arm and wrapped it around her shoulders. She snuggled against him, like it was the most natural thing in the world, and it *felt* natural. His head tilted, and, jeez, he caught himself sniffing her hair.

I am so screwed.

"I know we're not *just* friends," she added softly, huskily. "And I'm really glad about that, too." Her head turned toward him.

She had to have the most beautiful eyes in the entire world.

"I'm glad you were my first, Smith."

Baby, I want to be your only.

"When it comes to you," she added, voice soft, "there are lots of things that I'm glad about."

He had to kiss her. She was too sexy and sweet and tempting and—*mine. She is mine.* His mouth took hers, with more care than he knew he even possessed. Soft and gentle. "Me, too."

Something else he would be damn glad about?

When I find the bastard after you. When I stop him for good.

One thing Madelyn hadn't asked him about...she hadn't asked if Reginald had been right with his parting shots. Smith knew her stepfather had fully intended to kill the SOB who'd taken Madelyn so long ago. Reginald didn't want the guy in a cage. He wanted the man in the ground.

And that's exactly where I intend to put him.

CHAPTER FOURTEEN

"The honeymoon suite?" Madelyn spun around in the middle of the ginormous room, her hands waving in the air. "You booked us in the honeymoon suite?"

Smith had just lifted a bottle of champagne that yes, had been chilling in front of the electric fireplace. "Most of the rooms were booked. Had to get what I could on short notice." He didn't even seem mildly concerned. "Besides, it's a great cover. If anyone should come looking for you, I doubt they'd think to check here."

Her mouth opened. Closed. He had a point she couldn't deny.

"Good vintage," he said with a nod as he read the label on the champagne. "Want some?"

She marched toward the bedroom. Pointed inside. She'd gone in there moments before only to rush right out. "The bed is heart shaped."

"Cute."

Yes, vaguely, it was. "There are rose petals sprinkled all over it."

"Um." He popped the cork on the champagne. The bubbly poured out, and he expertly filled the two glasses.

"There are mirrors on the ceiling."

"Mirrors? As in multiple? Or just one big mirror?"

"I—does it matter?"

"Not really." He picked up the glasses and closed in on her. "Have a sip. You'll relax."

No, she would not. But she still snatched the champagne and *maybe* she downed it all in a couple of gulps. Fine, there was no maybe involved. She did drain it. Fast.

"Okay." Smith nodded, then sipped his champagne. "You must definitely be a fan of this vintage. Mental note. I'll be sure to keep it in stock for you."

She wasn't a fan of the champagne. She'd barely tasted it. From the moment they'd stepped foot off the private plane, her body had practically been humming with tension. Nerves. Vegas was like she remembered, but also different. So much different.

Same bright lights. Same crowds. Same hum of energy. But when she'd been a kid, everything had seemed so much bigger.

Sure, yes, the Ferris wheel in the middle of the city was still incredible. And they'd passed the replica of the Eiffel Tower. The fountains had been dancing and shooting lights in all of their glory. All of that was the same.

But...

Different.

The city felt darker. Shadows seemed to lurk everywhere. There were more buildings. More flashing signs. More shows.

But less...*I don't know what*. It just—it wasn't home any longer.

"Want more?" Smith asked her, voice courteous.

Madelyn shook her head. "No, I—"

A knock sounded at the door. The bellhop? Had he forgotten something?

"Right on time," Smith said. But he didn't head for the door. "You *sure* you don't want another glass? Might make this meeting go easier."

And, again, she shook her head.

"Got it." He strolled across the room, pausing to put the glasses back next to the champagne bottle. After glancing through the peephole, Smith swung open the door.

Craning her neck, Madelyn tried to get a glimpse of their visitor. Correction, visitors. Because when Smith moved back, three men stepped inside.

The first man wore battered jeans and a black t-shirt that stretched across his chest. His hair was dark, stubble covered his jaw, and his green eyes gleamed.

"Memphis Camden," Smith said with a wave toward the fellow. "Ice Breaker extraordinaire."

"Aw, don't go blowing smoke up my ass. You know I'm average at best." Memphis sent her a lazy grin as he dipped his head toward her. The faintest trace of the South whispered beneath his deep tone. "And you must be Madelyn."

She nodded.

The other two men followed Memphis inside before Smith shut the door.

Memphis pointed to the brown-haired guy behind him. The guy in the gray suit with polished shoes. "FBI Agent Oliver Foxx. Two X's on the end of his name, just because he's an extra asshole that way."

Oliver Foxx rolled his eyes even as he stepped forward and offered his hand to Madelyn. "I'm not an asshole. And it's nice to meet you, ma'am."

"You *are* an asshole," Memphis informed him. "Just ask anyone. Especially the other FBI agents. They don't like you much, and that's really why you should go freelance and work more with me."

She wasn't sure how to respond so Madelyn took Oliver's offered hand. His skin was warm, his hold careful, as he briefly shook her hand.

"I've been reviewing your case," Oliver told her. He released her hand. "Got to say, you sure did slip off the radar. And, ah, the name is *Madelyn* now?"

"Madelyn," Smith agreed, voice flat. "And she just moved out of the country with her mother. Not like a thirteen-year-old gets to control it when her mom makes a move."

Madelyn's gaze darted to their third visitor. His hair was even darker than Memphis's. He was big, wide in the shoulders. Like Memphis, he wore jeans, but he had on a button-down shirt with them. There was a faint bulge near his hip, and she wondered if he was armed.

"US Marshal Titan Everett. Kinda the quiet sort, so don't take offense if he just stands there and glares," Memphis added. "Only gets chatty when he's drunk off his ass."

Titan was pretty much just standing there and glaring. Not at her so much, but at the suite. His gaze seemed to be taking everything in, including the open champagne. Then his head turned toward her.

A long, white scar bisected his right eyebrow and climbed toward his forehead. A second scar sliced down from his cheekbone and slid along his jaw. His bright, bright blue eyes glittered.

Squaring her shoulders, she crossed to him. Madelyn offered her hand.

He stared at her hand, then at her. Without a word, he shook and let her go. In that brief flash, she'd felt the calluses that lined his fingers and palm.

"Didn't realize you were gonna be here, Titan," Smith said. "Long time."

Again, no words came from Titan. He just nodded.

Smith knows him? And he must know Oliver, too, since he hadn't introduced himself to the FBI agent.

Realizing that she hadn't shaken Memphis's hand, Madelyn turned toward him. "I—" She cleared her throat. Stuck out her hand to him. "Thank you for helping me. I appreciate it."

His slow smile came again. *Watch out with him.* Her instincts screamed that Memphis used that slow, easy smile to his advantage every chance he got. "My pleasure, ma'am," Memphis told her. "Got a thing about bastards who take kids—the thing is that those pricks really piss me off, and I do enjoy shoving them into cages for the rest of their miserable lives."

That sounded like a thing, all right. "I think I have that same thing."

He laughed. "I like you."

"Wonderful." A snap from Smith. He put his hands on Madelyn's shoulders and steered her a bit *away* from the other men. "We all like Madelyn. We all want to help her. So how about we get things moving?"

Memphis waved toward the champagne. "Don't I get some? Or is that reserved just for the couple in the *honeymoon* suite?" A low whistle. "Mighty *personal,* don't you think? Believe I warned you about that. Why can't people just listen to my warnings? I always know what I'm talking about."

"Eliza listens to you," Oliver pointed out.

Who was Eliza? Madelyn had no clue, but Memphis's face softened at the mention of her name.

Oliver put his briefcase on the table in the small dining area. "Isn't having her listen to you enough?" His fingers pushed the button on the side, and the briefcase snapped open.

As the top rose, Madelyn edged in closer.

"The original FBI agents who worked your case have retired," Oliver explained. "But after Memphis reached out to me, I did some digging and found your old file. Put in some calls to the retired agents, too—though they didn't have much more to add. As you know, your abductor was never found." He pulled out two files from the briefcase and put them on the glass tabletop.

She inched ever closer. The labels on the top file—her name, the bold, FBI stamp—sent tension humming through her. "My abductor and Heather Russell's killer."

Heather's file was there, too. She could see it beneath her own. Madelyn reached for the files.

Oliver closed his fingers around her wrist. "The pictures in there are graphic. They were never released to the public, and they aren't the sort of thing that you will ever forget once you see them."

Like forgetting had ever been possible. "My best friend was stabbed fifteen times. I know that already. I've never been able to forget it."

His lips thinned. "There's knowing and then there's seeing. You don't have to see that."

Yes, she did. "I'm not a scared little girl any longer." No, she was a scared grown woman, and she was so sick and tired of being scared. "I do have to see it. I want to see everything."

Memphis hauled out a chair for her. "Then how about you go first? You review the material, see if anything jumps out at you, then Smith and I will take our shot."

She sat in the chair. Curled her fingers under the seat and inched it closer to the table. After a long exhale, Madelyn reached for the first file. The one with her name on it. Not Madelyn Lake. Margaret Edgewood.

She opened the file.

And saw her thirteen-year-old-self staring back at her.

***

"Honeymoon suite, really?" Memphis muttered as he stepped back and gave Madelyn some space. "What the hell, man? Are you hunting her abductor or trying to make her fall in love with you?"

Smith sent Memphis a glare. "Don't make me kick your ass right now."

"Oooh. Scared. Oh, wait, I'm not." He grabbed Smith's arm and hauled him toward the bedroom.

Smith dug in his heels because he wanted to stay close to Madelyn.

"Titan and Oliver are right there. Your lady is good." Memphis kept dragging at him, and Smith gave in. Once they were in the bedroom, Memphis let him go and frowned at the bed. "Rose petals?"

"This suite has the best security in the whole hotel. And there's a damn convention in town so there weren't a ton of options—"

"When *isn't* there a convention in Vegas?"

"My choices were limited," Smith snapped. "Get off my dick, would you? I wanted her in a good place. A safe place. This was the best I could find on short notice."

Memphis didn't look convinced, but he did let the matter drop. Finally.

"What the hell is Titan doing here?" Smith wanted to know. When he'd last texted with Memphis, he'd only been told that the Ice Breaker and Oliver would be showing up. There'd been no mention of a blast from Smith's military past.

"Oh, what? You're not excited to see your old military buddy? Such a small world, isn't it? Imagine my surprise when I realized my friend Titan knew you, too." Memphis pursed his lips.

"Titan is considering joining the Ice Breakers, and I thought we might be able to use his skills on this case. Thought you also might like a friendly face, but I didn't exactly see a friendly reception in there when you two crossed paths." He jerked his thumb over his shoulder. The bedroom door was still open, but their voices were very, very low. No one else would overhear this conversation. "There something about Titan I need to know?"

"Titan is one of the most dangerous bastards I've ever met."

Memphis nodded. "I'm hearing good things. Keep going."

"I'd trust him with my life any day of the week."

"Again, nice. Tell me more because I'm not seeing a red flag."

"But he has demons that chase him. His own hell. Think of a volcano that is getting ready to erupt. That's Titan." A long exhale. "I don't know what's gonna happen on this case, and I need someone to have my back who will not—"

"*Smith!*" Madelyn yelled.

He bolted out of the bedroom. Rushed straight for her as his heart nearly lunged right out of his chest. She was still seated at the table, and Titan and Oliver were on either side of her. They'd gathered close and were both looking over her shoulder and down at the files.

He grabbed Oliver—he'd never met the FBI agent in person before, but Smith had chatted with the guy online and via texts—and lunged to Madelyn's side. He looked down and swore. "Baby, you shouldn't be seeing this." A young girl.

Blond hair. Knife wounds. Soaked in blood. Thick stab wounds covered her chest and her thin arms.

Her best friend. Heather Russell.

"I think he took her necklace." Madelyn's head swung toward Smith.

There were tear tracks on her cheeks. Did she realize that?

Madelyn motioned toward the photo. He noticed that she didn't actually look at it. "Do you see that she has a chain around her neck?"

He peered at the photo. Saw the thin, silvery chain.

"There was a charm on the end of her necklace. I know because she gave me the same necklace. One for me, one for her. Remember those old best friend charms? We each had one. I- I took mine off the night I was taken. I was crying before bed. Upset because I couldn't go to her party. So..." She sniffed. "I didn't feel like a good friend, and I took it off and put it in my nightstand. It was there when I went back. Heather—that chain she is wearing should have been connected to her charm. But it's not."

Smith's gaze flickered to Memphis. "I told you that we turned Madelyn's ring over to the cops."

"Yeah, and I briefed these two." He waved a finger toward Oliver and Titan. "We're thinking the perp is taking trophies? Jewelry? Madelyn's ring and Heather's charm?"

Sure seemed that way to Smith. "Did the family ever report Heather's charm as missing?" Smith asked Oliver.

Oliver reached for the file. Flipped through some notes. "I don't think so. I mean, it's not mentioned in here." He looked up. "I'll talk to them and find out. The mom is deceased, but the dad still lives in town. Brother does, too. He's the owner of the Night Gate casino." Frowning, he put down the file. "Anything else sticking out to you, Madelyn?"

Her hand reached up to her neck, as if to touch a necklace that wasn't there. "She screamed so much. On the ph-phone, when he called...the cops had it on speaker, and she *screamed*."

Fuck. Smith wanted to grab her and lock his arms around her and protect her from everything. *But you can't protect someone from memories.*

"There were defensive wounds on her arms," Oliver told her. His index finger jabbed toward the pics. "See those slices? Your friend was a fighter. She didn't make it easy on him."

Madelyn sucked in a hard breath.

Smith glared at him. "Do you think you're helping right now? Because you're not."

Madelyn snagged Smith's hand. "It's okay."

No, nothing was okay.

Oliver grimaced. "Maybe some of this intel will help, then. Just like at Madelyn's apartment, there was no sign of forced entry at Heather's home. He knew exactly how to get into her house. And that place did have a security system. A security system, and not just one dog, but two."

"Apple and Orange," Madelyn said quietly as her fingers released Smith's hand.

"Right. And Heather's parents were gone out of town on business, but her brother was there." Oliver scratched his jaw. "So, the original agents were working on the assumption that the perp took Madelyn, then, when she escaped, he turned his fury on her best friend."

Madelyn nodded. "I got away. He punished me by taking her. It was my fault."

"Fuck that," Memphis growled. "The only person to blame is that bastard."

Smith one hundred percent agreed. But...Oliver was frowning. *You'd better watch what the hell you say to Madelyn—*

"I don't know why they jumped to that conclusion," Oliver mused. "I can see a different possibility."

Everyone looked at Oliver.

"Uh, I mean, I don't know why they all assumed he took Heather *after* Madelyn escaped. That doesn't have to be the timeline." His stare sharpened on Madelyn. "You told the cops you were alone in that little room."

"I was."

"But do you know if there were other rooms?"

Madelyn shook her head. "I don't remember. I just ran out as fast as I could."

Oh, fuck. Smith knew where the agent was about to go, and he shook his head. One thing he was quickly learning about the FBI agent—Oliver had a big-ass mouth. Titan never talked, but Oliver seemed to talk too damn much. *Filter, man. Get a filter. Think things through before you—*

"She could have already been there," Oliver said as he scrunched his face. "That's what makes sense to me. I mean, think about it. He'd obviously been doing surveillance work on *both* of you. He must have if he knew how to get in her house without rousing her dogs. Maybe he didn't take her *after* you escaped. Maybe he already had you both. Best friends, a package deal. But when you escaped, he got pissed so he had to—"

Madelyn leapt to her feet. "Are you telling me I left my best friend with him?"

Oliver's mouth hung open.

And that, dumbass, was why I was shaking my head.

"I ran out and *left* her?" Madelyn put a hand to her mouth. "Why didn't the other cops tell me? Why didn't someone say—"

"Because no one knows that happened." Titan's gravelly voice. The first time he'd spoken since entering the suite. Titan's voice was always gravelly and rough. One of the reasons he didn't talk much. He'd once told Smith that just the sound of his voice had made little kids cry.

Pair that with his scars, and the kids went running from him.

"I read the files, too," Titan added, grunting.

Oliver frowned at him. "When did you get access to FBI files?"

"On the way here," Memphis answered for him. "We had to do something during our flight."

"Those are confidential—" Oliver blustered.

Titan rolled his eyes.

Memphis ignored Oliver's bluster. "We need to fucking find out which theory is correct. This is kind of a big damn deal. Because either Madelyn was the main target and her friend was collateral damage—sorry, I know that sounds callous as hell, Madelyn—"

She nodded. "Yes, it does."

He grimaced but continued, "Or if you were *both* the targets, then we need a new look at this scene. A new profile, too. Can't believe the FBI wouldn't have been jumping on every possible theory of the crime back in the day."

"Brother gave them the time." A growl from Titan. "The original Feds built the profile on that."

Oliver swung toward him. "How do you know that? I didn't see *anything* about that detail in the FBI files."

"Then the agents on the case weren't as thorough as they needed to be," Memphis cut in to say. "Because the local cops had that info. Titan and I got in town early, and we had some time to kill." He rocked forward onto the balls of his feet. "First stop was a dive on the edge of town. Retired cops like to gather there to drink coffee and relive their glory days. We chatted it up with retired Detective Noah Truce. He said that Heather's brother swore he checked on her at three a.m. Said he got up for water. She was tucked in, sleeping like an angel. That was the same time that headlights were hitting Madelyn as she ran down the road about five miles from town. Going by that timeline, no way could the cops think that the perp had taken them both together. *That's* why the theory isn't listed in the FBI files, anyway. The cops had a reliable witness who told them otherwise so they didn't consider that the girls might have originally been abducted as a package near the same time. The theory didn't fit so it was discarded."

But Smith realized Oliver still didn't look convinced. If anything, he appeared even more suspicious. "A sixteen-year-old teen is the 'reliable witness' in this picture?" A negative shake of his head. "Sorry, but I was a sixteen-year-old boy once. And when my parents were out of town, I was either sneaking my girlfriend *in* the house, or I was sneaking out to meet her."

Silence.

Fuck. He's right. Smith thought of all the times he'd snuck out over the years. Sometimes, he'd just crept out so he could keep an eye on a certain "good girl" who seemed so lost in town.

"You think her brother Quinn lied?" Madelyn finally asked.

Oliver looked back at the picture of Heather. "Doesn't she deserve for us to find out whether or not he did? One little lie could have changed everything."

"Gonna have one big problem with this talk-to-the-brother plan," Memphis warned.

Great. Smith knew this was going to be bad. The tone of Memphis's voice told him everything.

"According to my new retired cop best friend, the entire Russell family will not talk to authorities. At least, not without a wall of lawyers. They made it very clear—through a ton of press coverage—that they thought the local cops screwed up the case. You go at them, waving your FBI badge, and I suspect Quinn Russell won't give you so much as the time of day."

"Hmm." Oliver straightened his tie. "That's an annoyance. But I can—"

"He'll talk to me," Madelyn interrupted. Her voice was soft but certain, and it fell in the room with the force of a bomb.

Smith realized all of the men were locked and focused on her.

She squared her shoulders. He saw that her fingers slid over the closed file that belonged to Heather. Lingered. "He'll talk to me," she said once more. "Quinn and I both loved Heather. If I tell him that we're hunting her killer, he'll help."

Smith wasn't so sure of that, but he hated to rain on her parade, so he remained quiet.

"If nothing else," Madelyn said, "the shock of seeing me will at least allow us to have the chance to question him." She looked at Smith for reassurance. "Right?"

He stared into her eyes. Saw hope and determination. *Not gonna rain on her. Not ever.* "Right."

***

"Wrong, Smith. This is so fucking wrong." Memphis glared at him. "False hope is killer. If you're gonna be an Ice Breaker, the first thing you have to do is learn to *not* give families false hope. That shit wrecks them. When they reach us, they've already been let down more times than they can count. The least we can do is give them the truth."

They were in the hallway outside of the suite. "I am giving her the truth. I'll take her to talk with the brother first thing tomorrow."

"He might slam the door in her face. You *are* fully aware of that fact." Memphis exhaled on a gusty sigh.

Smith stiffened. "No one slams the door on Madelyn. Sure as fuck not when I'm with her." He'd like to see an asshole try.

Memphis shared a long, silent look with Titan. "You see what I mean?" Memphis appeared both satisfied and heavily annoyed. "Personal. You told me Smith *never* got personal. And I said, 'Oh, but you're wrong, he is personally involved all the way to his balls—'"

"What the fuck kind of an expression is that?" Smith demanded.

"It's the kind of expression that says you're fucking the client."

Smith lunged for Memphis, but Titan stepped between them. Titan shook his head.

Great. Now *Titan* was the one with control. Smith puffed out his cheeks and took a step back. At least the FBI agent was already gone. "She's gonna have new nightmares now."

Titan studied him, but it was Memphis who asked, "You suspected her friend might have been with her the whole time?"

He didn't speak. Mostly because speaking would make him feel guilty. He'd said he wouldn't hold anything back from Madelyn. *But I just didn't want to hurt her.* "It was a possibility that slid through my mind, yes. Only we have *zero* proof that event occurred, so I didn't want to give her a new hellscape until I had actual evidence one way or the other."

"The brother can give you that evidence."

Maybe. Or maybe not. "Too late to pay him a visit today, but you can damn well bet we'll be at his office door bright and early in the morning."

"We'll be working on other leads until then. Digging through some local case files. Seeing if anything shakes loose." Memphis slid his hands into the front pockets of his jeans. "If we had a perp who was taking trophies and was so organized that he managed to abduct two girls without being detected, there is no way that he decided to just retire. He would have kept going. Unless he *had* to stop."

Titan inclined his head in agreement. "He could be dead. Or in jail."

"That's why we'll be searching through old records to see if anyone stands out to us. Any SOB who might have spent too much time or paid too much attention to thirteen-year-old-girls. Bastards like that usually have a type." Disgust thickened Memphis's voice.

He was saying stuff that Smith knew. Sure, Smith didn't claim to be a profiler. Hell, no. But he'd read plenty of books and watched crime shows—didn't they always say that killers went after a certain type of victim? Yet... "If this perp likes teen girls, then why would he still be locked on her now? Wouldn't she have—fuck, hate to say it but—wouldn't Madelyn have aged up too much for his taste?"

"Oliver would say yes," Memphis replied after a brief pause. "He'd tell you that—typically—guys like him are attracted because of the youth, the innocence—whatever the hell it is that calls to these predators. But that is only *if* Madelyn was taken because she looked like the type of vic this guy desired. If she was taken for another reason—"

"What reason would that be?" Smith cut in to ask.

Memphis shrugged. "Maybe it was personal. If it was, and if he took her just because he wanted your lady in particular, then it wouldn't matter how old she was. He will always want her, no matter what."

Rage pulsed inside of Smith. "He's not getting her."

Memphis opened his mouth—

The suite door behind Smith flew open. He spun and found Madelyn standing in the doorway. "I have to get out of here," she told him, her words tumbling out too quickly. "Right *now*."

CHAPTER FIFTEEN

She'd been suffocating in that suite. Okay, fine, mentally, she knew the reaction was way, way over the top. The suite had been huge, after all. But Madelyn needed to get *out*. The revelations that Smith's friends had dropped on her—the possibility that she'd left Heather behind...

Get out.

Madelyn had thrown on fresh black pants and a matching top. She'd snagged black flats and yanked open the door to find Smith still huddled with Memphis and Titan. Smith had taken one look at her face, and he'd just nodded.

Now they were walking along the strip, lights were everywhere, voices rose and fell, and the city was so bright that she couldn't even see the stars when she tilted back her head.

I saw stars that night. A sky full of them.

Madelyn didn't even realize where they were going—she'd just been walking, but as the hulking exterior of the casino appeared before her, she realized that maybe, deep down, she'd always had a destination in mind.

Pausing near the edge of the sidewalk, Madelyn stared up at the casino. "This place used to be called Cowboy Luck, back when my mom worked here." The name had changed. The big, flashing lights showed her that now the casino was Midnight's Magic. Her head tipped back as she took in the sight of the big magic hat on the side of the building. The lights shifted and changed, and a rabbit appeared to jump from the hat. "But I bet you already knew that, didn't you?"

"I've done some digging, yes."

"Enough digging that you also thought I'd left my best friend in that terrible place?" Her head turned so she could see his reaction.

There was no reaction. No change of expression. Not so much as a flicker of his eyelashes. "No one knows if that happened. It's just a possibility."

"A possibility I never considered, but you did." Her gut told her this was true.

"Yes."

"And you didn't mention it to me." Pain slid through her. "I thought we were going to be honest with each other."

Smith stepped closer. Other people milled around them on the sidewalk, and he kept his voice low as he told her, "Why would I give you a new nightmare when I didn't have enough proof that situation had occurred? No one knows yet. It's possible you were the only one in that place. That after you escaped, *then* he went for Heather. Maybe the original timeline is correct. We'll find out the truth, together, and I will tell you everything that is discovered." His hand lifted.

His knuckles skimmed over her cheek. "I didn't want to hurt you unnecessarily."

Part of her just wanted to turn into his touch. She still didn't understand why he was doing so much for her, and it wasn't right for her to be angry with him but...she just hurt. And when you hurt, you sometimes lashed out at others.

Her eyes closed. "No one from my mom's past is going to be in that casino. There's no point in me heading inside. I have no idea why I even came to this place tonight."

"You came here because you're looking for answers. And someone from your mom's past *does* work here."

Just like that, her eyes flew right back open.

"Got the text about him from Memphis just as we landed. Memphis has reach like you wouldn't believe."

So she was realizing.

"When your mom was here, there was a bouncer named Troy Washington who kept an eye on the ladies who worked the late-night shift."

He meant the strippers. Because in the back of Cowboy Luck? A private club that catered to the wealthy.

"Over the years, Troy has moved up the ranks. He's head of security now. Don't know if he's working right now, but he used to love nights. Why don't we go inside and find out if he still does?"

Her head angled toward the grand entrance. "What if he doesn't remember her?" It had been so long ago.

But...

"What if he does?" Smith asked.

And with that, she found herself walking up the steps that led to Midnight's Magic. As soon as the glass doors slid open, she could hear the sound of bells ringing, various musical melodies playing from the slot machines, the rush of spins, and the excited—and disappointed—cries from the patrons. To the left, she saw rows and rows of slot machines. People were seated at the machines, drinks in hand. To the right, the tables waited. Poker. Blackjack. Roulette.

A massive staircase led to a second gambling area. Glass elevators were about fifteen feet away. She could see the entrance to a restaurant, and a big fountain flowed right in the middle of the lobby.

"This way." Smith took her hand and led her toward the security guard who stood near the slot machines.

The woman frowned at their approach, but after just a second, her frown turned into a smile. One of those professional ones that never reached her eyes.

"May I help you?"

"We're old friends of Troy Washington," Smith replied. "He on the floor tonight?"

The woman's brows rose. She also glanced briefly toward the second floor, and she touched the earpiece she wore for just an instant. "Old friends?"

Madelyn turned and glanced up at the second floor. There was dark glass covering part of that floor. A private room? And Smith saying they were "old friends" was a definite stretch. "He knew my mother," Madelyn said as she turned back toward the other woman. "He—"

"He says for you to come up." The woman pointed. "Take the stairs. Then go in the third door to the right. He'll be waiting for you."

Wow. That had certainly been fast. But Madelyn wasn't about to argue. She bounded for the stairs, with Smith right beside her.

But at the top of the stairs, she hesitated. Madelyn edged toward Smith. "Why would he agree so quickly?" She got that the security guard must have received a transmission from Troy via her earpiece, but the guard hadn't even said a word about Madelyn *to* anyone. She'd just received an order. *Maybe someone had been listening to the whole conversation?* Just how much could be picked up by the transmitter that the guard had worn?

"Washington was probably watching the door when we came in. Let's go find out just why he wanted to see you." But there was something about Smith's voice that was off. A tension that she didn't like.

He put his body in front of hers as they headed toward the third door. He reached for the handle, swung it open, and when they stepped inside, she saw a man standing in front of the dark glass on the far side of the room. His back was to her and Smith, and his focus seemed completely locked on the floor below him.

He had a broad back, one covered in a blue suit coat. Madelyn could see the faint hint of silver in his dark hair.

"I like to watch the door some nights because it gives me the chance to see trouble coming." His voice was warm and rich. "Tonight, I had to do a double take when I saw a ghost come inside my casino."

"I'm not a ghost," Madelyn denied.

"No?" He spun to face her. His gaze slowly took in her features. "Some differences, I suppose, but you could almost pass for your mother's twin."

He does know me. Or rather, he'd known her mom. Madelyn took a quick step toward him but stopped.

"How is she?" A wistful smile curved his lips. "Always hoped she'd come back to town and see me."

"I'm sorry." She could *feel* that something had been there. It was in his smile and in the gleam of memories that flashed from his dark eyes. "My mother passed away last year."

He sucked in a breath. Pain came and went on his face. "Was she—did she have a happy life? Her laugh, God, that laugh of hers used to light me up."

She didn't remember her mother laughing much. Not after they'd left Vegas. Not very much before, either. This man had known a different side of her mother.

And as he stared at Madelyn, he seemed to realize that. "I'm sorry," he said to her, and the words were genuine. "Your mother tended to carry a whole lot of secrets, and that weight could sure pull her down sometimes."

As shock rolled through her, Madelyn's head swung toward Smith. Secrets? Her mother?

"You the boyfriend?" Troy Washington asked.

Before Smith could reply, Madelyn shifted her focus back to Troy and answered, "Smith is my friend. He's helping me—we...we need information."

"Don't know if I have a lot of that to give you." Troy motioned to the two chairs that sat opposite his desk. He'd been standing behind the desk as he stared down at the floor below. "Why don't you take a seat?"

Sitting was a good idea. Especially since her knees had gone jiggly. Gratefully, she sat down. Smith eased into the chair beside her, and the two men seemed to take each other's measure.

Troy pulled out the chair behind his desk and let out a sigh as he settled in it. "Friend, huh?"

"I'm not particularly into labels," Smith murmured.

"Uh, huh. Bet you're not." Troy rubbed the back of his neck. "I don't know what kind of information you're looking for, Margaret, but—"

The name jarred her.

"But I'm not sure I can help. Haven't talked to your mother since she told me goodbye right after you—well, after that bad business with you." His lips tugged downward. "Scared the hell out of her, you know. Never seen Kat like that."

Kat. Her mother had been Kathleen. Kathleen Edgewood. Then she'd become Stephanie Guyer. *And we both had a new life.*

"Don't get me wrong, she was pretty shaken when I first met her, too. Shaken, but still brave. I knew she was running, but she was determined to start a new life for the two of you in Vegas. Told me it was the perfect place to vanish. It's Sin City. We can all hide here and forget what we did in the past."

Madelyn knew her mouth had just dropped open. She should close it and ask questions.

Smith beat her to the punch. "Did you just say that, uh, Margaret's mother was running from something when she first came to Vegas?"

"Something or someone. Never really told me which. Didn't ask." He shrugged. "If a woman wants you to know, she'll tell you. If she doesn't, I'm smart enough not to go digging."

Smith winced. "Yeah, I've heard digging can get you in trouble."

"It can." That was all. Troy didn't say anything else. Just sat there. But his gaze did return to Madelyn. His expression softened as he studied her. "You used to run around in the dressing rooms. Trying on every costume you could find. I didn't mind it, but eventually management said we couldn't have a kid back there."

Madelyn had no memory of ever running around in any dressing room.

"I let you stay at first because I hated the way you'd cry for your dad."

Her spine stiffened. "Excuse me?"

"You'd ask for him over and over. Sweet little kid, probably about four, and you just wanted to know where your dad had gone." Sadness swept into his eyes. "But Kat told me he'd died. *That* she did offer to me. Since I don't dig, I didn't ask more. Figured she'd tell me if she wanted me to know. Only she never did."

Madelyn's heart felt as if it might lunge out of her chest at any moment. "I was...four when we moved to Vegas?"

"Um." But he nodded. "Looked around that age to me, but I'm not exactly an expert on kids."

"And my dad had died? My mom told you that?" *Lies and lies and lies.* But...who had her mother been lying to? To Troy, when she said Madelyn's father was dead?

Or did she lie to me when she said he walked out before I was born, that he never wanted me?

"Yeah. She told me he'd died. And—" Troy stopped.

He couldn't just stop. Madelyn leaned toward him, almost falling out of her chair. "I'm digging right now."

"Thought you might be." A murmured response.

"The man who took me all those years ago was never caught."

"Crying shame. Someone should have dragged him from the dark and made him sorry he was ever born." His stare flickered to Smith. "That on your agenda?"

"Right at the top of the to-do list."

"Good. Figured as much."

She grabbed the edges of the desk. "I'm looking for something that might help me find him."

"Don't know anything about him." Troy rose. "Sorry I can't help you. Like I said, Kat hauled ass out of town. She disappeared. Never heard from her again. Always figured she'd just gotten herself another new identity. Started over like she'd done here in Vegas."

The room was spinning. To stay balanced, Madelyn held even tighter to the desk. "A new identity?"

His lips pressed together before he glanced at his watch. "I need to go check in with my people. Real nice to see you, Margaret. Again, sorry about your mother." He walked from behind the desk and strode toward the door.

Smith jumped into his path. "When Madelyn's mother came to work at Cowboy Luck, who helped her get a new identity?"

"You're in my way."

"Was it you?"

Troy's chin lifted.

Madelyn rose. "I think that's a yes."

Troy's head angled her way. "I'm warning you. Digging isn't the best thing to do. People leave the past behind for a reason."

"You thought she'd killed him," Smith said flatly.

Madelyn sucked in a sharp breath. No, no, there was some mistake—

Troy shrugged. "A beautiful woman comes to town. She's desperate for money but needs it to be under the table because she can't afford a paper trail. Got a cute kid with her, one who is begging for her dad, and every time little Margaret asked for him, Kat's whole face would lock down." Another shrug, but this time, it seemed as if he attempted to push the past away. And failed. "Kat had bruises on her arms when she arrived. The kind of bruises you get when someone grabs you and digs in. The ones that look just like fingerprints."

Madelyn stumbled against her chair.

"Beneath her makeup, I could see the black eyes. So, no, I didn't ask her questions. Second week she was here, she offered me all of her tips if I could help her get a new ID. I happened to know someone, and he gave her a two-for-one special." He didn't look back at Madelyn. "It took a few years, but eventually, she started to smile and laugh again. Like I said, Kat's smile could light you up." He stepped around Smith. "Got things to do. A casino to guard." His fingers curled around the doorknob.

"Who was I before?" Madelyn asked him. "Before I became...Margaret?"

Who am I now?

"Kat wanted to keep the first names. Said it would be easier for you and her that way. You *were* Margaret. She was Kat. But she told me your last name was Smith originally, and I'm sure that was bullshit."

Yes, Madelyn suspected it had been.

Troy yanked open the door. "Be careful in Sin City. It wasn't so good to you before." He swept her a quick, final glance. "You might not think it's so good now, either."

Smith edged to the right, blocking Troy's view of Madelyn. "Are you threatening her?" A low, lethal tone had entered his voice.

"No. Never that. I was warning her. This city wasn't safe for her when she was a kid, and her mom sure as hell cut out fast. Maybe the trouble is still here. If so, you'd better be a real good *friend* and stick close to her."

"Don't worry. This *friend* knows how to kick the ass of anyone who comes to hurt her."

CHAPTER SIXTEEN

He didn't like it. Smith had tried to keep silent—as much as he could, not like he was Titan, the bastard who could stay silent for freaking ever—during the chat with Troy Washington, but the meeting had left him feeling more than a little uneasy.

It was just so damn convenient. Walking into the casino and immediately being given the all-clear to meet with Washington. It was almost as if the guy had been waiting for them.

And how could that be? Unless someone tipped him off that we were in the area. Someone who had been, say, watching Madelyn.

Like the bodyguard her stepdad hired? Or the bastard who has been stalking her since she was thirteen years old?

"Do you think she killed him?" Madelyn suddenly asked.

They'd snagged a cab back to their hotel. During the drive over, they'd both been quiet. Not like he wanted to share all with the cabbie. The short elevator ride up had been quiet, too, but he'd been able to practically hear the thoughts screaming from Madelyn. "I don't know."

They were once again in the honeymoon suite. Madelyn stared out at the city, with her arms wrapped around her stomach. Her back was to him, and she seemed delicate and beautiful. When she turned her head to glance at him, her eyes were shrouded in secrets, and he wanted to pull her into his arms. Promise her that everything was going to be all right.

But he couldn't make that promise, not yet. Memphis had been right. Ice Breakers shouldn't give false hope. It was cruel as hell.

"My mom told me that he abandoned us. As soon as he found out she was pregnant, he left." She turned to fully face him. "My mom told me—over and over again—that my father didn't want me. That we were better off without him."

He surged to her, helpless. Her pain ate at him. "If he was abusive, then you were better off without him." His hands closed around her shoulders. "And as far as killing him..." Fuck. Sure, it could be a possibility. "We need to find out who you were. Who you *really* were." Margaret Edgewood had just been another alias. Margaret Smith? Smith was always a convenient BS name. But... "This is all happening under the assumption that Troy Washington was telling us the truth." A pause. "We both know what they say about assuming."

Her brows shot up. "You think he was lying? Why would he do that?"

"People lie for a million reasons, but it's usually to cover up something they don't want biting them in the ass." His fingers slid down her arms. "I think he was involved with your mother at some point."

"So do I. I could see it in his eyes. Hear it in his voice when he said her name."

"They were involved, but when she cut out of Vegas, she didn't tell him where she was going. She didn't ask him to go with her. She started a new life far, far away, and never came back."

Her eyes widened. "You think she was running from Troy?"

"I don't know what to think yet. But I had the feeling he was waiting for us to walk into that casino. Guys on Troy's level don't waste time watching doors. He was waiting for you. Specifically." Something that made tension knot in Smith's gut.

"How could that be the case? No one knew we were coming to Vegas."

Someone might have known—the bastard who'd been arranging the attacks on Madelyn. *Or maybe her stepfather's goon.* "Your stepfather had people watching you."

"You think my stepdad told Troy?"

One option. "I think it's possible someone else has been watching you, too."

"The man who's trying to hurt me."

Yes. "I don't trust Washington. I don't know him. That's why I *will* be having Memphis and Titan find out as much intel on him as possible." He let her go. Stepped back.

"You'll also try to get them to figure out who I am, too, won't you?"

There were ways to speed the process along. "You don't remember anything at all about your dad?"

Her eyes seemed so stark. "I thought I'd never even met him."

And yet Washington was saying she'd begged for him over and over. "Guessing you never did any of those online DNA tests?"

"Of course, not. I was supposed to leave my past behind. Not try to unearth some long-lost relatives."

Might be time to change that. "Do you have anything of your mother's? Something that might have her DNA on it? A lock of hair? Something that—"

"Reginald got rid of everything, and my mom wanted to be cremated."

Fuck. "We'll find out who she really was. Who *you* were. We'll pull in Oliver and get him to see if the FBI can turn up anything."

"There might not be anything to turn up. My mother reinvented herself as Stephanie Guyer. She must have reinvented herself as Kathleen Edgewood, too. There is no telling who she was before. I don't think I ever knew her at all."

On this, she was wrong. "The woman loved you."

Madelyn swallowed.

"I don't care what her real name was—she loved you. She fought hard to protect you, and, no, you might not have liked her rules and you are damn right on that—but you did know her. She was your mom. She would have done anything for you." *And maybe she did. Maybe she killed to keep you safe.*

But the day had been filled with enough pain already.

He backed up a step. "You should get some rest. I'm gonna call Memphis and brief him on what we found out tonight." *And see if he can start investigating to see what's truth and what's bullshit.* "In the morning, we'll hit the brother's office and find out exactly what he remembers about that night and Heather's abduction."

Her gaze slid toward the bedroom door.

"You can sleep in there," he told her, aware that his voice had turned rough, "and I'll take the couch. It's huge. Plenty of room for me."

Her eyelashes flickered. "I can sleep in there," she repeated his words but—

Her tone was off. "Madelyn?"

She stepped around him. "You've been more than kind, and I don't think I can ever repay you, but I will try, I swear it."

His head craned as he watched her walk away. "Thought we covered that I don't do much to be kind. No repayment is necessary."

She looked back at him. Held his gaze.

Do not move. Let the woman go to bed. Do not fucking pounce on her because you are not that much of a bastard.

Her lips pressed together, and Madelyn marched away. She opened the bedroom door. Closed it a moment later with the softest of clicks.

Smith expelled the breath he'd been holding. *Fucking honeymoon suite.* He yanked his phone from his pocket and called Memphis. Of course, the guy answered immediately.

"How goes life in the honeymoon suite?"

"Fuck you."

Rumbling laughter.

"We had a meet and greet with Troy Washington tonight."

That stopped the laughter. "You did? Already? Someone moves fast. Got to say, I am impressed with your initiative. Tony was right. You'll be one hell of an Ice Breaker."

"He was waiting for us the minute we walked into the casino."

"That's...odd."

"Tell me about it. Ready for the next part?" Didn't matter if he was or not. "Washington says that he got a new identity for Madelyn and her mom. Madelyn isn't really Margaret Edgewood. Her mom was never really Kathleen Edgewood."

"Then who the hell are they?"

"That's what we're going to find out." He paced toward the window. Vegas at night—beautiful. A million lights. "And while we're at it, we're going to find out one more thing."

"Is it who abducted your girl? Because we're kinda already on that case."

"No, we're going to find out if Madelyn's father is still alive. See, while Troy Washington was being chatty, he let drop the little tidbit that he thinks her mother might have killed her father."

"Shit."

"It was rather a shitty night, thanks so much for asking." He rubbed at the tight muscles in the back of his neck. "Madelyn thought she'd never met her dad, that she'd lived in Vegas since she was a baby, but Troy said she was four when she moved here—and that she called for her dad all the time."

"Hell."

Yeah.

"Kids that little don't remember a lot." Memphis's voice was halting. "I don't remember jack from that age. It would have been easy enough for her to forget."

Especially if her mom had been "helping" her to forget. "Titan used to be hell on wheels when it came to trailing prey. Can you get him on Troy? I have a feeling that Troy might have just been feeding us lines, and I sure as hell would like to know who told him to throw out the bait."

"On it, man."

"Great, I—" His phone beeped. Smith glanced at the screen and saw that he was getting a call from Aiden. "Hey, this is Aiden. Give me a second, will you?"

"I'll get Titan moving. You tell Aiden congrats for me."

The easy words caught him by surprise. "You know already?"

"Dude. It's me. I know everything."

Smith switched to take Aiden's call. He began by saying, "Memphis says congrats."

Silence. Then, "You told him about Tony?"

"No, guy is just creepy like that. He knew. He's also on the other line—"

"Then I'll make this fast. We've got another dead body."

That *was* fast. And blunt. And so not the news Smith had been expecting. "Who the hell is dead?"

"The mysterious elevator repairman. We found him. Turns out the bastard died of a drug overdose two days after he left that damn device in my elevator."

The knots in Smith's neck got thicker. "That's one hell of a coincidence."

"Tell me about it. I don't like it, and Tony is pissed because the body was already released to the family. She wanted to take a look at it, but that doesn't seem to be happening."

Tony could usually make the dead talk, but not in this case. Not if she couldn't get access. "Someone is tying up loose ends." The elevator repairman. The bastard who'd been set up to attack Madelyn. "This isn't a damn thing like what happened to her before."

"Yeah, be sure you're passing that on to Memphis, would you? *I don't like this.* I feel like Madelyn is in the middle of some massive trap, and I'm worried as hell about the two of you. Memphis needs to watch your six at all times, and whatever you do—don't let Madelyn out of your sight."

He glanced toward the closed bedroom door.

***

Thought we covered that I don't do much to be kind. Smith's words replayed through her mind for about the twentieth time.

Madelyn threw off the bed covers. Rose petals fluttered in the air. She'd tried to get rid of them earlier, but there had been so many that shoving them all away had been impossible. She'd ditched her clothes and changed into a silky black gown that someone had packed in her magically-appearing-on-the-jet bag. The night gown had been brand new, and it fit her perfectly.

Another mystery associated with Smith.

There were truly too damn many mysteries in her life these days. Or maybe, always. There had always been mysteries, ever since she'd been four years old. Madelyn just hadn't realized the truth.

Her bare feet curled into the lush carpeting, and she crept toward the door. So much was happening and just closing her eyes and drifting off to sleep wasn't an option.

Not when she had to get answers. And there was *one* answer that she absolutely could get that night. After taking a deep breath, she closed her fingers around the doorknob and turned it. The door opened with the softest of creaks. She stepped over the threshold and spotted Smith.

"You think I like this shit, either? I don't. No way. Aiden just gave me the update, and I'm passing it along to you. Hell, yes, I'll stick to her like glue."

She stepped closer. She didn't think she'd made a sound, but Smith suddenly whirled to face her. His eyes widened as he seemed to drink her in.

The air seemed colder in there, and her nipples pebbled against the silky material of her gown. The gown skimmed the tops of her thighs and only had small spaghetti straps that slid across her shoulders, so it wasn't as if it provided her with a whole lot of covering.

Maybe she should have thought more about that lack of covering before coming to confront Smith.

Or maybe I'm lying to myself, and I wanted to come out like this to see what he'd do.

"Got to go," Smith barked into the phone. "Something came up. Hell, screw that. It's always up with her." He hung up, stalked toward her, and tossed the phone onto the couch as he closed in. His fingers flexed and fisted. Flexed and fisted. "You should be in bed."

"What's the update from Aiden?"

A muscle jerked along his jaw.

"No secrets, remember?"

That muscle jerked again. "I remember," he gritted. "The elevator repairman who probably planted the device to sabotage the elevator? Turns out the poor bastard OD'd two days after that little visit. Aiden and I happen to think that is convenient as hell."

Her mouth opened as she sucked in a shocked breath.

"Someone is getting rid of loose ends." His stare never left her face. "He will *not* be getting to you. I swear it. Whatever happens, I will protect you."

He meant it. Madelyn understood that truth with one hundred percent certainty. Smith would risk his life for her. And it just— "You're a liar."

He didn't deny the charge. His eyes glittered.

"You told me that you didn't do much to be kind."

A little furrow appeared between his brows. "You think it was kind just dropping the little bombshell about that guy's death? Sweetheart, we need to revisit what that term means."

Screw that. She'd wanted the truth. He'd given it to her. She couldn't think too much about that man's death. Not now. Her mind was already as tangled as her heart. Everything was so jumbled and twisted. The one thing that wasn't? *Smith.* "I wanted the truth. You gave it to me. That is kind."

"If you fucking say so. Rather thought it was a cold bastard thing to do."

He wasn't a cold bastard. At least, not with her. "You've done nothing but be kind to me. It doesn't make sense. *Why* would you do this for me? All of this?" She gestured to indicate the massive suite. "And bring in the Ice Breakers? Why?"

"You're in danger."

"Yes, but I think I've been in danger a long time. Not like it's new for me." Safety had been another lie. "Why are you helping me? If you're not kind, then why do it?"

"What am I supposed to say?" He stepped closer.

"You're supposed to say..." Madelyn wet her lower lip, and *she* inched closer, too. "That you're a good man. You hide it, but I can see it. I know exactly what you are. You're taking off time from your job. You're turning your life upside down, and you're doing it to help me. You act like you're some badass."

"Thanks for noticing. Wasn't sure you'd caught that part."

"*Stop* mocking! Stop teasing! You do it all the time because you don't want people to see who you really are." Her breath came faster. "But I see. You're the best man I've ever met, and I am more grateful to you than I can ever say."

"I don't want your gratitude."

"No, I get that. That's too bad, though. Because you have it."

His eyes swept over her. From her head to her toes, then back up. Seemed to glitter—no, burn—ever brighter. "Go to bed."

"I'm telling you that I think you're a hero—"

His mocking laughter cut her off. "That is not what I am. You should know better."

She could see right through him. "I do know better. I know exactly what you are. You're helping me so much because—"

"Because I want you, Madelyn. I've always wanted you."

Her breath caught.

"But I don't exactly want you fucking me out of gratitude. Not what I'd call a major stroke to the old ego. So how about you turn around and you go back into the bedroom, you shut the door, and you go to bed?"

She made no move to retreat. "I thought you didn't want to have sex with me again."

Surprise flashed on his face. "What the hell are you talking about?"

"You've been standoffish."

He gaped at her.

Crap. She wasn't explaining this well. Mostly because she'd never had to explain anything like this before. Most women her age could seduce a man easily. Meanwhile, Madelyn felt as if she was basically begging him to come into her bed.

"Standoffish?" His lips twisted, but the smile was mocking, with no gleam of amusement appearing in his eyes. "That's what I get for being a gentleman. I was worried you were sore, sweetheart. Trying to give your body time to adjust seeing as how I am the lucky bastard who got to have you."

She backed up a step.

"Oh? Did I not mention that I'm a territorial asshole?" he groused. "My bad. But, I think my control might just be reaching its limit. Probably because I *tried* to get you to leave, but you came back out looking like my best fantasy ever, and all I want to do is put my hands on you. Put my dick *in* you. Fuck you until you claw my back."

Madelyn swallowed.

"You came out here because you thought I didn't want to have sex with you again?" His head tilted. "Let me help you out. I *always* want to have sex with you. I see you, and my dick gets hard. You smile, and I want to carry you to the nearest bed. You kiss me, and I want to be balls deep inside you. Sort of basic facts of life for me where you're concerned."

She really should say something. She would, as soon as she managed to untangle her tongue.

"But your life is hell. Figured you didn't want a horny, territorial bastard like me coming at you again." A pause. "Because here is the thing, when

I say I'm territorial, that's something reserved for *you*. I was your first. I want to be your only."

Madelyn shook her head.

His expression hardened. "That's why I'm trying to keep my hands off. I know you're not playing for keeps. You'd never want to be with me long term, but the more I have of you, the more I will want you. I don't want any other SOB near you. I want you to be mine, always, and that is *not* what you want, so go back in the bedroom. Shut the door. Pull those covers up to your chin and—"

Madelyn rushed at him. Her hands flew out and curled around his powerful, upper arms. "You're the only one I've wanted. How could you think I would want to go to someone else? Smith, even when we were kids, it was you."

His eyes widened.

"It was you," Madelyn said again.

His mouth crashed onto hers.

CHAPTER SEVENTEEN

There would be no control.

Smith knew it on a deep, primal level. His control had been shredded to hell and back because of three little words. Not "I love you"—no, he didn't think she loved him, but fuck, he wished she did.

For now, she wanted him. That was enough.

It was you. Those were the three words. Words that told him he wasn't alone in his madness of lust and need. She'd wanted him before. She wanted him now.

He was going to fuck her like a man possessed.

He kissed her with a frantic need. A stark demand. Smith hadn't been lying when he told her that he was possessive. The thought of another man touching her, taking her—*no*. Madelyn's moans and sighs, her pleasure—that was all for him. She was for him.

He'd known it for years.

You weren't supposed to fall in love at sixteen. Not real love. At least, wasn't that what people said? But he'd met Madelyn at sixteen, and she'd been in his dark heart ever since. Even when he'd been facing hell in war zones, she'd been there. The dream that he just couldn't give up no matter how hard he tried. The hope that wouldn't die.

"I want you," Madelyn whispered against his mouth.

Yeah, dammit, he wasn't sure he'd be able to make it to the bedroom. He wanted to be in her, right the hell then. Smith's hands clamped around her hips, and he lifted her up against him. Her legs locked around his hips, and her silky gown shoved up to her waist. His dick rubbed against her, wanting *in*. He wanted in her so badly. Smith surged forward, and he pinned her to the nearest wall.

Have to be in. Have to touch her.

His left hand curled around her hip, but his right snaked between their bodies. She wore a pair of black panties—just as silky as the gown—and his fingers dove under the panties.

"Smith—"

"I need *in*." He shoved the panties to the side. His fingers rubbed over her clit. Dipped into her. She was wet and hot and so unbelievably tight. He withdrew his fingers, thrust them into her again, and she moaned his name.

He could make her come just like this. He knew it. A few more thrusts of his fingers, the hard rub of his thumb over her clit, and Madelyn would be coming for him. But he wanted his mouth on her core. Wanted to lick and lick and lick and feel her pleasure on his tongue.

He was frantic for her. Wanting every single bit of Madelyn.

Growling, he pulled his hand from between her thighs. He carried her to the bedroom, hating each step. *But don't take her against the wall. Fucking try for her—try—*

Try to be what? A gentleman? That shit wasn't going to last, but Madelyn needed care.

He lowered her onto the bed.

She needed—

Madelyn yanked the gown over her head and tossed it onto the floor. Rising to her knees, she reached for him. For the buckle of his belt.

His hands clamped down on hers. "Baby..."

The bedside lamp threw a soft glow onto her. "I want you to be the first everything for me." She tugged against his grip. "Let me—"

"I will lose my mind." Ragged. "You put your mouth on me, and I won't be able to hold back. I don't want to hurt you."

"You never have." She pressed a kiss to his neck. "You never will."

"Madelyn."

Once more, she tugged against his grip. "Let me..."

Like he could tell her no to anything. Especially the temptation of putting her mouth on him. Her hand slid from his hold. She unbuckled the belt. Eased down the zipper. The zipper's hiss seemed extra loud, and then she was carefully, hesitantly, shoving his boxers out of the way. The briefest of hesitations came from her before she began to lower her head.

"You don't have to," he rasped.

Her mouth was on him.

Still hesitant. Still careful. She started with a soft kiss right over the head of his dick. One of her hands curled around the thick length of his cock as she lifted it toward her. Madelyn bent and feathered another tender kiss over him.

Smith tilted his head back, squeezed his eyes shut, and knew he was going to lose his mind. Those feather-light kisses were akin to torture. So good. So tempting, but he desperately needed more and—

Her lips parted. Her mouth opened fully over him. Hot. Wet. Her tongue swirled around him. She sucked—and he was gone.

Fuck it.

"Can't." That was all he managed before he tumbled her back onto the bed. She still had her panties on, and he yanked them away. The fabric tore, and he tossed it aside. He left her only long enough to strip. Then Smith shoved her thighs apart and put his dick right at the entrance to her body. He thrust into her. Heaven. So tight and wet and...

Nothing between us.

He grabbed the sheet. Fisted it. "Sorry." Dammit, no. He couldn't do this.

Madelyn with my baby. Madelyn with me, always.

No, no, *no.*

Smith began to withdraw.

Her legs locked around his hips. "I'm covered," she told him. "There's no risk of a child."

His gaze flew to pin hers. He could barely think because she felt so freaking fantastic. And since he wasn't thinking clearly, he didn't speak clearly, either. No filter as he blurted, "Not a risk. I would love a baby with you."

Her eyes widened. "Smith?"

"Because I fucking love you."

Fuck. Dammit. *Fuck.*

Too late. The words were out, and there was no going back. He couldn't. Primal need exploded between them. Sex to sex. Nothing between them. All he felt was her, and she was paradise. Slick. Hot. Wet. *His.* He pounded into her again and again. He grabbed her legs and lifted them over his shoulders because he wanted to go in deeper. Harder. Wanted to own her.

As she owned him.

She'd owned him since they were sixteen. *Sixteen.*

She arched up against him, and he saw the pleasure sweep across her face as her orgasm hit. "Smith!" Her hands grabbed his arms. Her nails dug into him.

Hell, yes.

He rocked into her. Plunged. He could feel the delicate contractions along the length of his dick, and he erupted. A long, hard surge of release that had the mattress shaking. Her name tore from him even as—

Even as rose petals fluttered in the air?

He ignored the rose petals and drove into her again. She gasped and twisted up against him, and Smith didn't know if she was still coming or if she'd rushed into a second release. He kept thrusting because he could not get enough of her, and yes, hell, *yes*, her neck arched as she cried out again.

A second release. Definitely. He kissed her. Drank in her pleasure and knew that he would never, ever get enough of Madelyn.

He also knew that he'd made a confession he couldn't take back.

Talk about being fucked.

***

Rose petals were everywhere. In the, ah, heat of the moment, some had even been fluttering in the air. Now some stuck to Smith. Some stuck to her. When she'd tried to get rid of them before climbing into bed earlier, obviously, Madelyn had done a half-assed job.

But she wasn't particularly worried about the rose petals.

Her heart still hammered in her chest, but over that thunder, she could swear that she still heard the echo of Smith's words. *Because I fucking love you.*

Probably not the most romantic declaration ever. Mostly because of the "fucking" part. And she was sure that he hadn't meant what he said. Must be one of those heat-of-the-moment situations. Maybe Smith said those words to all his lovers.

Her body tensed. Anger burned inside, replacing what had been a rather pleasant—okay, *incredibly pleasant*—afterglow. She glared at Smith.

Concern immediately flashed on his handsome face. "I was too rough." He cursed himself even as he started to withdraw. "Baby, I'm sorry. I'll get a tub of warm water—"

"You didn't mean it."

He rolled from the bed. "Of course, I mean that I'll get warm water running in the bathroom for you. A soak will make you feel better."

"You didn't mean it when you said you loved me."

He stilled, halfway between the bed and the bathroom doorway. And *why* was she having this conversation right now? Why hadn't she just ignored his words? Madelyn sat up, pulling the sheet with her and holding it to her chest, right over the heart that ached.

"So you *did* hear that part," Smith rumbled.

"Guess you say that to all your lovers."

He spun in a flash. Took a lunging step toward the bed, then stopped himself. "No." Clipped. "Actually, you're the only person I've ever said those words to. I might lie about other things, but I don't just tell a woman I love her for shits and giggles—or for the best sex of my life."

There was a whole lot to unpack from those angry lines. So it took her an understandable minute to process things.

You're the only person I've ever said those words to.

Really? And her heart was back to drumming too fast because...

I don't just tell a woman I love her for shits and giggles.

Well, she certainly hoped that he didn't. But if he'd meant the words, then—then—

"Let me be clear," Smith began. Naked, aroused, hot, he stared straight at her. "I love you, Madelyn Lake. Or Margaret Edgewood. Or whoever the hell you are. I've loved you for a very long time, and I suspect I will love you until I die." A shrug of his broad shoulders. "My problem, not yours. I'll deal with it."

His problem?

Her eyes narrowed. "You said you wouldn't lie to me."

Was it her imagination or had his eyelashes just flickered?

"Madelyn..." Rough.

"You don't need to tell me I'm the best sex of your life. I get that I have a—a learning curve, clearly."

A furrow appeared between his eyes.

"I'm sure your other lovers have been fantastic." Her voice held a decided snap. "I get that I'm not them and I'm sure—" *I was awkward as hell when I went down on you.* Okay. She just couldn't say that. She was already confused and embarrassed and probably sounding crazy enough as it was.

"Screw anyone else," Smith snarled. "As far as I'm concerned, there is only you." He stalked toward her. Leaned over the bed. "For me, there is *only* you." Smith leaned forward, as if to kiss her, but he stopped. A muscle flexed along his jaw. "I'll get the tub ready." He swung away.

Her hand flew out and caught his wrist. "Forget the tub." She dropped the sheet and rose to her knees. "You can't say you love me one moment and then tell me it's a problem you'll *deal* with. Love isn't a problem. Love is supposed to be the best thing in the world. Doesn't every single greeting card tell you that? *Why* am I a problem for you?"

As if she had to ask. Her life was a mess, and he was in danger trying to help her sort it out. She brought danger wherever she went, and she knew that. He didn't want to stay close to her. She'd warned him what happened to people close to her.

Her hand snatched back. "I'm sorry. Forget it." Her gaze fell to his chest. To the tattoo that covered him.

Smith doesn't get scared. Wasn't that one of the many reasons she'd trusted him with all of her secrets? And yet...

Yet he turned away without a word. He headed into the bathroom while she crouched on the bed. He'd torn off her panties and thrown them. Maybe she should search for her underwear?

Madelyn climbed from the bed, but her legs felt shaky beneath her, so she threw out an arm to brace herself. Her palm flattened on the nightstand even as she heard the sound of running water.

Then she heard the pad of his footsteps.

Get it together, woman.

Her chin lifted. Her head turned and eyes locked on him. Still naked. Still far too sexy. And...glaring at her. Wait. Why was he glaring? Shouldn't she be the one glaring?

He went straight to her and scooped Madelyn up into his arms. "You are a problem in so many damn ways," he bit out.

Wonderful. Just the after-sex talk that a woman hoped to hear. One of her arms was around his neck, and her grip automatically tightened.

"You drive me crazy. Something you've done for years. Ever since you were sixteen years old, and you told me that you certainly hoped I didn't bite."

Her brows flew up. "I have no idea what you're talking about."

A soft laugh rumbled in his chest.

And then he lowered her into the biggest tub she'd ever seen. Steam drifted in the air, and rose petals—apparently, they truly were everywhere—floated on the surface of the water.

Smith climbed in with her. Eased behind her. His legs stretched around hers, and his arms curled over her mid-section, pulling her back against him.

"You drive me crazy because every single thing about you is sexy. I don't think you even try to be sexy, you just are." He pressed a kiss to her shoulder. "You're a problem because I'm not going to stop loving you."

The steam was making her eyes teary. That had to be it. Steam.

"Loving you is what I do. It's what I've done for years." Another kiss on her shoulder. "Do you know how much it wrecks me to know you were afraid, for so long, and I didn't know?"

Her eyes closed. "It wasn't your burden to know." *Just mine.*

"Any burden you have is mine. *You* are mine."

"Smith—"

"Just like I'm yours. I get that you don't love me. *That's* the part I'll deal with. My problem. Maybe one day you will. I hope like hell that you will, but until then, we'll take things helluva slow. We'll find the bastard after you. We'll let you finally live a life without fear, and then we'll go from there. Sound like a plan?"

No, it didn't. She spun toward him. Water and rose petals sloshed over the edge of the tub. Her legs were all twisted, so—screw it. She straddled him.

Smith's brows rose. "Baby..." A warning edge.

She didn't need a warning. Not from Smith. Her hands locked around his broad shoulders as she steadied herself—and brought her body even closer to his. In this position, his cock pushed against her sex. If she just angled down a little more, he would slide inside of her. Before she could, his hands clamped around her hips. He held her still.

"I don't like your plan," she told him.

His head moved in toward her. "What part?"

"You don't know how I feel about you."

"I've been back in your life for days. You don't love—"

"I met you when I was sixteen. You brought me my English book. When anyone would say so much as a harsh word to me, you'd tell them to back the hell off." Her lips wanted to tremble, so she clamped them together. After a tense moment, she made herself continue speaking. "You think I didn't know? I saw you, Smith. When Trevor Hollows was dodging my steps and saying that I had my nose in the air—"

CYNTHIA EDEN

"Trevor was a dick who wanted in your pants. Hell, yes, I was going to tell him to back off."

"What about when I didn't have anyone to sit with at lunch? And you got Hillary to invite me to her table? You think I didn't know that was you?"

His hold tightened on her. "It's really hard to concentrate when you're straddling me."

Was it? Really? Her hand reached down between them. Fumbled a bit because she was way not confident at this. But her fingers curled around him, and she guided his thick, thrusting cock to the entrance of her body. The water let her hips rise up easily, and when she pushed against him, he slid inside of her.

They both gasped.

She was still sensitive from her release, and he filled her completely. Perfectly.

"*Madelyn.*"

"Is it, ah, harder to concentrate now?"

His eyes glittered at her. "*Yes.*" A hiss. He used his grip to lift her up, then drive her back down. Water and rose petals sloshed over the tub's edge. He lifted her again.

"You got me in to see Aiden." A rush of words from her.

His fingers bit into her hips. "What the hell?"

"When I wanted to set up my business." Deliberately, she clamped her inner muscles around him as tightly as she could.

He swore. His eyes blazed with dark fire.

"My original ap-appointment wasn't going to be for three more weeks. I g-got a call..." He lifted her up, jerked her down. More water went over the edge. "You got me in s—*sooner!* Aiden told me—you said he should meet me—" She couldn't finish her sentence. Words were just beyond her because one of his hands had dipped down and was feverishly stroking her clit.

"So what?" His mouth moved to her ear. He bit her lobe.

She shuddered.

"So I got you in earlier." His fingers rubbed faster. Her hips rocked like crazy. "So—what? You avoided me after you got the deal from him. Ran every time you saw me coming. Can't run now, though, can you?"

Her hips slammed down on him. "I ran because I wanted you."

His hand pulled from her clit.

No! "Smith!"

"You ran because you wanted me? Explain that in terms I can understand."

Her breath heaved in and out. Explaining would be easier if he wasn't in her. She'd done this to herself. And to him. And it felt so good.

He nipped her ear lobe again and pulled back. "Hard to concentrate?" A sensual taunt.

She managed a jerky nod.

"Then let me help out." Both of his hands went back to her hips. He began thrusting in a feverish, desperate pace. Her hands flew to grab the sides of the tub, and her back arched. Water went everywhere. His mouth latched onto her throat. He kissed her. Licked. Sucked. Bit—

She came. A keening cry burst from her as her sex throbbed and throbbed on waves of pleasure so intense that Madelyn was sure she was just going to sag back and slip into the water and be done. The pleasure was too intense. It hollowed her out, and she'd had no idea—never suspected—that sex would be as consuming as it was with Smith. No one had ever told her it would be like this.

"That's because sex with another man won't be like this." A growl.

Her eyes flew open. She'd squeezed them shut when the orgasm hit. Embarrassed, Madelyn felt the flush in her cheeks because she hadn't realized she'd been speaking out loud.

"It's only this good with me. *With us*. Remember that." He lifted her up and down. Up and down. Up and—

He sank deep. Came inside of her. She saw the pleasure blast across his face. Pleasure that she'd given to him.

Only this good with me. "With us," Madelyn whispered. She grabbed his jaw. Dragged his face toward her. And kissed him.

***

"Why did you run from me?"

She was in bed, his arm was around her, and sleep beckoned. She'd been drifting off when his rasping words reached her.

"If you wanted me, why run?"

Madelyn licked her lips. She could still taste him. Feel him everywhere. *Inside and out.* "Because I did want you."

"Doesn't make sense."

It did if you were her. If you were worried that the people you cared about would get taken away. "I didn't think I was your type."

"You're my only type."

"The boring, good girl who never went out with anyone in high school?"

He rolled her toward him. "The hot girl who melted my heart with her incredible eyes."

"I wasn't in your league."

"No, I wasn't in yours." His head tilted against the pillow. "You ran because you were afraid."

She opened her mouth but couldn't deny the words. She was afraid that people close to her would be hurt. "The elevator repairman..." Madelyn sucked in a breath because she'd been trying not to think about his death. "Is he just someone else who died because of me?"

"Not because of you. *Never that*. We don't know if it was a real OD or if more was involved, but if his death *was* related to what he did in that elevator—"

She suspected it must have been. Those two events occurring so closely in time? Couldn't be a coincidence.

"The guy set you up to be terrorized, Madelyn. For all he knew, that remote could have made your elevator plunge twenty floors and you would have died."

She flinched.

He swore. "Fuck, I'm sorry. I don't want you scared, but you don't need to be beating yourself up over him. *You didn't do anything wrong*."

"I don't want anyone dying because of me." That burden had been one she carried for far too long. "Promise me, Smith, no matter what else happens, you will *not* die." Because that was what terrified her the most.

"And there it is," he said, sounding satisfied.

She hadn't heard a promise.

"When I said you ran before because you were afraid, I meant you were afraid of how you feel about me."

No denial came because...*he's right. I'm afraid of how I feel with him. I'm even more afraid of what would happen if I lost him.*

"You know I can take care of myself, baby. I'm not scared of the bastard out there." His hand lifted, and his finger traced along her lower lip. "It's been so long since you let go, you're afraid of how I make you feel, aren't you?"

He knew her so well. "Yes." A breath against his fingertip.

A nod. "It's okay to be scared. Be as scared as you want. But don't leave me, got it?"

She kissed his fingertip. His nostrils immediately flared. "Don't leave me," Madelyn told him.

"Baby, there's no way in hell that would ever happen."

CHAPTER EIGHTEEN

"Mr. Russell is fully booked for the day and will not be taking any unscheduled appointments. He's recently been traveling and has a great deal of work to catch up on." The receptionist had perfectly highlighted, blonde hair, clear blue eyes, and a serious no-one-gets-past-me vibe. "I'll be happy to take down your name and number, and I'll call you later for scheduling." Her smile flashed in dismissal as she focused on Madelyn.

As Smith watched, Madelyn just straightened her shoulders. "I'm an old friend of the family."

The smile didn't dim. "Mr. Russell gets a surprising number of those. Oddly enough, most aren't friends of his family at all."

Madelyn didn't seem even mildly daunted. "I need you to pick up the phone and tell Quinn that Maggie Edgewood is here to see him. If you don't and I walk out of this office right now, you'll lose your job when he finds out that you didn't tell him I was here."

Damn. Impressive. Smith almost whistled. It was just after eight a.m., and they were in the lobby of Night Gate Enterprises. Not the actual casino, but the business office—the place where they should find their prey. Provided, of course, they could get past the blonde who seemed to very much not like Madelyn.

After a tense moment, the receptionist narrowed her eyes...and reached for her phone. Her eyes remained on Madelyn as she said, "Mr. Russell?" Her icy tone defrosted as if by magic. The warmth was palpable. "I am so sorry to interrupt, but there is a woman here who claims to be a friend of your family. Her name is..." She covered the mouthpiece on the phone. "What was it again?"

"Maggie Edgewood."

The blonde removed her hand. "Maggie Edgewood—" She stopped. Swallowed. "Yes, sir. I'll send her up on the private elevator. Absolutely." Hurriedly, she hung up the phone even as she sprang from her seat. "My apologies, Ms. Edgewood. You wouldn't believe the number of visitors that we have here at Night Gate. Ever since that article about Mr. Russell appeared in *Forbes*, he's had a flood of women trying to catch his attention." She rushed around the lobby's check-in desk.

"What article?" Madelyn asked blankly.

"Oh, the one about him being one of the top forty entrepreneurs under forty." She sent a quick, considering glance Smith's way.

He just stared back at her.

Clearing her throat, she headed toward a bank of elevators. After swiping a keycard on one of the exterior control panels, the doors slid open. "This elevator will take you straight to the top floor. Mr. Russell will be waiting there for you.

He's in his penthouse today on the sixtieth floor, but he said for you to come straight up."

"Sixtieth?" Madelyn peered into the elevator. "Wonderful." Her voice said it was anything but wonderful.

Smith caught her hand. Threaded his fingers with hers. "We got this."

Madelyn nodded quickly. They both entered the elevator. The walls, the floor, and the ceiling were all mirrored, tossing their reflections back at them.

The doors closed. Madelyn instantly stiffened.

"Want me to distract you?" Smith asked her, already doing just that. "Imagine how fun it would be if I went down on you right in here. With all the mirrors, you could see what I was doing from every single angle. Which reminds me, when we were making love in the bed, did you peek at the mirrors? Because I did."

"Smith."

"Or you could go down on me right now," he considered. "You know, seeing as how you did such a stellar job the last time. I could watch you and go insane with pleasure." He turned his head.

She gaped at him.

So freaking gorgeous.

She was staring at him, not worrying about what floor they were on, so he continued, "Option three would be a regular fuck. I'd have to make it fast, though, because we are—"

The elevator dinged. The doors opened.

"Here," he finished in satisfaction.

Her eyes widened. She looked toward the open doors, then back at him. Understanding dawned in her gaze.

"You're welcome," he told her. "But just remember for the ride back, all three options are on the table."

"Maggie?"

Through the open doors, Smith saw the man barreling toward them. Brown hair, carefully styled, expensive suit, and eyes completely and totally locked on Madelyn.

Smith exited the elevator first, and he took stock of the man before him. Memphis had texted him intel on Quinn Russell. The former lawyer had bought a casino-slash-hotel a few years ago. He'd turned the biggest failure in Vegas into a sensation. Every night, packed crowds came to see his performers, and the high rollers always stopped at his place. He had connections left and right, and Memphis had suggested that some of those connections might just be to criminal elements.

If you wanted a business to succeed in Vegas—especially as spectacularly as Night Gate had—then you needed to have the *right* connections. Or, rather, the wrong ones.

"My God." Quinn staggered to a stop as he seemed to drink in Madelyn. "It is you. After all of these years." He stepped toward her. Reached out as if to touch her.

Yeah, so... "Hi." Smith inclined his head toward Quinn. "I'm Smith Sanders, and I'm her bodyguard."

Quinn's mouth dropped open. "What?"

"You can call me Smith. Everyone does." He tucked Madelyn's hand into the crook of his arm as he led her a few steps away from the elevator. "How about we go *inside* the penthouse to chat? My client and I aren't exactly big fans of hallways."

"I don't understand what's happening here." Quinn didn't move.

"We're standing in a hallway when we should be speaking privately." Smith thought that was pretty easy to understand. What he didn't understand—or like—was the way Quinn kept sweeping his stare over Madelyn. And letting that stare linger a little too long in certain places.

So Smith stepped fully in front of her. "My client and I need to speak with you."

Quinn's forehead furrowed. "About what?"

"About Heather's murder," Madelyn answered before Smith could say anything else. "If you have a few minutes, I really think we need to talk."

Those words got Quinn moving. "Follow me." He spun on his heel and marched down the elaborately decorated hallway.

As they passed what looked like a Monet, Madelyn paused a moment. "Should have consulted me," she whispered to Smith. "I could have told him that is a fake." Her voice was a little breathier than normal, and he knew nerves were pushing hard at her.

But she had on a brave face, and he freaking loved her even more for that. "You're always fantastic at seeing the difference between the real deal and the bullshit out there."

Her stare slid slowly over his face. "Yes, I am."
A tender smile. One just for him.

Then she turned her head. And they followed
Quinn Russell into his penthouse.

***

"I've got eyes on the house," Titan said as he
settled back in his front seat and surveyed the
home across the street. A quiet street. Sidewalks.
Manicured yards. Big houses. His focus was on
house number four-oh-five on Spring View Lane.
The house that belonged to Troy Washington.

A house that had been purchased and paid for
in full just a few months ago.

"Stay on him today," Memphis ordered, his
words carrying easily through the phone. "Smith
is convinced the guy knew that he and Madelyn
were in town, that Washington was waiting for
them. If that's the case, then I want to know who
tipped him off. Hopefully, he'll lead you right to
our prey."

"He won't lose me." Titan never lost a target.
His gaze slid to the driveway. *Nice.* A blue Benz
waited beneath a carport. Troy's car. If the car was
there, then Troy should be there, too.

"I'm getting Oliver to see what he can possibly
turn up on Madelyn's mother. Maybe there's
some old missing person's report on a woman and
a child fitting Madelyn's description in ViCAP.
There are grandparents out there, family
members—someone who must have missed them.
A woman and child shouldn't be able to just
vanish."

But it happened. Titan knew people vanished every single day.

"Keep me updated on Troy Washington. I'm with Smith, I think it's too damn convenient that the man was just seemingly waiting for Madelyn to appear. He must have been tipped off about her arrival. Unless he *is* the perp we're after." Memphis's voice grew thoughtful. "Smith told me that Washington might have once been involved with the mom, but she left and cut out with Reginald. Could be that she and Washington had a volatile relationship. Could be he might have been a whole lot more involved in things years ago than anyone suspected."

Titan was hearing a whole lot of "could" talk from Memphis. They needed less of that and more cold, hard facts.

"Smith and Madelyn are meeting with Quinn Russell right now," Memphis revealed. "Smith texted just a few moments ago, saying the guy had escorted them into his penthouse. I'll let you know what shakes loose from the sit-down."

Titan's gaze lingered on the front door of house four-oh-five.

"As always, it's amazing chatting with you, Titan," Memphis mocked. "But, damn, bro, try to stay mission-oriented, would you? You can talk a bastard's ear off."

"There's no movement," Titan said.

"Uh, excuse me?"

"I'm going closer to the house."

"Troy Washington works the late shift! He probably came rolling in around five a.m. You aren't going to see movement for a while. Just be ready to roll when he comes out, got it?"

Titan got that he wanted to make sure his prey was actually in the house. The car was there, but that didn't mean his prey *had* to be inside. Washington could have left on foot. If Washington was one of their main leads—and, clearly, he was—then no chances could be taken. "Bye."

"Titan—"

Titan hung up. He checked his weapon, put it in the holster, and shoved open the door to his ride. No one else was out and about on the street, but he still made a point of sticking to the shadows and near the edges of the high bushes that marked the property line for Washington's house. He'd do a quick recon check to make certain his prey was, in fact, sleeping and contained.

In his experience, you just couldn't take chances.

***

"Maggie Edgewood." Quinn motioned toward the plush, white couch. "Please, take a seat." He shook his head, seeming dazed. "After all these years, I can't believe it's you." His watchful gaze swept over her face as she slowly lowered herself onto the couch. "You look the same." A rough, quick laugh. "Different, of course, but the eyes are the same. Chin, too. You're just—you know, all grown up now."

Smith settled onto the couch next to her. His leg brushed against hers. "That's what happens when people age." Curt.

Quinn blinked. Grimaced. "Right. Of course." He cleared his throat and lowered into the brown, leather chair across from Madelyn. His gaze remained focused on her.

She shifted a little, uncomfortable. His stare was so penetrating. And his eyes—they hadn't changed over the years, either. He and Heather had the same eyes. So deep and dark, but with flecks of gold inside. Heather's eyes had always gleamed when she laughed. She'd laughed a lot.

Madelyn wished she could remember more of Heather's laughter and less of her screams.

"Where did you go?" Quinn leaned forward. His hands fisted over his knees. "One minute, you were living in that apartment with your mom, and the next, you were gone." His jaw hardened. "Was it witness protection? Did they take you away?"

She shook her head. "No, I—" She didn't know if witness protection had ever been an option. If it had, her mother had certainly not mentioned it to her. *But I guess there's a lot she didn't mention.* "My mother remarried. We moved to be with my stepdad."

A furrow appeared between his brows. "That's it? You go missing one day, my sister dies, and your mom just remarries some guy immediately? *That's* where you went?" Anger hummed beneath his words.

Smith moved, a deceptively lazy movement as his body shifted to the edge of the couch. His arm slid against hers. "You seem awful tense, Quinn."

Quinn blinked. His gaze shifted to Smith. "I'm sorry." He didn't sound sorry. "You're the...bodyguard? Why exactly does Maggie need a bodyguard?"

"Oh, lots of reasons," Smith replied easily. "Reason one would be because I think she's in danger, and my job is to make sure that danger *never* touches her again." From the corner of her eye, she saw Smith send a smile to Quinn. A very shark-like smile.

The furrow between Quinn's eyes deepened in the face of that smile. "I don't understand."

She needed to take control of this conversation. Or, at least, try to get it back on track. "I need to ask you a few questions about that night."

His stare jerked back to her. "And I need to ask you questions." Flat. "Would have asked them one hell of a lot sooner, but you disappeared. You ran away, and you left us all here to grieve and pick up the pieces." He surged to his feet.

So did Smith. They stood almost toe-to-toe.

Madelyn stayed on the couch, but her eyes were on the men having a stand-off.

"That's an awful accusing tone you're using with her." Smith's voice was pleasant, but...chilled. "She was a kid when her mom took her away from this place. Not like Maggie had a choice. And she was a victim. Getting the hell away from the man who abducted her was a necessary step."

"My sister was a victim, too." Quinn's chin lifted. "Did you know he stabbed her fifteen times? Did you know one of the local channels got an audio copy of the phone call the bastard made to the cops? And that the producers thought it was okay to air that shit so I—and everyone else—could hear my sister's dying screams?"

Madelyn flinched. She rose, too, aware that her legs were shaky. "I am so sorry."

Quinn didn't speak.

"She was my best friend. I loved her, and if I could change the past, I would. I never, ever wanted her hurt. I didn't know it was even a possibility. When I woke up in that room, I just—I thought of escape. I didn't know he would hurt her. If I had..." She sucked in a breath. "I would have stayed."

Quinn's eyes glittered at her. "You would have traded your life for hers?"

"You think I haven't ever wished I had been in her place so she could live? I have. More times than I can count." But this wasn't about dying. This visit was about getting justice. "I'm trying to find the man who killed Heather." She curled her fingers around Smith's arm and felt the tension in his body. "Smith and I are working with some investigators."

A mocking laugh came from Quinn. "You think you're going to find him after all of these years? What—you believe no one else tried? You think I didn't spend a fortune trying to find my sister's killer? I loved her, too." He released a ragged breath as his mocking laughter faded, and he suddenly just appeared deflated. "I never forgot her or what happened to her. Not for a second. I've *tried* to find him, but he's like a ghost. Or, hell, maybe he *is* a ghost by now. Long dead and rotting in the ground." His face twisted for just a moment with rage. Hate.

"Don't you want to know for sure?" Smith asked. Again, his tone was cool. "I have resources that you don't."

"Oh, right, because a bodyguard knows tons of shit that someone with my money and power doesn't."

It was Smith's turn to laugh. "You really shouldn't judge people by what they say they are. Everyone is more than you think." He rolled back his shoulders. "When did you notice your sister was missing?"

Quinn took a step back. "That old question again? So much for blowing open the investigation."

"When did you notice her missing?" Smith repeated.

"This is bullshit." Quinn whirled away and stomped toward a table to the right. His hand reached out and curled around a picture frame.

Inside the frame? A photo of a younger Quinn and a smiling Heather.

"All of that information is in the old reports." Quinn stared at the image. "You know what? Fuck it." He put down the photo and spun to face them. "I have questions, too. For each answer you give me, Maggie, I'll give you one, too. Sound fair?"

She nodded.

"Did you ever see the bastard's face?"

She opened her mouth.

"That information must have been in the old police reports," Smith returned.

"Fuck you, bodyguard."

Smith just shrugged.

Her hold tightened on his arm. "Smith."

His head turned toward her. Immediately, his expression softened.

"I'm okay," she whispered. Then she focused on Quinn. "No, I never saw his face. He wore a mask and bulky clothing, so I have no idea what his face or body really looked like."

"But you stabbed him in the eye, right? So his eye would have been fucked. Maybe he needed to go to a doctor."

Maybe. "Yes, I stabbed him in the eye."

"Which eye?" Quinn demanded.

She blinked. "Right."

"That's three questions," Smith rumbled. "Our turn. When was the last time you actually saw your sister?"

"Saw her at three a.m. I checked on her because I wanted a glass of water. She was sleeping." Gritted. "Maggie, was anything about his voice familiar to you? Any accent?"

Familiar to her? "I don't think so."

"What did he say to you, exactly?"

Smith's phone beeped. She saw him pull it out of his pocket and frown at the screen.

"Maggie?" Quinn prompted.

"When I ran, he yelled that he'd punish me."

"And he did. He killed my sister because you got away."

Her chest ached. "I—"

"By my count," Smith cut in to say, "you've asked around six questions. We've asked one. Our turn again. Actually, it's our turn for the next five rounds."

She wet her lips. What question should she ask now?

Smith casually asked, "Are you familiar with a woman named Harmony Ramos?"

Quinn's face tensed.

"I'll take that as a yes," Smith decided. "Funny thing, an associate of mine recently had a talk with Harmony."

Madelyn let go of Smith's arm. She'd just realized she still held it. "Who is Harmony?" The name meant nothing to her.

"She was the girlfriend of sixteen-year-old Quinn Russell. Oliver was good enough to discover that info for us. He just texted it to me." His stare remained on Quinn. "Oliver Foxx is an FBI acquaintance who is assisting us in the investigation. We were talking recently, and he happened to have a flashback to himself as a sixteen-year-old boy. He raised the point that, at sixteen, he was busy sneaking off to see his girlfriend every chance he could get." A pause. "So I guess that made him curious. In the old reports, Harmony Ramos was questioned briefly because she was someone who moved in your family's circle. She moved in that circle because she was dating you. Back then, she told the officers that she was at home, asleep, during the abduction."

Quinn's expression didn't alter.

"But she just told my FBI acquaintance that she wasn't actually asleep. She was having sex with you. You'd snuck over to her house that night—her parents were on the same out-of-town trip that your parents took. A business conference, I believe it was. You were with her until nearly four-thirty that morning."

His Adam's apple bobbed. "It's been a long time. Harmony's memory is faulty."

"Or yours is." Smith took a step toward him. "The authorities have worked one timeline forever because *you* told them that Heather was in bed at three a.m. But is that the truth? Do you *know* that she was home then? Because according to Harmony, that would be impossible, seeing as how you weren't in the house yourself."

"You need to get the hell out." Flat. He pointed to the door.

"And you need to tell the truth," Smith snapped right back. "You want to find your sister's killer? Work with us. Tell me if you actually know when she was taken."

Quinn paced behind the leather chair. His hands flew down and grabbed the back of the chair.

"If you weren't at home then, you can't know if she was taken *after* Maggie or before," Smith continued relentlessly. "You can't know how long she was gone from the house. You can't know—"

"If my sister screamed for help when the bastard broke in and took her? I can't know that? I can't know if she screamed for me to help her, but I wasn't there?" Torment. That was what thickened his voice. "I can't know that if I had just kept my fool-ass at home...my sister might never have been taken? She might still be alive, but she isn't." Each ragged word seemed torn from him. "And I'll never fucking know if I could have saved her."

CHAPTER NINETEEN

Madelyn hurried toward Quinn. As Smith watched, she put her hand on Quinn's arm. "I'm sorry."

Quinn's head turned toward her. His gaze seemed to drink her in.

I don't like the way he looks at Madelyn.

"It's not your fault," Madelyn told Quinn, voice sympathetic and comforting.

"I could have saved her."

"You don't know that. He got past your dogs. I heard the neighbors told the cops that they never made a sound." She shook her head. "I remember your room was all the way down the hall from hers. You might have been home and never heard a thing. *You didn't do this.* He did."

Interesting that Madelyn tried so hard to comfort someone else yet she still tried to take the blame for Heather's death onto herself. She didn't want Quinn feeling guilty. Smith wished she'd stop blaming herself, too.

Quinn kept drinking her in. That needed to stop. She was showing sympathy. Not that she wanted to screw the guy. "You lied to the cops."

Both Madelyn and Quinn turned to stare at him.

"You weren't home that night. You have no idea when Heather was taken, do you?" Madelyn could be the comforting one. Smith would stick to being cold. Their good cop/bad cop routine would work for them.

At first, he didn't think Quinn would respond, then his shoulders slowly sagged. "No, I have no idea." A long exhale. "And this is the first time I've admitted that to anyone." His eyes squeezed closed. "God, *I wasn't home*. Why the hell wasn't I home? Because I wanted to fuck my girlfriend? A woman I don't even talk to these days? My sister died. She *died*." His eyes opened. "On my watch."

Their whole timeline had just changed. Both girls could have been in the cabin together that long ago night. Hell. "When did you notice she was missing?"

"When the cops came to the door. She was already dead by then. They came *after* that terrible phone call from him." His lower lip trembled. "I didn't even look in her room when I finally got home from Harmony's because I thought Heather was sleeping. Our parents were due back later that day. Heather's birthday was coming up that weekend. I just—I didn't even look. Why didn't I look?"

Madelyn's hand was still on his arm.

"If they were taken together," Smith said, keeping his voice emotionless, "then we don't know which girl was the original target. The cops believed it was Maggie and that Heather was taken as some kind of punishment, but that might have been the wrong idea. The whole profile on the killer could be off."

Madelyn's hand began to slide away from Quinn. In a flash, he caught her wrist. "It was about you."

Smith stepped toward them. Quinn had better not be holding her too tightly.

"It was you. I heard the recording—he punished her because you weren't good. *It was you.* It had to be. Heather didn't have any enemies. She was good and sweet, and it wrecked my parents when she died."

Smith advanced another step. "Wrecked them so much that you couldn't tell them the truth? You couldn't admit you weren't home when she was taken?"

He kept holding Madelyn's wrist. "They would have hated me." He stared down at Madelyn. "Just as much as they hated you."

Okay. Enough. "Your hold is too tight. Let her go, now."

Quinn frowned and glanced down at his hand. His fingers encircled Madelyn's delicate wrist. Far too tightly for Smith's peace of mind.

"I believe I said 'now' in my order." Smith was almost on them. If Quinn didn't move his hand, Smith would be moving it for him.

But Quinn let her go and backed away.

"Excellent." Smith reached for her wrist. His fingers skimmed lightly along her pulse point, then he released her. "Anything else you didn't tell the cops back then? Some info that you might realize you need to share now?"

But it appeared Quinn had clammed up.

Smith sighed. He looked at Madelyn. Taking the cue, she cleared her throat. "I have reason to believe that the man who took me all of those years ago may be stalking me now."

Quinn's eyes widened. In that flare, Smith saw something that worried him—eagerness. Excitement.

Shit. This guy wants his own revenge.

"He's made contact?" Quinn asked.

"In a manner of speaking," Madelyn said.

Quinn surged toward her—

But Smith blocked his path. "You told us that you'd hired plenty of investigators over the years. They never turned up anything?"

"No."

"Your sister's body was found in the middle of the highway on the outskirts of Vegas. No DNA evidence was on her. No material that could be useful to cops at all."

Quinn's jaw locked.

"Your PIs didn't find anything that pointed to the killer? You never picked up any similar crimes? Nothing that you could use?"

"Not a damn thing. After Madelyn vanished, he did, too. The bastard has been *gone* all this time, and I want him back. I will do whatever it takes to find him and stop him." Each word was gritted out from between his clenched teeth. "So if you are really hunting him, if you think he's stalking *you*," he craned around Smith to see Madelyn, "then I want to help. Consider me all in. Every resource I have will be at your disposal."

"That's very generous of you," Madelyn said. "Thank you."

After Madelyn vanished, he did, too. Smith's body wanted to tense, but with an effort, he kept his muscles relaxed. Smith sent Quinn a cold smile. "Very generous." He inclined his head. "We have an appointment now, but we'll be in touch very soon." His fingers threaded with Madelyn's. "Thanks for your time." He tugged Madelyn toward the door.

"That's it?" Quinn demanded. "You're leaving already? But—"

"Got to meet with that FBI acquaintance I told you about. He's expecting us. Don't worry, you'll see us again soon." Smith let go of Madelyn's hand and wrapped his hand around her waist. The better to urge her forward. He wanted her out of that penthouse, right the hell then.

They were almost at the door when—

"*I know we can find him together,*" Quinn called out. "I know you've always been the key."

Smith looked back at him. "She's not your key for anything."

"Uh, Smith," Madelyn whispered. "We need—"

"To go," he finished. "Agent Foxx won't wait forever." He yanked open the door and they double-timed it down the hallway. But when they got to the elevator...

The fucking thing wouldn't work without the keycard.

Sonofabitch. Sonofabitch.

"Smith, what's wrong?" Madelyn asked, voice low.

He yanked out his phone. Fired off a quick text to Memphis.

"Smith?" Worry threaded through his name.

He jabbed the button near the elevator again, but the doors weren't opening. The receptionist downstairs had used that freaking keycard because it was a private elevator. His gaze slid to the left. At the end of the hallway, he saw the bright EXIT sign over the stairwell door. If they could get down those stairs and to the next floor, they could get on an elevator at that level. Only one elevator came to the penthouse level, but other floors were accessible via a bank of elevators. "Come on."

He was aware that Quinn was leaving the penthouse.

"What is happening?" Madelyn whispered.

They were practically running. His instincts were screaming. He needed to get her to the stairwell. "He called you Madelyn."

"So? That's my name—"

"He should have only known you as Maggie. You never introduced yourself to him as Madelyn. He shouldn't have known—" They were almost at the stairwell door. He let her go and rushed toward it. But it wouldn't open.

Locked. Sonofabitch.

"Smith?" Fear hitched her breathing. "What's happening?"

He whirled back toward her and just as his eyes locked on hers, Smith felt something slam into his chest. His stare whipped away from her. He had a fast image of Quinn racing toward him, of the SOB holding something small and black in his hand and then—

Smith hit the floor.

"*Smith!*"

Her scream was the last thing he heard.

***

Titan peered through the back window of the house at four-oh-five Spring View Lane. He saw no movement inside. Heard no sounds from the interior. Sure, a guy on the nightshift could be sleeping in, but something felt off.

Titan had learned to never ignore his instincts. The last time he'd ignored them, he'd wound up with two wicked scars on his face.

He noted the condensation along the window as he leaned forward. Yeah, he looked like a Peeping Tom, but he needed to see in that bedroom. If he got caught, Memphis would chew his ass out for not keeping a low profile. But...

But I'm worried.

Because Titan was good at seeing patterns. One of his things. He could always detect a pattern, and the more he learned about Madelyn, the more he worried.

The man who'd sabotaged the elevator had died of an OD.

Her attacker had been set up so that it *looked* as if the man had committed suicide. If Tony hadn't been there to examine the body, maybe Andrew Bryson's death would have gone down as suicide, and no one would have ever suspected the truth. You get an overworked ME with too many cases, and things often slipped through the cracks.

Two deaths. Both designed to look as if they weren't murders.

Two men who'd been in Madelyn's orbit. Who'd done things to set her up. To terrify her.

And Smith told Memphis he was worried that Troy Washington was waiting for them. That he was feeding Madelyn information.

Another setup?

He—

He thought he saw movement. The faintest shadow inside the bedroom. As if someone had risen from the bed, only to fall.

Up, then down.

Titan tensed, but there was no more movement from inside. The house went back to being quiet. Still.

He slipped toward the back door. Pulled out his lockpicking set. This could be a major clusterfuck. If he got caught now, it wouldn't just be about pissing off Memphis. He'd lose his job with the Marshals. You didn't just get to break into someone's house.

Be sure of this.

His fingers reached for the knob, but to his surprise, it twisted easily in his grasp.

If you've worked in security your whole life, do you really leave your back door unlocked?

His jaw locked. Titan swung the door open. He slid inside. Could have sworn the air felt and smelled stale.

He heard a groan. Immediately, Titan ran toward the sound, realizing fast that the groan had come from the bedroom he'd been viewing moments before. The bedroom door was already open, and through that open doorway, he saw a man on the floor. Troy Washington sprawled close to the bed. Vomit covered the carpeting near his mouth.

Titan lunged toward him. The man barely seemed to be breathing, and Titan's first fear was that Troy had choked to death on his own vomit. Titan flipped him over, cleared Troy's air way, and tried to figure out what the hell he was facing.

An OD? Like the elevator guy?

"D-dizzy..." Troy muttered, not opening his eyes. "Head...h-hurts..." He started retching again. "H-help..."

Titan's gaze swept the room. Something was way off. And it wasn't just the dazed and sick man on the floor. Titan assessed the scene and saw...*Wait just a damn minute.* A smoke detector hung from the ceiling in the hallway, just outside of the bedroom. He could see it through the open doorway. He'd rushed into the bedroom and hadn't noticed it before. A thin wire dangled from the ceiling, stopping the detector from falling completely. When he rushed closer and grabbed for detector, Titan realized that it was one of those duo devices. A smoke detector and carbon monoxide detector all in one.

Only someone had ripped it off the ceiling and yanked open the back. The batteries were gone.

Batteries are gone. Fuck. A wave of dizziness hit Titan even as he surged back toward the man on the floor. They had to get out, now. Because he was pretty sure someone had set the scene so that Troy Washington would be dying. He hauled the man up, heaved him over his shoulder in a fireman carry, and rushed for the back door.

You would only disable a carbon monoxide detector if you didn't want it to sound an alarm. He burst out of the house and sucked in a deep breath of air. Moving as quickly as he could, Titan rushed about twenty feet from the house. He lowered Troy to the ground and whipped out his phone. "Breathe," Titan ordered him. Then he looked at the phone's screen. He'd missed a text from Memphis. As he read it, Titan's body stiffened.

Smith just sent me a nine-one-one. His last known location is Quinn Russell's penthouse. On my way. Meet me there. STAT.

His gaze flew to the man who was gasping and wheezing. Shit. Titan couldn't just abandon Troy. Dammit. Titan called for help.

"*Nine, one, one, what is the nature of your emergency?*"

He tilted his head. "Pretty sure I got a vic of carbon monoxide poisoning here."

"*Get out of the house. If you suspect that there is a carbon monoxide leak on the premises, you need to immediately evacuate.*"

"Did that." He rattled off the address. "Hurry. Got other places to be." *And an old friend who had better not be in trouble.* But those patterns were swirling in his head again. Titan leaned over Troy. "You with me?"

Troy blinked at him. "Who...are...you?"

"Your hero."

Troy heaved some more. "Spinning...everything is..."

"Who told you that Maggie Edgewood would be back in town?"

Troy vomited.

Fuck. The guy was in a bad way. "The person who told you is probably the one who just tried to kill you."

Troy shook his head.

"Fine. Keep trusting him. I won't be around to save you next time." He turned away.

"W-wait! It w-was..."

But he had a guess. Titan looked back. "Quinn Russell?"

Troy's head bobbed in a nod.

Dammit to hell.

Then Troy started having a seizure.

CHAPTER TWENTY

Everything stopped. Her heart. Her breath. The world. Nothing was moving at all because Smith had fallen before her. He'd been shot, and he'd gone down and her whole body had frozen. The ice coated her, tried to choke her and imprison her, and a guttural scream rose in her throat as Madelyn stared down at him.

No. Not Smith. She would not lose him. She couldn't. She'd made him promise that he wouldn't die.

No, no, I asked for the promise, but he never gave it. He never—

"Smith!" His name broke from her on a scream. She fell to her knees beside him. Frantic, her fingers flew over his chest, and when she realized that he was breathing, her whole body shuddered. *Still alive. Still alive. Still alive.*

"Of course, he's still alive. That was a tranq. Not a bullet to the heart. Do you know what a pain in the ass it would be to clean up all that blood from the hallway?"

Her head whipped toward Quinn.

Quinn smiled at her. "Hi, there." He lifted the device in his hand. It *looked* like a gun, but with a thicker, more snubbed nose. He pointed it at her. "Got another dart in here. I can knock you out and carry you from the building. After all, you're a whole lot lighter than him, so transport would be easy. But wouldn't it be more pleasant to walk out with me like a civilized human being?"

He couldn't be serious. Her hands fluttered over Smith's chest. The rise and fall pushed strength through her body and drove back the enveloping cold that had tried to drag her under. "Why are you doing this?"

Quinn exhaled on a long sigh. "I believe it was Robert Burns who wrote, 'The best laid plans of mice and men often go awry.' Or, you know what? Maybe that wasn't the direct quote, but I figure it's close enough."

He was quoting literature to her?

"The point, my dear, is that I had a brilliant fucking plan in place, but your dumbass bodyguard picked up on something. I could tell by the way he was trying to haul ass and get you out of here. He realized I was a threat." He kept pointing his tranq gun at her. "What was it? What did he know?"

"You called me by the wrong name."

He frowned at her.

"You called me Madelyn, but I never introduced myself to you that way." How long would Smith be out? *Wake up. Wake up.* Her fingers slid under the edge of his shirt. He had his gun holstered near his hip. She could grab it and—

"I don't remember calling you Madelyn. I couldn't have done that. Not made such a stupid mistake when I had set everything up so beautifully."

"You did make such a stupid mistake." *Why is this happening?* "And guess what?" She sent him a disgusted glare. "That Monet hanging on the wall? It's a stupid mistake, too. Seriously amateur-hour forgery."

His head whipped to the side, and he laughed when he looked at the painting. "That forgery brought me to you."

What?

"When a man acquires wealth as I have done, he's supposed to collect beautiful things. I started picking up art. A friend of mine told me that I had to be careful. Lots of forgeries were out there. He said he'd used the services of an incredible authenticator down in Miami. A woman who used to work for the Smithsonian. She dealt with antiques as well as art pieces. A real eye, that's what he said. You had a real eye." More laughter. "I saw a picture of you. Like I said before, you're just an older version of the girl I once knew. One look, and I knew I'd found my Maggie."

"I'm not your Maggie."

He took a gliding step forward. "You had a real eye," he repeated the line again. "Thought that was like a sign because you took the eye of the man who abducted you, didn't you Maggie? Stabbed him with a spoon and twisted and took out his eye."

Smith's eyes were still closed. His body slack. "No." Soft. "I attacked him with the spoon because that was all I had. I don't know if he lost his eye. I just ran." Her fingers carefully slid down Smith's right side, toward the holster she wasn't sure if Quinn had noticed. *Almost there. Almost.* A couple more inches, and she could grab Smith's gun.

"*You ran and let my sister die in your place!*" Fury exploded in Quinn's voice.

He's going to kill me. She shoved her hand down fast, going for Smith's gun.

"*Nope.* You're not going to fire that at me. Cute, though, that you think you can try. Don't move a muscle, understand?"

She froze because he'd closed in with his tranq gun, shoving it against her, and in a flash, he'd taken Smith's weapon. But he didn't use Smith's gun on her. Just thrust it into the back waistband of his pants.

Then he pulled out a phone and started barking orders to someone. His words buzzed past her. He wanted the building secured. Wanted to be sure the limo was ready.

Her racing heartbeat was so loud it drowned out some of Quinn's words. *Smith has more weapons.* He must have. Smith probably had a knife hidden on him. She'd lost the gun, but she could find something else. Her hands fluttered over Smith once again, and when Quinn snarled into his phone, she shoved her fingers into Smith's pockets. *Keys.* He had keys to the rental car. She grabbed them, fisted them, and shoved her hand behind her back just as Quinn turned his head toward her. He'd finished his call, and now his angry eyes were locked and loaded on her.

Smith was out cold. Unconscious, Smith couldn't fight. He would just be easy pickings. *I have to get Quinn away from him.*

"This isn't about Smith." Her left hand lingered on his chest. She felt his chest rise, then fall. More strength seemed to pour into her. Her right hand remained hidden behind her back. She stared directly at Quinn. "This is about me. What I've done."

"It's about you." A nod. "Stand up, Maggie or Madelyn or whatever the fuck you want to be called."

She stood up.

"We're walking out of this building. You're going to put your arm around me, and you're going to act like we are the best of friends." A shrug. "Or lovers. Whatever. I don't give a shit. We're leaving together, and we are leaving now."

"And you won't hurt Smith?"

His lips pursed.

"If I walk out with you, you won't hurt Smith?"

"He's not a very good bodyguard, is he? I mean, the man is clearly asleep on the job."

She lunged toward Quinn.

He lifted his hand and the tranq gun pointed dead center at her chest. "I can shoot you. Carrying you from the building is still an option."

Her mind sought desperately for a way out. If she fought him now, he would just tranq her. Then he could kill Smith while she was out cold. If she pretended to go with him, then as soon as they got to the lobby, she could scream for help. She could fight him. "I'll come with you."

"Of course, you will. No hesitation at leaving someone behind. But I suppose he is just the bodyguard. Not someone you actually care about."

"I love him." Holy crap. What a time for those words to come out, but they just did. *I love him.* "And if you promise not to hurt Smith, I will do whatever you want."

He smiled at her. "Smith isn't my bait. You are. You give me exactly what I want, and I'll even let you go when this is all over."

"I don't understand."

"I know. It's rather sad. But you'll get the full picture soon enough." He puffed out his cheeks on an exhale. "Let's get going before that bruiser wakes up."

That means Smith won't be out for long. I just have to keep Quinn away from him, and Smith will be okay. He'll come for me. He'll kick Quinn's ass. On that last point, she was certain.

She surreptitiously tucked the keys into the pocket of her pants. "Where are we going?"

"A fun spot I picked out just for you. Don't worry. You'll love it. No, scratch that, you'll hate it." He grabbed her arm, his fingers digging deep, and hauled her with him toward the elevator.

Just as they reached the elevator, Smith let out a ragged groan.

"Fuck, he's already waking up. Guess I need to send the bastard back to bed." Quinn let her go and turned to aim at Smith once more.

"No!" She jumped in front of Quinn. Put her body between him and Smith. "Leave him alone.

You said you would, if I came with you. You said you wouldn't hurt him."

His eyebrows shot up. "Did I say those specific words?"

"He's unconscious. Leave him alone. Let's get in the elevator, and I'll do what you want. Be bait—be whatever. Let's just go."

He pulled a keycard from his back pocket. Slid it against the control panel on the outside of the elevator. "You go in first." The doors opened.

"No, we'll go together." She didn't trust him. Not for a second.

Smiling, he motioned her forward. Cautious, no, terrified, she went with him. They crossed into the elevator together.

"Madelyn?" Rough. Ragged. Smith. He was awake.

"Fucking too fast," Quinn muttered. "Knew he was so big I'd need a higher dose. Should have shot him twice." He jammed the button on the elevator and the doors started to close.

Her heart raced, her stomach flipped, and right before those doors closed, she saw Smith's face.

Smith.

He grabbed out with his hands, trying to stop the doors from closing, but it was too late. They sealed shut.

She sucked in a breath. *Smith is okay. He's safe. He's going to come for me.*

The elevator descended. Her stomach dropped. Her breath heaved in and out, and Madelyn thought she might be hyperventilating. "Why are you doing this?"

"For Heather."

"Heather wouldn't want you to hurt me."

"Well, Heather wouldn't want to be dead, either, now, would she?"

Madelyn flinched. "I never wanted that, either."

"No? Then maybe you shouldn't have run."

They were almost to the lobby. The floor numbers flashed so quickly as they descended. When the doors opened, she would rush out and scream like hell for help. Smith was trapped in the penthouse. She had to get someone up there. She had to do *something*. "You've killed people."

He leaned his shoulders back against the wall of the elevator. "I have no idea what you're talking about." His gaze raked her as he kept the tranq gun pointed at Madelyn's chest. "You're sweating and shaking. Don't like elevators, do you? One of my investigators turned up that fact in one of the FBI's reports. Someone noted that you had been trapped in a very tight room. According to your recollections, one barely bigger than a closet. The agent recommended therapy for you. She worried you'd develop severe claustrophobia." A pause. "Did you ever get that therapy? Because it looks like that answer is a big no."

Her hands twisted together. "You knew I was in Miami. You knew all about my authentication business." Her chest seemed to ache as her heart raced. "You set up the elevator sabotage, didn't you?"

"Um. I needed to set the stage."

What was that supposed to mean? "And the man who attacked me? Did you send him to my house, too?"

Quinn smiled. "Again, more scene setting. Unfortunate, but necessary. If we want to draw out the target, we have to make the bait look good."

"I don't know what the hell that means, but I *do* know the man who attacked me in my house is dead." Chill bumps chased up and down her arms. "You murdered him?"

"Don't act like you're upset. He was garbage and needed to be disposed of."

The elevator doors slid open. Madelyn didn't hesitate. She raced through them. "Help!" The high-pitched cry tore from her. Her eyes latched onto the receptionist. "Call the police!"

The blonde rose from behind the desk.

A security guard stepped forward from his post on the right.

"A man is injured in the penthouse—get the police, get an ambulance, get—"

"Get back in your chair, Rhonda. Clayton, hold your position." Once more, Quinn's fingers bit into her arm. "My building. My employees. My rules. They're not doing anything without my order."

Stunned, her gaze swept from Rhonda to Clayton. "He's—he's a killer!"

Rhonda paled but sat down.

"A man is hurt upstairs!" Madelyn yelled. "Do something!"

The security guard looked away.

"A car is waiting," Quinn told her, all fake solicitous. "Got a drive ahead of us. Don't worry, it's not too far. And I think you'll get a kick out of our final destination."

Bullshit. She *kicked* him. As hard as she could in the shin. Surprised, swearing, he let her go. She ran for the main doors of the building. She'd almost reached them when another security guard stepped into her path. "Ma'am, I think you're supposed to stay with Mr. Russell."

Not happening. She shoved him, and he stumbled aside. With a burst of speed, Madelyn burst through those doors. "Help!"

Arms closed around her from behind. Madelyn was lifted up and carried toward the limo. Before she could shout again, she was tossed inside. Quinn followed right behind her. The door slammed shut, and the limo raced away.

She'd landed on the floorboard, and Madelyn pushed herself up.

Quinn smiled down at her. "I lied." He put the tranq gun down beside him.

"What?"

"Some of my employees are already on the way up to the penthouse. They'll take care of your bodyguard. I can't have loose ends, now, can I?"

Her hand drove into her pocket. She positioned the key between her fingers, just like she'd been taught in her self-defense classes. Then she yanked her hand out and flew toward him, driving her fist—and that sharp key—right at his smiling face.

CHAPTER TWENTY-ONE

The elevator dinged, and the doors began to open. Smith didn't hesitate. He'd been waiting for the moment to attack, knowing that someone would be coming back for him. Like Quinn would just leave Smith alive? *Hell, no. He'll send goons for me.* As soon as those elevator doors parted, Smith launched forward with his fists raised and fury in his heart. Still groggy, still dizzy, but he knew he would fucking destroy whoever was—

"*On your side!*" A fast yell from the man standing inside. His hands went up.

That was when Smith noticed two unconscious security guards on the floor of the elevator.

"I am not here to attack you." The man—with his hands still up—inclined his head toward Smith. "How about you take a breath and don't punch me in the face?"

Fuck taking a breath. Smith stepped into the elevator and jabbed the button for the lobby. "Who the hell are you?"

His hands slowly lowered. "D'Angelo Bryant." He wore a gray suit, one that had a little blood on the shoulder. "I believe you know my employer, Reginald Guyer."

"You work for her stepdad?" Smith rubbed his chest. It freaking ached where he'd been—what? Shot? No, there was no bullet wound. No blood soaking his clothes. And he just felt weird. He had to sag against the wall of the elevator because his legs seemed weak.

Drugged. I feel drugged, dammit.

D'Angelo's dark gaze hardened. "I screwed up before. That bastard should never have gotten into Madelyn's house. Reginald sent me after you because he wanted you to have backup. Told me that if I ever saw her get separated from you, I was to step in."

"*Where is Madelyn?*"

D'Angelo looked at the two unconscious men on the floor. "Pretty sure they were coming up here to kill you."

Smith agreed with that assessment, but he had other priorities. "*Madelyn.*"

D'Angelo's head angled up as he grimaced. "She was tossed into a limo. I was across the street. Couldn't get to her fast enough. Saw no sign of you, so I figured you still had to be inside the building. When the guards rushed up here, I, uh, managed to hitch a ride with them."

Tossed into a limo. "Fuck," he ground out from between clenched teeth. "Why didn't you stay on her?"

A shrug. "Because I figured there were already two dead bodies in Miami. Trying not to have a third. You're welcome for my heroic efforts."

"Madelyn matters, not me." He'd let her down. He'd promised to protect her, and she'd just been taken from him. Right before the elevator doors had closed, he'd caught a glimpse of her with Quinn. After waking on the floor, Smith had dragged his body down the corridor, trying desperately to get to her. His legs hadn't wanted to work. His normal coordination had been gone.

But he'd seen her. Just for an instant.

She'd been terrified.

"I tagged the limo when it arrived. Didn't like the look of the driver. He seemed more like a hired thug than a chauffeur. Tagged the back, so we can track them."

Smith jerked away from the wall. "D'Angelo, I fucking love you."

The doors opened. He leapt out—or did as much leaping as his still sluggish body would allow—only to see Memphis barreling toward him.

Memphis's eyes widened as he took in Smith. "I was coming to save you!"

So the guy had gotten his nine-one-one text. "We're going to save Madelyn."

"Madelyn? Where the hell is she?"

Smith grabbed his new best friend and hauled him forward. "D'Angelo knows."

D'Angelo had already pulled out his phone and was tapping on the screen.

"What is happening right now?" Memphis demanded to know. "Gonna need to be brought up to speed."

"Quinn Russell drugged me." *I think that's what he did.* "I also suspect he's the one behind the attacks on Madelyn in Miami. I think he blames her for what happened to his sister." Smith sucked in a breath. "If he was behind the attacks down there, it stands to reason he was behind the murder of Andrew Bryson, too." *And maybe he'd helped the elevator repairman with the OD?*

"Got them," D'Angelo announced.

"Who the fuck is he?" Memphis asked.

"A friend."

"Uh, you sure? Because I don't think you should trust any of Quinn Russell's friends—"

"I'm not with Russell." D'Angelo kept staring at his phone. "I'm D'Angelo, and I work for Reginald Guyer." He tapped the screen again. "We can follow the limo. They have a lead, but we'll catch them," D'Angelo added, but a little furrow appeared between his brows. "Provided we don't lose the signal and they don't realize I tagged the car—"

"I-I know where they went." Soft. Hesitant. Scared.

They whirled to see the blonde receptionist standing behind her desk.

"Where are the guards?" she asked, wrapping her arms around her stomach.

"Unconscious in the elevator," D'Angelo replied.

She bit her lower lip. "More will come."

"Good." Memphis stepped toward her. "I'm feeling a little jealous because I missed out on the action."

Smith ignored Memphis and D'Angelo and closed in on the receptionist. There had been a hint of intimacy in her voice when she first made the call to Quinn Russell. "You're sleeping with Quinn."

A flinch. "Did he—did he kill people?"

Smith wished the freaking lingering weakness would vanish from his body. "Seems that way." He was in front of her. Only the desk separated them. "You saw him take Madelyn, didn't you?"

A jerky nod.

"That's called kidnapping," Smith told her, keeping his voice gentle. "And if you didn't help her—"

"You don't know how much power Quinn has!"

"If you didn't help and you know where he took her and Madelyn winds up dead, you will go to jail."

A tear trailed down her cheek.

"We can protect you," Memphis assured her as he joined Smith in front of the desk. "We can make sure that the guy never hurts you or anyone else, but you need to work with us."

Another tear fell. "I wondered why he wanted the property. When I first heard him making the deal, it made no sense. He can't build out there. And that cabin is so old and rundown."

Cabin. "Give me the address."

She bent down, grabbed a sheet of paper, and scribbled the address. "Don't let him hurt me?" She extended the paper.

He took the small slip of paper. "By the time I'm done, he won't be hurting anyone ever again."

Smith turned away, heading for the exit. He saw a door open to the side, and a man in a brown security guard uniform rushed out.

The guard went for his taser as he ran for Smith, like he'd been given an order to make sure Smith did not get out of the building. The guard was a locked-and-loaded missile heading right for his target.

Only before that missile could fire, Memphis slammed his fist into the man's face. Then his elbow. And Memphis followed up that hit with a vicious kick that took the guard down. "Not feeling so jealous now," Memphis announced, sounding pleased.

Smith shoved open the door. He reached for his car key but...gone. Hell. Had Quinn taken the key to his rental?

"I think we need to take a minute and plan," Memphis said as he closed a hand over Smith's shoulder.

Screw that. "What I need is your ride."

"My ride is a motorcycle, and you're kinda weaving on your feet. Not so sure you should be driving anything." He squinted at Smith. "What happened up there?"

He rounded on D'Angelo. "Your ride?"

D'Angelo pointed to a black Suburban. "Let's roll."

Hell, yes.

"Wait!" Memphis barked. "Dammit, Smith, we need a plan. You can't go in with guns blazing!"

An excellent point. "I need a gun. Give me yours." Because, after waking, he'd realized fast that his gun had been taken from him.

"You can have my *backup*, but you need to *breathe*."

He couldn't breathe. Madelyn was gone. And he had a sick suspicion of just where Quinn had taken her.

"You're acting like you plan to go out there and kill the bastard." Memphis glowered. "We need to call the cops. Hell, let's at least get Oliver to help. He'll bring in the Feds. On my way to you, I heard from Titan—he has his hands full with an emergency situation, but Oliver can meet us at our destination."

"I'm not acting." He marched for the waiting Suburban.

"Uh, what?"

D'Angelo had unlocked the ride. Smith climbed in the passenger seat. He sent a glare D'Angelo's way. "You'd better be who the fuck you claim to be. If you're not, Memphis and I will be taking you out."

"Understood." D'Angelo hopped in the driver's seat.

Swearing, Memphis climbed in the back. He also shoved a gun up at Smith. "From my ankle holster. You are *lucky* I am such a prepared bastard." A pause. "And what do you mean you aren't acting?"

"I fully intend to kill Quinn Russell. He set up attacks on Madelyn. He terrified her. He took her. The man won't be walking away."

Grim silence filled the interior of the Suburban.

"Start the vehicle." Smith tapped the address into the Suburban's GPS. The location filled the screen. "Fuck."

"A cabin in the middle of nowhere?" D'Angelo pulled away from the curb. "Why take her there?"

"The same reason he's done all the other shit to her. Because he likes to make Madelyn relive her nightmares." Smith's hands fisted. "The bastard is taking her back to the scene of the original crime."

***

The limo pulled to a stop. Madelyn's breath heaved in and out, and she lifted her hands—hands locked in zip ties.

"You didn't have to wear those." Blood still dripped from the long scratches on Quinn's face. Scratches that had come courtesy of her attack with the key and her fighting feverishly even as he punched at her. Quinn had overpowered her. He'd taken the key and wrestled her phone from Madelyn. The phone had been tossed during the drive to who the hell knew where.

The right side of Madelyn's face throbbed, but she ignored the pain. "Heather would be terrified of you."

"Never know, will we? Considering that she's been in a grave for a long time." He slid across the seat and pushed open his door. "Come on out, you'll want to see this."

She didn't move.

A long sigh slipped from Quinn. "Drag her out, would you?" he said to someone else.

And rough hands grabbed at her. She kicked and twisted, using her bound hands to grab at the seat. Her foot hit the man's nose, and she saw blood spurt. He growled and locked his hands around her kicking feet. He yanked her out of the limo and tossed her onto the ground.

Madelyn rolled her body, sprang to her feet, and started to run—

To the cabin?

She froze. Her gaze locked on the dilapidated structure. Sagging roof. Sun-bleached wood. A window with broken glass at the front. A porch that leaned to the left.

Two steps lead off the porch. She knew it before she even looked down at the steps.

Two steps off. Then run across the dirt toward the twisting trees. Trees that look like thin monsters, shriveled and dying.

Her head turned. She followed the dirt. Saw the remains of trees that were even more twisted than in her memories.

"Want to go inside?" Quinn asked, voice courteous. "Because I think your old room is waiting for you." He moved to stand in front of the house. His hands lifted into the air. "Welcome home, Maggie."

CHAPTER TWENTY-TWO

"Where is my daughter?" Reginald Guyer's voice filled the interior of the Suburban.

"Quinn Russell took her, and we're currently hauling ass to kill him," Smith replied.

From the back seat, Memphis cleared his throat. "Could you stop saying we're killing people? Less talk, more action. Doesn't bite you in the butt so much in court."

There was a swift inhale from Reginald. "*You lost her?* I thought you were going to protect her! I thought you would keep her safe, I thought—"

"I'm getting her back." Grim. "Verify that D'Angelo Bryant is your guy and not some plant from Russell so I don't kick him out of the vehicle."

"Uh, I'm driving," D'Angelo pointed out. "You don't throw out a man who is driving—"

"He works for me," Reginald retorted instantly. "How are you getting her back? Do you know where he took her? Do you—"

"We can't trace Madelyn by her phone." He'd tried. Failed. "Good thing the receptionist turned on her lover—and that D'Angelo tagged Quinn's vehicle." Smith pulled in a breath. It did nothing to settle his rage. "Quinn took her back to the scene of the crime. I think it's the same cabin where she was held all of those years ago."

Silence. Sometimes, silence could say so much.

"Okay, from what I'm gathering the guy seems to blame Madelyn for what happened to his sister," Memphis said, raising his voice. "The man got money and power and connections and instead of—I don't know, being a good fucking human being—he went off the rails and turned into a psycho who terrorizes women."

D'Angelo's hands were tight around the wheel. He had the gas pedal pressed to the floorboard.

"I don't get it," Memphis continued. "Why unleash all of his hate on Madelyn? She was just as much of a victim as his sister. Dammit, you don't hurt victims. You hurt the guilty. You hurt the predator."

Reginald still wasn't talking. And something he'd said to Smith in their last meeting kept nagging at him. "Why did you say Madelyn would hate me?"

"*You said you'd protect her.*" A snarl from Reginald. *Not* an answer to Smith's question.

Yes, he had vowed to protect her. And he would. *I fucked up. I have to get back to her.* "I'll be killing for her."

"*Stop* saying that shit!" Memphis blasted. "I texted Oliver. The FBI is coming in hot, and just so you know, he thinks he did get a lead on Madelyn's mom. There was a dancer who went missing from Chicago that *might* have been her.

The dancer and her daughter, though the daughter was listed as being a year younger than what we *think* is Madelyn's age—"

"Her mother was so beautiful when she danced." Sorrow deepened Reginald's voice. "She was meant to light up a stage, not hide in the shadows."

He knew. Reginald had known that Madelyn's mother had been hiding out in Vegas. "Did she kill Madelyn's father?"

More silence. Then, rasping, "Some people need to be killed. The world is better off without them in it."

"Did she kill Madelyn's father?" Because that hadn't been an answer. A simple "yes" or "no" would be fabulous.

"Thirty minutes away," D'Angelo said. "Doubt they're hauling ass as fast as we are in that long limo. We should pull up right behind him."

"Don't go in the front," Reginald ordered. "They'll see you coming long before you arrive and will kill Madelyn. You're going by what's on standard GPS. Don't. Ten minutes from the cabin, you'll want to turn on a dirt road next to an abandoned gas station. There used to be a sagging, metal gate blocking that road. Move it. Drive through it. Do whatever you need to do. That road will take you back behind the cabin. Kill your motor when you get closer. Go in on foot. He won't see you coming."

Smith tightened his grip on the gun Memphis had given him. "Been there before, have you, Reginald?"

"Some people just belong in the ground." Flat. "Bring Madelyn home." He hung up.

"*Fuck,*" Memphis breathed. "Uh, D'Angelo, did your boss just confess to—"

"All my boss did was give us some directions." His eyes cut to Smith. "We following them?"

Did he trust Reginald? Would that intel get him close to Madelyn? Whatever else Smith believed, he knew one thing. Reginald loved Madelyn. "We're following them."

"Fuck," Memphis said again.

Exactly.

***

"Memories coming back?" Quinn asked as he kept one hand clamped around Madelyn's shoulder and pushed her forward. Forward into the tiny room that haunted her nightmares.

It was more of a closet than anything else. There had been three locks on the outside of that door. *Three.* Old and faded. A sagging bed sat in the corner. Dirt and spiderwebs covered it. A poster was still on the wall to the right.

A poster that she'd had in her own room, at the apartment. Her favorite band from a lifetime ago. The other posters had fallen to the dirty floor.

"Ah, I can tell by your face that you do remember." He spun her around. "Tell me everything."

She already had told her story. Again and again. To the cops. The Feds. To her mother. To Reginald. To Smith. "I woke up in here. He came in wearing a mask. I attacked him with the spoon that he'd brought me with the soup."

"Your favorite soup. Chicken noodle."

Her brow scrunched even as she retreated from him. Not that there was anywhere to run in that little room. "I never tasted the soup. I have no idea what kind it was."

"It would have been your favorite. Just like he put your favorite posters on the wall. Just like he took your favorite *friend*. He did everything to make you happy."

"H-he said he'd been watching me."

Quinn's smile nearly split his face. "Of course, he had. That's why you're the bait. Why I had to do those things to you in Miami. If you are threatened, I think he'll run to the rescue. He didn't just forget you, Maggie. He's never been able to forget you."

"Madelyn." The name emerged from her. Maggie was someone else. A girl who'd been trapped in this little room.

"He couldn't forget you. After all, he eventually tracked you down to Vegas the first time, didn't he? He never forgot about you. Took him a while, but he found you and your mom after she fled Chicago.."

Madelyn shook her head.

"Don't know about that? Didn't realize you were born in Chicago? Don't feel too badly. It took me a long time to discover it, too. To discover that and all sorts of interesting things about sweet, little Maggie."

He didn't have Smith's gun on him any longer. She'd seen Quinn give it to the hulking asshole who'd dragged her from the limo. Quinn had the tranq gun tucked into his front waistband, but he made no move to pull it out. He just glared at her while she stared at him in silence.

The silence seemed to anger him even more. "Know what I found out about you and your family?"

She had no freaking clue. "If I knew, would I be standing in this godforsaken cabin with you?" She'd thought he was a grieving family member. Not the villain.

His lips twisted. "I discovered that when you get money and power, people talk more to you. In fact, they can get damn chatty. Troy Washington got chatty with me. I made sure he received the promotion he wanted, and he spilled on his ex-girlfriend. Did you know he dated your mom back in the day? Nothing too serious. Troy said your mom kept everything about herself so secret. They were kind of a friends-with-benefits thing, so he never pushed her, but secrets have a way of spilling out."

Her gaze darted around the small room. Surely there was something in there she could use as a weapon.

"Troy grew up in Chicago, until he was about fifteen. One day he was talking with her about this pizza joint he missed, and he remembered how she knew the place, too. Said she told him sometimes she jonesed for a slice so badly she could taste it."

Her stare shifted back to him.

"And Troy realized she'd lived in Chicago before coming to Vegas. Also said he'd sometimes catch her dancing, twirling around, going up on her toes. Spinning over and over. Figured she'd been trained before. Said she could have been on a big stage somewhere, the main attraction, but she kept hiding in the dark." His lips pursed. "You don't get why she was hiding, do you?"

"She killed my father." That was what Troy had said. Or implied or—

"No, she was *running* from your father. Your father—the man who was obsessed with her. The man who was obsessed with you. The man who hunted you down and took you because he wasn't going to let her steal you away from him."

Her knees buckled. She almost went down, but Quinn grabbed her.

"Your father..." His eyes bored into hers. "The man who abducted you all of those years ago. The man who killed my sister when you ran away from him. The sick fuck whose blood runs in your veins—that's the man she was running from. And that's the man you will help me to kill."

"No."

"Yes. Took me some time to piece it all together, but Chicago—and your mom's dancing—was the info that I needed. Once upon a time, Kathleen Kennedy was quite the ballerina. But she fell for a bad boy." He made a tut-tut sound. "And by bad, I mean your dear old dad was an enforcer—and hit man—for the mob. Oh, sure, I'm quite certain that wasn't how he introduced himself to her. By all accounts, he could be quite charming. One of those tall, dark and good-looking types that women enjoy so much. He also reportedly had money to burn. She didn't discover the truth about where his money came from until much later."

Madelyn shook her head.

"He had a specialty. Want to know what it was? He would use a person's loved ones against them. He learned that he could get anyone to do anything with the right motivation. He'd study his prey. Learn what they valued most. Then use it against them." His voice roughened even more as he added, "I must confess, I have learned to mimic his style. I discovered what he valued most, and I certainly intend to use you against him."

Wrenching herself from his hold, Madelyn backed up. One step. Two. Three. She hit the edge of the small bed. "You're wrong."

"No, I'm not. Your father is a psychotic killer. He abused your mother, but she stuck around until he turned his fists on you. That's what my investigators discovered, anyway. You made her run. But your dad wouldn't let go. He eventually found you. Took you. When you escaped, he killed my sister to punish you. He always enjoyed taking the things his prey loved. That's what you were—prey, not just a daughter. *Prey.*"

There was no window in that little room. The only escape was behind Quinn.

"You vanished, and for years, I thought you might be dead. I was fine with that."

She saw no weapon in the room. Just the old bed. And—something on the faded cover over the bed. Something small. Her eyes narrowed on the little object.

"I didn't learn that your father was the killer, not until I had established my own business. It took money to hunt him. Money and ties with the wrong people. But those people turned out to be the *right* ones for me."

Nothing was right about what he was saying.

My father? My father?

She reached for the object on the bed as her breath shuddered out.

"When I could afford PIs and I had the *wrong* people giving me connections—you know those people, the ones your father worked for—I was able put everything together. Got the intel from Troy Washington, got leads from the mob in Chicago. See, turns out, the people in power there were pissed with your old man. They didn't like that he just disappeared one day. They had work for him to do, but like you, he just up and vanished."

The small object bit into the palm of her hand.

"But I got a list of his kills. Or at least, some of them. My, my, but he was busy. And it was when I was looking at the dead that I realized one of his vics owned this old cabin. A place close to Vegas. A place that matched the description you'd given so long ago. I came out with my team, and we ripped this cabin wide open. Every board you see on the floor? We tore them up. That's when I found your ring."

The ring that had been sent to her stepdad.

"Kept it for a while because I had no freaking clue where you were—or if you were still alive. I found your ring, and I found my sister's charm."

The charm that Madelyn held in her palm. Half of a heart. The half with the letters "BE" and

"FRIE" engraved. The other half would have "ST" and "NDS."

Best friends.

Madelyn squeezed her eyes shut.

"The possibility that your father had killed you was really strong, but then, like a gift from God, I found out that you were alive and well and living in Miami. I started planning. If you were alive, then he must be, too. And he wouldn't walk away from you. He *had* to be close."

"No." She lifted her chin and opened her eyes.

"Oh, it's all true. I've got files that can prove it, but they're not exactly on hand right now. Most of them are back at my penthouse."

"No, he's not watching me. You were the only one doing that. You had eyes on me in Miami."

Quinn shrugged.

"I don't know who the man was that kidnapped me—"

His face darkened. "He was your father, Maggie. I just told you that shit. Are you not listening?"

"But he's long gone," she blasted right over his words. "He won't appear to save me." Monsters didn't save anyone. She kept her chin up. "But Smith will. He will come for me."

Quinn burst into laughter. "A dead man can't save you."

"Smith isn't dead." No, he couldn't be.

"Sure, he is. The minute we left, my guards threw him down the stairs. I didn't shoot him with his own gun in that hallway because I truly can't stand a bloody mess. And that mess would have been harder to explain away. But I already had another plan in place. I'm very, very good at staging scenes, you see. My men were going to make it look like he had a terrible, terrible fall. By the time his body is discovered..." He made freaking air quote marks around "discovered" as he smirked at her. "By then, the tranq I used will be out of his system. Not like this is my first time. He'll have broken his neck. Have a ton of injuries consistent with a tragic fall. And your hero will just be gone."

Rage blasted through her. Deep, dark, consuming rage. "No."

"You're going to stay here, and when your dad comes, you can watch me kill him."

"He's *not* coming."

"He will, sooner or later. If he wasn't keeping eyes on you, don't worry, I do have a backup plan." He pointed to the small camera on the right wall. Mounted high up near the ceiling, a red light glowed from the bottom of the camera. "I have connections to the same people who used to know your bastard of a father. A video feed of you will go live on the dark web. If he's out there—*and I know he fucking is*—he'll learn about you. He'll recognize this place. He will come for you."

"Monster," Madelyn breathed.

A grim nod. "Absolutely, he is. But I will put him out of his misery."

"I meant you." And Madelyn erupted. She rushed right for him.

But he backed away, and he swung the door closed as he jumped back over the threshold. The door slammed shut. A lock flipped. Then another. Another. Madelyn slammed her fists into the door. "You bastard, let me out! *Let me out!*" And even as she screamed, agony burned through her heart. Smith wasn't dead. Smith *wasn't* dead. "Let me out!"

***

"The Feds are on the way," Memphis said, voice low. "ETA of seven minutes."

"I'm not waiting," Smith returned. His eyes were on the back of the small cabin. The place from Madelyn's nightmares.

"Sure, don't wait. Just stand there, still weaving a little, and plan to go in and face who the hell knows how many men."

D'Angelo lowered the binoculars he'd taken from the back of his vehicle. "I don't see anyone guarding the back. Did catch a shadow moving in front. The place is so small, can't imagine there are a whole lot of guys inside."

"I'm not waiting," Smith said again. He couldn't wait. Being in that cabin had to be hell for Madelyn. And he didn't know what Quinn was doing to her. The bastard could be hurting her. He could be torturing her.

I'm getting her out.

Once more, his gaze swept the area behind the cabin. They were crouched beneath the branches of a western honey mesquite. He recognized the damn thing because of his grandmother. The woman who'd taught him about jasmine had loved talking for hours about all kinds of plants and trees. They'd been her passion.

More of a shrub than a real tree, the mesquite was still freaking huge. The fragrant scent from the flowers was heavy. Cloying. But the mesquite provided good cover so...

A car engine fired to life. The limo? He heard the crunch of gravel. Hell, yes. The driver was leaving. One less bastard in his way. "You got my six?" he asked Memphis.

"You know it."

"Good." He glanced at D'Angelo. "If things go badly—"

"If I go back to Miami without Madelyn, my boss will kill me."

Smith did not think D'Angelo was kidding.

"Rest assured," D'Angelo continued in a low voice barely louder than a breath, "I will do whatever it takes to make sure she gets home safely."

"So will I." He didn't say more. He didn't have to. Smith went toward the cabin. He went in low, and he went in fast. When he got to the back door, he saw the pathetic lock. Barely took a second to get it open.

He could have kicked in the bitch. Gone in with guns blazing but...

Can't let Madelyn get caught in the crossfire. Until he knew exactly where she was, he had to be careful. For all he knew, Quinn had a gun to her head right then.

His heart drummed in his chest as Smith opened the door. It squeaked faintly, and the sound seemed so loud to his ears. He rushed inside, still staying low, and he saw Quinn huddled over a computer in the far right of the room. Another guy—a big, hulking fellow with a gun on his hip—sagged against the wall near Quinn. There was no sign of Madelyn.

"Let me out!" A scream. Her scream. His blood iced. He heard a pounding. Fists hitting wood. "Let me out now! Now, dammit, let me out!"

"Go gag that bitch," Quinn ordered without looking up from the computer. "I don't want her screaming all day and night."

Grunting, Quinn's goon straightened from the wall. He headed for a small door on the right. One with three freaking locks on it. *Screw this shit.* Smith leapt forward.

"You're not gagging her." Smith put the gun dead center at the back of the man's head. "And I don't like it when people call Madelyn a bitch."

"What the *fuck?"* A snarl from Quinn. "You're dead, dead!"

Clearly, he was not. Smith slammed the butt of the gun into the back of the goon's head. He heard a grunt escape from him as the man fell, but Smith was already whirling. Quinn rushed at him, yanking out a familiar, black, gun-like object from the waistband of his pants. *Tranq gun.* Yeah, Smith knew what it was now. "Not this time." Smith pulled the trigger of his own weapon. The gunshot blasted straight into Quinn's chest. The SOB went down, crying out in pain.

"Guess what?" Smith snarled. "That was a real bullet, asshole."

CHAPTER TWENTY-THREE

The boom of a gunshot echoed in Madelyn's ears. For an instant, she stopped pounding her fists against the door. Terror tried to choke her. *No! No!* In a frenzy, she drove her fists even harder into the door and it was—

Suddenly thrown open. It almost hit her, and she stumbled back. Her mouth gaped open because standing in the doorway—looking strong and dangerous and so handsome that it almost hurt to look at him—was Smith. Her Smith. Alive and well and *her Smith*. With a quick cry, she launched at him.

Smith caught her. His arms wrapped around her and held her tight. She'd leapt into his arms, literally jumping at him, and her legs wrapped around his hips. Her arms flew over his head and slid down to his neck. She still wore the damn zip ties, but Madelyn wasn't letting them slow her down. She held him desperately, and never, ever wanted to let him go.

"You're alive!" A desperate cry from her. "He said you were dead, but I knew you'd come. I didn't want to leave you at the penthouse, but he was going to tranq you again. He promised not to hurt you, but it was a lie. Then we got here and he said you were dead." Her words tumbled out. She knew she wasn't making any sense, and it didn't matter. The only thing that mattered? Smith. Warm. Strong. Alive. "I love you. I told him I loved you. Nothing was supposed to happen to you. You didn't promise not to die, I asked you to promise..." Her head lifted, and she stared up at him with tears clouding her vision. "Promise now. Right now."

He kissed her. His mouth crashed down on hers. Frantic and desperate and so *real*. The cold and fear shattered around her. Smith was with her. He'd found her. He was *alive*. Everything was going to be all right now.

He pulled his mouth from hers. "You just said you love me."

"I love you with everything that I am." Her legs and arms tightened around him. "Now get me the hell out of here."

One of his hands was on her waist. The other—she realized he held a gun. She remembered the booming blast she'd heard moments before. "Smith?"

"I love you with everything I am, too, sweetheart." He carried her out of that little room.

She clung to him even as her desperate gaze flew around the cabin.

Memphis stood over a man who appeared unconscious. A big, burly fellow—one that had been waiting inside the cabin when she and Quinn arrived. Memphis had cuffed the guy's hands behind his back. Memphis swept his stare over her and lifted one eyebrow. "You good, Madelyn?"

Good wasn't the word. Alive. That was what she was. What Smith was. What—

"Yeah, he's bleeding out like a bitch," a man that she didn't know announced. There was a whole lot of blood on his gray suit as he crouched beside Quinn's prone form. "Don't know that an ambulance is gonna get here in time."

She shuddered. Her legs slowly lowered, but her hands were caught behind Smith's neck. "I have zip ties on me. Get them off?"

Smith put the gun on a spindly table beside them. He caught her arms. He bent and lifted them over his head. His face hardened when he caught sight of the zip ties. Memphis stalked forward and offered him a knife.

The knife sliced through the zip ties. They'd been so tight that pinpricks immediately shot through her fingers.

Smith began rubbing her fingers. "Baby, you're okay, you're safe. I'll never let you go again. I fucking *swear* it." He released her fingers and reached once again for the gun. Stark determination hardened his face. "You will never need to fear—"

"*No!*" A guttural cry from Quinn. He'd shoved the man in the gray suit aside, but not before grabbing a gun from a holster on the guy's side. Quinn lifted that gun and pointed it straight at her.

Smith shoved her to the side even as Memphis grabbed her arm and yanked her hard toward him. And then—

Boom.

Boom.

Boom.

Just like before. Only louder. Blasting right next to her ear and for a minute, she couldn't hear anything at all after the last boom died away. Her eyes were on Quinn, as they'd been since his shrieking cry. She'd seen the bullets slam into him. He hadn't even had a chance to fire. Smith had been too fast. Blood exploded from Quinn's chest, spurting into the air. The sight was horrific. Chilling.

She saw the life leave his eyes. One second it was there. The next, just gone.

"Look away, baby," Smith urged her.

Quinn fell back against the floor.

The man in gray had even more blood on him. "Freaking bastard." He jerked at his suit coat and glared at Quinn. "No damn way is that ambulance gonna arrive in time now." He stood up, stripping off his suitcoat. He dropped it onto the dead man. His head swung toward Smith. "My fuck up." Flat. "Thought he was too weak to do anything. Was trying to save the bastard's life when he—" He stopped. "Reginald is going to fire my ass. Damn glad you're fast on the draw. Only seen shit like that on TV."

She hauled her gaze away from Quinn and found Smith staring at her.

The gun was still gripped in his hand.

"I was trained really well." His tone was off. Too stilted. Cold. "Told you once, I'm a really good killer."

And again, without hesitation, she threw her body against his and held him as tightly as she could. "And I'm pretty sure I told you that you were my hero." If she hadn't, she'd make sure he got the point now. "*That's* what you are." What he would always be. "Now can we please get out of this cabin?"

Before Smith could speak, she heard the scream of sirens.

"That'll be the FBI," Memphis said. "Always late to the party."

Smith put his gun on the floor. He lifted her into his arms and carried her out. Sure enough, the FBI was swarming. They'd come with the local cops. A whole rescue squad. Everyone had come to help her.

This time, she wasn't running out alone.

No, she wasn't alone at all.

"I love you," Smith whispered.

And she felt those words all the way to her soul.

***

The honeymoon suite had never seemed more beautiful. There were fresh rose petals on the bed. More champagne chilling. Soft music playing in the air.

"I don't think anyone realizes what happened today," Madelyn said as she collapsed on the side of the bed. "Anyone here, I mean. The staff still just thinks we're a couple in love." She lifted some of the rose petals and let them fall back onto the comforter.

"Aren't we?" Smith asked from his position in the doorway. He wanted to rush to her. To sweep her into his arms. Hold tight. Never let go.

Never.

But he didn't move. It took all of his control, but he did not move.

They'd been interrogated by Feds for most of the day. When one of the most influential men in Vegas wound up dead, courtesy of a chest riddled with gunshots, there were bound to be questions. And when it was discovered that the influential man in question was linked to several murders, there were even *more* questions.

Troy Washington had survived the attempted carbon monoxide poisoning at his house, thanks to Titan. Troy had been able to tell police that Quinn had shot him with a tranq—must have been the man's MO. Quinn had gone to Troy's house, saying he wanted to know everything Troy had told Madelyn. After he'd gotten the info he wanted, Quinn blasted Troy, then got his men to help him set the scene so it would look like an accidental death.

Accident, my ass.

The Feds had turned up plenty of info at the cabin. The computer Quinn had been using had been a fount of intel. Plus, when the authorities had gone in Quinn's penthouse with a warrant, they'd basically found a whole crime planning room where the man had been chronicling his hunt for Madelyn. They'd gotten evidence to tie him both to the OD of the elevator guy and to the murder of Andrew Bryson. Quinn looked guilty as hell, and Oliver had told them that Smith would be free to go. No charges would come his way. After all, several witnesses could attest to the fact that his shooting of Quinn had been justified.

He was dead the minute he took her, justified or not. But Memphis had advised Smith to stop saying shit like that out loud.

As he watched Madelyn, she picked up a few more rose petals and let them fall. "Quinn said the man who took me was my father."

He'd heard her recount those words to Oliver earlier, when she'd gone over every moment of her ordeal with Quinn.

"He could be lying, couldn't he?" She peered up at him, with hope in her eyes. "Quinn was all twisted up inside. The hate—I think it made him crazy."

"The Feds believe Quinn Russell was involved with illegal activities up to his eyeballs, baby. Oliver says the guys in organized crime have been tracking him for a while. His whole upstanding businessman routine was BS. The man was dangerous. Completely in bed with the mob."

She blinked. "He said my father worked with the mob. That he was some sort of enforcer. That my father's MO was to use the people his victims loved against them. Like he used Heather."

Smith lumbered toward her. He just couldn't stop himself from getting closer.

"Do you think it's true?"

He'd seen the evidence on Quinn's computer. A peek that Oliver had allowed that went against protocol. Smith stood over Madelyn but didn't touch her. Not yet. She'd asked him not to lie to her, and he wasn't supposed to hold back any longer. "Yes. I'm sorry, but I do."

She swallowed. "My mother ran from him. Because she was terrified of what he'd do? To her and me?"

Again... "Yes."

"But he found us. He took me. He—you know, I remember him saying that he wanted to take care of me. That I just had to be good."

She'd told Smith those words before. Only he realized that now—to her and to him—they made sick sense.

"A father," Madelyn whispered as a tear snaked down her cheek, "wanting to take care of his daughter."

Helpless, Smith reached out. His index finger caught her tear.

"He was a killer. Twisted and evil." Her lower lip trembled as she stared up at him. "What if I'm like him?"

Oh, fuck that. "Never." Utter certainty. "You are everything good in this world. You are not a damn thing like him. You understand me? *Nothing like him*."

"I-I killed Heather, I left—"

"There were no other rooms in that little cabin, baby. There wasn't even a damn bedroom. Just the open den-slash-kitchen with a pullout couch that looked fifty years old. The little closet you were in. And a bathroom. Your room was the only one with locks." *Not a room. A cell. Prison.* "There are no signs that he took her at the same time that he took you. There is no real proof of that. You have to let the guilt go. *You didn't hurt her*. He did."

"But he was my father, and she died because she was my friend."

She'd found Heather's best friend charm. Smith had seen her give it to one of the cops on scene, and the half heart had been bagged and tagged as evidence. Her pain seemed to live and breathe in the room with them. Voice low, he asked, "Do you blame Heather for what her brother did to you? For what he did to me?"

Her eyes widened. "What? Of course, not! She had nothing to do with—" She stopped and sucked in a breath.

"Right, baby." His knuckles skimmed over her silken cheek. "She didn't have anything to do with his actions. You didn't have anything to do with your dad's. You were a kid. Let go of the guilt. Just remember how much you loved her. Remember how happy the two of you were. And remember that you have to keep living." He was standing right in front of her, and he wanted to offer her a new life. "You don't need to be afraid any longer. You don't need to hide who you are. You can live the biggest life you want to live."

Her lashes fluttered. "But he was never caught. My father is still out there. And Quinn has just been waving me like a red flag. You heard what the FBI crime techs said—he posted about me online."

Yes, Quinn had. And the cyber techs were working to use his posts to track down other criminals and work on a ton of linked cases. Quinn's death and all the evidence he'd left behind had been like a dam bursting for the authorities.

"My father may come for me one day. It won't be safe around me."

He lowered to his knees so he could be on eye level with her. "He's not coming."

"You don't know that."

He did. "I want Tony to search the area near the cabin."

"Tony? But why?"

Smith could hear her stepfather's voice echoing in his head. *Some people belong in the ground.* And Reginald had known all about the cabin. Had known how to sneak up the back way to catch the occupant by surprise. "Because I think your biological father is dead. I suspect he has been for a long time."

She sucked in a breath even as her hands flew out and grabbed for his arms. "Is it wrong that I hope he's dead?" Her fingers dug into him.

"Nothing about you could ever be wrong."

She crumpled before him. Deep sobs. Smith didn't know if she was crying for the friend she'd lost. For the father who'd turned out to be a monster. For the fear and horror she'd experienced that day. He didn't know why the tears came. He just knew he wanted to comfort her.

Smith pulled Madelyn into his arms and held her tightly. "You don't need to be scared anymore."

Not ever again.

CHAPTER TWENTY-FOUR

The pounding at the door came just after midnight. Smith hadn't been sleeping. He'd been holding Madelyn while she slept. Watching her. Stalkerish? Maybe, but after nearly losing her, he'd needed to keep his eyes on her. She'd cried then slept, and he knew that a turning point had come for her.

The past was uglier than she'd dreamed, and he knew her dreams had been pretty freaking nightmarish already. What did you do when you discovered the real devil was your blood? Your father?

The pounding came again.

Carefully, Smith slipped from the bed. He'd changed earlier and now wore sweats and a t-shirt. Barefoot, he padded to the door. A quick glance through the peephole showed him the identity of his late-night visitor. Smith swung the door open. "I expected you sooner."

Reginald Guyer just shook his head. "Flight was freaking delayed by weather. Should have been here at least two hours ago." His chin lifted as he glared at Smith. "The honeymoon suite? Did you marry my daughter?"

"Would there be a problem if I had?"

"Do you love her?"

Smith heard the faint creak of a door behind him. Madelyn was up. Considering her stepfather had been pounding on the door loudly enough to wake everyone on the floor, he wasn't exactly surprised she'd stirred. Voice clear and dead serious, Smith replied, "With all that I am."

Reginald grunted. "Good." He stepped over the threshold and shut the door behind him. "You put a bullet in Quinn Russell?"

"Several actually," Smith told him.

Another grunt. Reginald's hand shook as he smoothed down his slightly rumpled dress shirt. His gaze slid toward Madelyn.

Smith turned to look at her, too.

Like him, she'd changed. Yoga pants. An oversize shirt. She looked beautiful yet fragile. Only, she wasn't really fragile. How could she survive all that she had and be fragile? Strength just looked different on some people.

Madelyn took a slow step away from the bedroom. "Smith told me that you helped him get to the cabin."

Smith had told her, as he held her and she cried. She'd wondered how he'd found her.

"He also said you had a bodyguard tailing me," Madelyn added.

Yep, he'd mentioned D'Angelo, too. "Your bodyguard saved my ass," Smith told Reginald. "I'd give him a raise."

"The same bodyguard who let Quinn take his gun?" Reginald retorted. His gaze didn't waver from Madelyn.

"Same man. A good man. He was trying to save Quinn's life at the time. Thought the guy was so injured he couldn't fight back."

"Some people don't need saving." The lines on Reginald's face deepened. "Some of us are just bad." There was something in Reginald's voice that Smith had never expected to hear. Guilt.

Madelyn slowly advanced. "You knew where the cabin was located. When Smith and I came to see you in Miami, you said you'd hired a ton of people to work my case over the years. You already knew that the man who kidnapped me was my father, didn't you?"

"That man wasn't your father. He was evil. He hurt your mother and he hurt you, and he hurt dozens of other people over the course of his life." A ragged sigh. "Your mother told me about him. After you were taken and Heather was killed, she feared it was him. She was so scared, and she wanted to get you to safety. She was desperate. That's when I stepped in."

"You sent us out of the country." She stopped about two feet away from him.

Reginald nodded.

Smith crossed his arms over his chest. "While they were gone, you went hunting."

Reginald's gaze softened as he stared at Madelyn. "I loved your mother. She didn't know who I was when we first met. When I was in Vegas, I used a false name. No one knew who I really was. I was so sick of people pandering to me because of my money that I just tried to be anonymous for a while. And I didn't meet her when she was dancing. I met her at a coffee shop.

She worked there some, did you know? She worked there because it was close to your school, and she liked to be close during the day."

Madelyn's lips parted.

"She didn't tell me about you. I learned that she often didn't talk about the things that were most important to her. But I discovered the truth when you were taken. The first time I saw you, you were so pale. Your eyes were like windows to hell, and all I wanted to do was make sure you never hurt again." His nostrils flared. "I got you and your mom out of town as fast as I could. I sent you far away. I tried to give you everything you could ever want."

Madelyn swallowed. The small click seemed so loud. "Then you brought us back."

Reginald's gaze dipped to Smith. "You know, don't you?"

A nod. "You brought them back when he was dead."

"Took me some time to figure things out. I knew her father was the man I had to take down, but I didn't know where he was. Two years and ten months later, I had an address. Another potential *victim's* address, someone I had discovered because I'd been building a profile of kills that I thought related back to Benny Thomas."

Smith saw Madelyn's hard jerk at her biological father's name.

"Benny Thomas," she repeated.

"Benny the Blade." Reginald's hands clenched. "You can guess how he got the name."

Her hand rose to her mouth.

Heather had been stabbed fifteen times.

Reginald said, "Benny liked his knives."

Reginald, you are not helping shit right now.

"I found the cabin. Did surveillance for a time. At first, I thought it was just abandoned, but I kept a guy watching it because I was sure it was the place you'd been held. Then one night, my man on the scene called. Said there was movement." His nostrils flared. "This is the part where you'll probably think I should have reached out to the police. But the movement my guy saw? It was Benny getting rid of a body. He was digging the grave. When I arrived, I-I sent my man away. I watched Benny dig for almost an hour. He dug so deep." A long exhale. "I walked up behind him. I had a gun. I told him that he would never hurt you again."

Fuck. Smith edged closer to Madelyn. He positioned his body right beside hers even as he twined their fingers together.

"Benny laughed. Said he would find his daughter again. That he was gonna teach you to be good." His voice had turned raspy. "I fired without another thought. It just happened. He was right in front of that grave. A body was already inside it. I fired, and he fell back. The grave was waiting for him." A heaving sigh. "I just put the dirt back in place. I wiped down the shovel. And I walked away."

Madelyn backed up a half-step. "You brought us back to the states after that."

"It was safe. He wasn't going to hurt you or your mother ever again."

"But...the rules. I had to change my name. I couldn't get close to anyone. My mom said I had to keep everything secret."

Reginald blinked quickly, and Smith realized the older man had tears in his eyes. "That was for me because she knew what I'd done, and she was so afraid someone would find out. Your mom tried to protect me, and she tried to protect you, but I only realized later we were putting you through hell, too." His nostrils flared again. "I am sorry. I am sorry for what you lost. I am sorry I hurt you. I'm going to tell the cops everything."

To Smith, that sounded like one fucking bad idea. "You'll go to jail. You give them the story you told us, and they'll say you were shooting an unarmed man. Self-defense will be a real stretch, despite the shit he did."

"Madelyn doesn't need to follow rules any longer." A nod. "She needs to live and be free. Happy." His shoulders fell. "Just wanted to tell you everything first." He turned away.

Madelyn pulled her hand from Smith's and grabbed for Reginald. She spun him back to her. "Why did you kill him?"

"Because he hurt you. And no one hurts my daughter."

She hugged him. Tight. Smith knew she wasn't letting go. Reginald was gonna need to rethink that whole confession scene. But for the moment, Smith stayed silent. Madelyn needed this time with her dad. Her *dad*.

Not the maniac who'd taken her.

Her real father. The man who had been willing to go to any length to keep her safe.

***

"I don't want you going to jail." Madelyn sat on the couch, with Reginald by her side. "You are the only family I have."

Reginald pointed to a watchful Smith who sat across from him. "That man is going to be your family. He's going to love you forever, and you'll have kids, and maybe you can tell them that I'm not as much of a bastard as the world thinks."

Smith was going to be her family. Reginald was right. But she turned toward her dad. "I don't want you going to jail."

Reginald opened his mouth to respond.

"Not gonna be a whole lot of evidence left after all this time." Smith's voice was musing. "What did you do with the gun?"

"Put it somewhere that it can't ever be found. Hell, I couldn't even get to it if I wanted."

A nod from Smith. "And you wiped down the shovel. Did you leave anything else at the scene?"

"No."

"And your men weren't there? No one actually saw you shoot him?"

His lips pressed together, then Reginald replied, "No."

"If only you and Benny were there, then you're the only one who can tell the story of what happened. A shovel was on the scene. For all we know, Benny lunged at you with that shovel. You confronted him. He tried to take your head off with it." A roll of Smith's shoulders. "It would be easy for a lawyer to spin that version of the tale.

Considering who you are, I'm assuming you have the best lawyer that money can buy."

She knew that Reginald did.

"Benny's remains come up, the remains of his last victim are found, and my buddy Oliver will be able to solve a ton of old FBI cold cases that I suspect will link back to the SOB. You'll work out some plea for tampering with human remains or some such shit, claim you were emotionally wrecked and not thinking clearly at the time, but the recent attack brought everything flooding back for you and you just had to go to the cops." Smith leaned forward. "The body *will* be found. Hell, I already know where it is, and I'm strictly an amateur at this thing, but when I was out at the property, and I saw that freaking huge honey mesquite, I got suspicious. See, my friend Tony has been sharing a few forensic tips with me. She told me that when she's looking for bodies, she always searches for heavy areas of growth with vegetation or trees. Decomposing bodies give life somewhere else."

Madelyn tried not to flinch, but his words made her stomach churn.

"The story won't be a full lie," Smith added softly. "Because maybe the events of that night are a little cloudy for you. Only you and Benny know exactly what went down. Considering who Benny was and all that he did, I don't think the cops are gonna cast him in the role of victim."

Reginald didn't speak.

"Choice is yours," Smith told him with a careless shrug. "But if you ask me, Benny already caused enough pain. No one else needs to suffer. Think it might be time for us to all look forward."

"And you're okay with that?" Reginald demanded, voice cracking. "With keeping my secret? Both of you?" His gaze jumped between Madelyn and Smith.

"Yes." Madelyn didn't hesitate.

"Yes." Neither did Smith. "You protected the woman I love. How the hell could you think I'd want you locked away for that? Not when it's something I understand so completely."

Reginald's lips trembled. "I need to think about this. I—" He inhaled. "I love you, Madelyn. I loved your mother. You *are* my family, and all I want is for you to be happy."

"I am going to be happy," Madelyn assured him. "Very, very happy. Because it's time not to be scared any longer. I don't need to look over my shoulder, and you don't either. Let's put the past to bed. Let's move forward. All of us." Her right hand curled with Reginald's. Her left extended toward Smith.

Smith rose immediately and took her hand.

"No more fear," Madelyn said. "The past might not stay buried, but we aren't going to let it hurt us. Nothing is going to hurt us." Her head turned, and she found Smith staring at her. There was no missing the love in his eyes.

"Not ever again," he vowed. "Nothing will hurt you again."

***

"You're not confessing to murder. Fuck that shit."

Reginald stiffened, then spun around. He'd just pressed the button for the elevator. Obviously, the man had not realized Smith had followed him out of the honeymoon suite. Also, something else pretty obvious? Reginald wanted to run straight to the cops.

"You confess, you get locked up, and that hurts Madelyn." Smith stalked forward and kept his voice low. They were the only ones in that hallway, but he still intended to be careful. No one else could overhear this particular talk. "I don't want *anything* hurting Madelyn. Get over the guilt. You took out a fucking monster. He would have kept coming for her. He would have killed her if he could. He would have killed her mother. He would have killed you." All true. "During all of my fun chats with the cops and Feds, I learned more about Benny's MO. The Feds had a giant file on him, but they had no clue he'd been Madelyn's biological father. Or that he was the freak who'd killed her friend."

The elevator doors opened. Smith glanced inside. No one was there.

Reginald made no move to enter the elevator. After a few seconds, the doors closed.

"You want to throw the rest of your life away for a sadistic prick who *would* have killed you if you hadn't fired that gun?" Smith shook his head. "Seems like a stupid fucking decision to me. Especially when you could be using that time to, oh, I don't know, play with the half dozen grandkids you'll be getting." He considered the image of those kids. "I would like a big family, but that's totally Madelyn's call. How many kids do you think she'll want?"

"I don't want her hating me," Reginald rasped.

"You're her dad." A deliberate phrasing. Not stepdad. Dad. "She loves you. If you get sent away, you'll wreck her." A pause. "Don't you think she's been through enough?"

"Y-yes."

Smith stared into Reginald's eyes. "Your memories of that night are blurry because of the emotional trauma. Let me help you out. Repeat after me. Benny came at me with a shovel."

"Benny came at me with a shovel."

"He was going to kill me."

"He was going to kill me."

Smith nodded. "I had no choice but to defend myself."

Reginald licked his lips. "*I-I had no choice but to defend myself.*"

"Excellent." Smith slapped him on the shoulder. "Get your lawyer with you before you talk to anyone, understand?"

"Yes."

Smith punched the elevator button. The doors opened almost instantly. Reginald stepped inside, but he threw up his hand before the doors could close again. "You really love my daughter?"

So much that I'm keeping your ass out of jail and so much that I killed a man for her. "She's my world."

"Will she always be?"

"Until I take my last breath."

Swallowing, Reginald nodded. "My memories of that day are blurry. Because of the emotional trauma." He lowered his hand. The elevator doors began to close. "*Benny came at me with a shovel...*"

Smith waited until the elevator descended, then he turned and headed back to the honeymoon suite. Before he could reach for the door, it swung open. Madelyn stood there, with her beautiful eyes gleaming. "My dad—"

"Got him covered, baby. He'll be around to play with the grandkids."

Her body slammed into his as she hugged him tightly.

He picked her up—with her still hugging him—and carried her back inside. He kicked the door shut. "Brings up a good question, though. Just how many kids do you want to have? Or, do you even want kids? Because I will be deliriously happy either way. It can be just you and me forever if that's what you want."

"It will be you and me forever." She stared up at him. "And I don't care how many we have. I want a home and a life and a family with you. I want healthy and happy kids that never know fear. I want a love that lasts. I want *you*."

"You have me." His head dipped toward her. "You've always had me, and you always will." His mouth took hers.

EPILOGUE

"Madelyn? Uh, Madelyn? Yo!"

Madelyn blinked and turned her head to find Memphis squinting at her.

"You okay?" His squint shifted into a full-on frown. "Because I swear, I called your name like twenty times." His assessing gaze swept over her. "You look great, by the way. Serious fairytale-princess vibe going on with that dress. Smith will lose his mind." Grimacing, he yanked on his black tie. "Not that he isn't already losing his mind. He sent me in here to check on you even though the wedding march is going to play in like, five minutes. I told the man to chill, but he was worried. I don't think he'll stop being a tight-ass until he actually has the ring on your finger."

Memphis wore a dashing tux, the same one that all the groomsmen had donned for the wedding. Aiden was Smith's best man, of course, and a very pregnant Tony was Madelyn's matron of honor. Memphis was one of Smith's groomsmen, as was the ever silent Titan. The last member of the little group was a seriously intense man named Saint. Oliver was a guest, too. She'd seen him poking around earlier.

"Madelyn?" Memphis whistled. "I think you're phasing out on me again. Is this a bridal-jitters thing? Shit, don't be jitters. Do you know what Smith would do if you changed your mind?"

"That would never happen. I'm marrying Smith. I love him." She'd just been taking a minute to realize how much her life had changed in the last six months.

There was no more hiding. There was no more fear. She'd laughed more with Smith in these last six months than she'd ever laughed in her life. She'd started therapy. She'd let the guilt drift away. She'd grabbed onto hope.

A soft knock sounded at the door. It creaked open, and Reginald poked his head inside. "You ready?"

Her stepfather had worked out a deal, as Smith had predicted. The charges had all been vague, something about tampering with a corpse, and the authorities had never questioned his story of self-defense. Considering that Benny the Blade was currently suspected in over *forty* murders, no one seemed too interested in looking at Benny's own death too closely.

My father was a hit man. A murderer. He kidnapped me. He terrorized me.

No, no, her *father* was smiling at her as he entered the dressing room. Reginald wore a tux very similar to Memphis's.

The past was over. It was her future that waited.

She'd actually gotten a little surprise news earlier that day. One of the reasons she'd, ah, phased out, as Memphis called it.

I'm pregnant. Smith didn't know yet. She'd tell him soon enough. He wouldn't just be marrying her. *He's marrying us.*

Her fingers fluttered over her stomach. "I'm ready." More than ready.

"Thank Christ." Memphis wiped his forehead. "I will go cue the music. Maybe you can do a double-time walk so Smith will breathe easier?" He scooted around her dad and hurried off.

Her dad offered his arm to her. Without a hesitation, she took it.

"I wish your mom could have been here," he said, eyes a little misty.

"Me, too," Madelyn told him.

The music had already started to play. Memphis had certainly been fast. Before Madelyn knew it, she was walking down the aisle.

She'd be getting a new name. Her choice. Smith hadn't cared if she kept her maiden name or if she took his. But she wanted his. She wanted to become Madelyn Sanders.

A new name.

A new life.

Smith smiled when he saw her, and she knew that she had never, ever been happier.

***

"Happy endings make me feel teary as shit," Memphis confessed as he snagged a champagne flute from a passing waiter. He couldn't help but notice Madelyn had been avoiding the champagne, and he had a pretty good idea why. Smothering a smile, he slanted a glance at Titan.

Honestly, he'd been a little surprised the guy had been picked to be a groomsman. Titan's relationship with Smith seemed...complicated.

Most things about Titan were complicated, though.

"They make you teary, too?" Memphis asked before he gulped down his champagne. His beautiful wife Eliza was currently chatting it up with Madelyn. No shock at all, those two had become fast friends. Two survivors. Like to like.

Titan didn't answer.

Again, something that was no shock at all.

"Does it work for you?" Memphis asked, truly curious. "With the ladies, I mean? This strong, dangerous, silent routine?"

Titan glared at him.

Memphis winked. "Dude, can't help myself. You have *got* to learn how to open up a bit."

Titan took a glass of champagne from a waiter.

"There you go," Memphis praised him. "Starting to be wild, I can feel it. You are just going to break loose soon, and no one will know what the hell to do with you."

As Memphis watched, Titan took a small sip of champagne.

"So..." Time to get down to business. "You gonna continue working with the marshals? Because I keep hearing rumors that you're going freelance. If that's the case, I've got some work to offer you with the Ice Breakers."

Madelyn and Smith walked onto the dance floor. Smith's eyes were on Madelyn, and he looked at her as if she was the only person who existed for him.

Memphis caught the quick flash of envy on Titan's face. He clapped a hand on the guy's shoulder in sympathy. "Don't you worry. One day, some poor, unsuspecting woman is going to fall hard for your dangerous and untalkative self."

"Fuck off."

Ah, now they were getting some place. "I really...*really* could use someone who is good at tracking down a runaway witness. Any chance you might be interested? You know, if you're going freelance?" He waited. Waited and...

"*Yes.*"

Hot damn. "This is the right decision, my friend," Memphis assured him. "It is one that is going to change your *life.*"

THE END

A NOTE FROM THE AUTHOR

I love cold cases. I'm addicted to watching true crime shows and listening to podcasts, so, of course, I couldn't wait to write my own cold case mysteries! But, of course, I had to mix up the stories with lots of romance—and thus my Ice Breakers were born.

Thank you so very much for taking the time to read TRAPPED IN ICE. I hope that you enjoyed Madelyn and Smith's story. Madelyn's life was far from easy, and I wanted to give her a hero who would take on the world for her. Smith is the kind of guy who loves with his whole heart, and, for Madelyn, he was a true hero.

If you'd like to stay updated on my releases and sales, please join my newsletter list.

https://cynthiaeden.com/newsletter/

Best,
Cynthia Eden
cynthiaeden.com

ABOUT THE AUTHOR

Cynthia Eden is a *New York Times*, *USA Today*, *Digital Book World*, and *IndieReader* best-seller.

Cynthia writes sexy tales of contemporary romance, romantic suspense, and paranormal romance. Since she began writing full-time in 2005, Cynthia has written over one hundred novels and novellas.

Cynthia lives along the Alabama Gulf Coast. She loves romance novels, horror movies, and chocolate.

For More Information
- *cynthiaeden.com*
- *facebook.com/cynthiaedenfanpage*

HER OTHER WORKS

Wilde Ways: Gone Rogue

- How To Protect A Princess (Book 1)
- How To Heal A Heartbreak (Book 2)
- How To Con A Crime Boss (Book 3)

Ice Breaker Cold Case Romance

- Frozen In Ice (Book 1)
- Falling For The Ice Queen (Book 2)
- Ice Cold Saint (Book 3)
- Touched By Ice (Book 4)
- Trapped In Ice (Book 5)

Phoenix Fury

- Hot Enough To Burn (Book 1)
- Slow Burn (Book 2)
- Burn It Down (Book 3)

Trouble For Hire

- No Escape From War (Book 1)
- Don't Play With Odin (Book 2)
- Jinx, You're It (Book 3)
- Remember Ramsey (Book 4)

Death and Moonlight Mystery

- Step Into My Web (Book 1)

- Save Me From The Dark (Book 2)

Wilde Ways

- Protecting Piper (Book 1)
- Guarding Gwen (Book 2)
- Before Ben (Book 3)
- The Heart You Break (Book 4)
- Fighting For Her (Book 5)
- Ghost Of A Chance (Book 6)
- Crossing The Line (Book 7)
- Counting On Cole (Book 8)
- Chase After Me (Book 9)
- Say I Do (Book 10)
- Roman Will Fall (Book 11)
- The One Who Got Away (Book 12)
- Pretend You Want Me (Book 13)
- Cross My Heart (Book 14)
- The Bodyguard Next Door (Book 15)
- Ex Marks The Perfect Spot (Book 16)
- The Thief Who Loved Me (Book 17)

Dark Sins

- Don't Trust A Killer (Book 1)
- Don't Love A Liar (Book 2)

Lazarus Rising

- Never Let Go (Book One)
- Keep Me Close (Book Two)
- Stay With Me (Book Three)
- Run To Me (Book Four)
- Lie Close To Me (Book Five)
- Hold On Tight (Book Six)

Dark Obsession Series

- Watch Me (Book 1)
- Want Me (Book 2)
- Need Me (Book 3)
- Beware Of Me (Book 4)
- Only For Me (Books 1 to 4)

Mine Series

- Mine To Take (Book 1)
- Mine To Keep (Book 2)
- Mine To Hold (Book 3)
- Mine To Crave (Book 4)
- Mine To Have (Book 5)
- Mine To Protect (Book 6)
- Mine Box Set Volume 1 (Books 1-3)
- Mine Box Set Volume 2 (Books 4-6)

Bad Things

- The Devil In Disguise (Book 1)
- On The Prowl (Book 2)
- Undead Or Alive (Book 3)
- Broken Angel (Book 4)
- Heart Of Stone (Book 5)
- Tempted By Fate (Book 6)
- Wicked And Wild (Book 7)
- Saint Or Sinner (Book 8)
- Bad Things Volume One (Books 1 to 3)
- Bad Things Volume Two (Books 4 to 6)
- Bad Things Deluxe Box Set (Books 1 to 6)

Bite Series

- Forbidden Bite (Bite Book 1)
- Mating Bite (Bite Book 2)

Blood and Moonlight Series

- Bite The Dust (Book 1)
- Better Off Undead (Book 2)
- Bitter Blood (Book 3)
- Blood and Moonlight (The Complete Series)

Purgatory Series

- The Wolf Within (Book 1)
- Marked By The Vampire (Book 2)
- Charming The Beast (Book 3)
- Deal with the Devil (Book 4)
- The Beasts Inside (Books 1 to 4)

Bound Series

- Bound By Blood (Book 1)
- Bound In Darkness (Book 2)
- Bound In Sin (Book 3)
- Bound By The Night (Book 4)
- Bound in Death (Book 5)
- Forever Bound (Books 1 to 4)

Stand-Alone Romantic Suspense

- Kiss Me This Christmas
- It's A Wonderful Werewolf
- Never Cry Werewolf
- Immortal Danger
- Deck The Halls
- Come Back To Me
- Put A Spell On Me
- Never Gonna Happen
- One Hot Holiday
- Slay All Day
- Midnight Bite
- Secret Admirer

- Christmas With A Spy
- Femme Fatale
- Until Death
- Sinful Secrets
- First Taste of Darkness
- A Vampire's Christmas Carol

CPSIA information can be obtained
at www.ICGtesting.com
Printed in the USA
BVHW081915220623
666267BV00011B/561